MEN IN BLACK II

Also published by Ballantine Books:

INSIDE MEN IN BLACK II by Brad Munson

MEN IN BLACK II

The official novelization
by Esther M. Friesner

Based on the screenplay
by Robert Gordon and Barry Fanaro

Story by Robert Gordon

BALLANTINE BOOKS • NEW YORK

A Ballantine Book
Published by The Ballantine Publishing Group
Copyright © 2002 by Columbia Pictures Industries, Inc. All Rights Reserved.

All rights reserved under International and Pan-American Copyright Conventions. Published in the United States by The Ballantine Publishing Group, a division of Random House, Inc., New York, and simultaneously in Canada by Random House of Canada Limited, Toronto.

MEN IN BLACK™. All Rights Reserved.

Ballantine and colophon are registered trademarks of Random House, Inc.

www.ballantinebooks.com

Cover photo by Michael O'Neill

ISBN 0-345-45066-3

Manufactured in the United States of America

First Edition: June 2002

10 9 8 7 6 5 4 3 2 1

ONE

New York, New York. Don't let anyone tell you different: It's all about the out-of-towners.

No man is an island, but Manhattan is. Key word: *insular,* meaning a little bit exclusive, meaning the people who live here can be particular about who gets in, and who had better stay the hell out.

Ask that friendly cabbie who's driving you around. Go ahead, ask him, about your chances for getting into this smash-hit Broadway musical, or that red-hot nightclub, or even a taping of the David Letterman show. Just ask. He could probably use a good laugh—right before he says, *You wanna do* what? *Into* where? *You want it* when?

Yeah, riiiight. Lotsa luck, Tourist.

But hey, don't feel dumb for asking. Nobody expects a lot from an out-of-towner.

Psst. Want to know a secret? What the cabbie tells you, fahgeddaboudit. Here's the truth about New York: It's *all* about the out-of-towners. Always has been, right from the start. Always will be.

New York's got a funny effect on folks who come here for a visit. A lot of them wind up spending the rest of their lives. It's like there's something in the water, besides the plutonium. Something that puts a crazy spin on the whole evolution thing, the way out-of-towners manage to meta-morphose themselves from tourists, to transients, to the types who act like they've always had their roots sunk deep into New York City bedrock. Like they own the place.

That's what you call nerve. That's what you call chutz-pah. That's what you call New York attitude. That's why you can kick a New Yorker where it hurts, but you can never keep him down.

The first significant bunch of out-of-towners to hit the Big Apple were the Dutch crowd headed by Peter Minuit. He's the man who had the bright idea of buying the is-land of Manhattan from the locals for a bunch of baubles, bangles, beads, and gewgaws, stuff on a par with those "genuine" Rolex watches you can buy out of an attaché case in Herald Square, or the Theater District, or some-where along Fifth Avenue, three steps ahead of the cops.

The whole schmear set the Dutch East India Company back a few guilders, which broke down to about twenty-four bucks American after you did the math and allowed for the exchange rate. Sneaky Pete probably figured he'd got a real steal. In a way, he had.

As for the Native American sellers, sure, maybe they could've scared up a better price for Manhattan if they'd posted it on eBay, but whaddayagonnado? Right place, wrong time. Besides, it turned out that these Native Ameri-can guys, New York's first documented real estate moguls, actually belonged to the Canarsie tribe, which meant they maybe had the right to sell off part of Brooklyn, a little of Queens, but absolutely no legal claims to Manhattan what-soever. Not that it stopped them from selling it to the Dutch anyhow, thus kicking off another grand old New York custom, as both parties in the deal walked away from it, each one convinced he'd played the other for a sucker.

Twenty-four bucks' worth of twinkly things may not seem like a heck of a lot these days. That's because it isn't. Twenty-four bucks won't even buy a seat on one of those rolling tourist traps, the double-decker sight-seeing buses. Straight from London, they're ubiquitous in Manhattan: Rain or shine, day or night, summer, winter, spring, and fall they go looping up and down the island, showing off the big buildings and the bright lights for the out-of-towners.

The best seats are on the top deck. Sure, unwary tourists are going to get soaked if it's raining, freeze if it's cold, or suffer from sunstroke if it's summertime, but when they go back home, they'll boast and brag about how they had the best damn view of the best damn city in the world.

Of course, not everybody likes to make his way around Manhattan on the bus. There are alternatives available to everyone, natives and out-of-towners alike. There are the subways and regular buses for people who don't think money grows on trees, taxis and car services and limos for the high-ticket crowd. Some folks even swear by skateboards, in-line skates, and their poor cousins—the common or garden-variety roller skate. In a pinch you can even get where you're going by what you call Shank's Mare.

Don't let the name fool you, though. That's one mare that doesn't have anything to do with the horse-drawn hansom cabs that go clopping through Central Park or park outside the Plaza Hotel. Naaaah, it's just French for "walking."

Tourists who get tired of seeing the sights by land can take to the water, sign up for one of those tour boats that circles the island, or do it on the cheap by grabbing a quick ride on the Staten Island Ferry.

What really drives people crazy, so to speak, is the way some people drive even after they've hit the Big Apple. It's like it's open season on pedestrians. It's a mystery why people bother with cars at all, what with the cost of garages, alternate-side-of-the-street parking, and all the other ways to get around New York. Why would even an out-of-towner want to get into the driver's seat at all?

Of course, some of them do it because that's how they got here in the first place, behind the wheel of their own personal vehicles. And if they sideswipe everything that gets in the way, from squirrels to parked cars to little old ladies, they don't seem to give it a moment's notice. Take it from the natives, they're the worst.

The sleek, swift starship was gold and glittering. Deadly, alluring, and in its own way beautiful.

It careened at breathtaking speed through the star-filled blackness of the void, spreading carnage wherever it went. Unsuspecting worlds, many of them inhabited, exploded into lifeless debris under the merciless assault from its weapons. Fire burst gleefully from its guns, leaving a trail of debris and chaos in its wake.

But from its purposeful path, it was apparent that none of these unfortunate planets was the intended target, that its pilot was seeking another, unknown destination. Picking up speed, it streaked toward a single star, past the outermost, frozen planets. Past the gas giant, and its ringed neighbor, ever onward.

Finally, almost imperceptibly, it slowed as it approached the Third Planet from the sun, and veered to drop down through the atmosphere. Strangely enough, it easily found a parking spot—a landing site in a place green and leafy and serene.

A tree grows in Brooklyn, but in the heart of New York City's famed Financial District a flower bloomed. In the middle of the night, in a section of the city where the hustle and bustle of countless feet was certain to trample any unfenced bit of greenery to a sticky pulp, this exquisitely formed, daintily colored blossom protruded from the sidewalk, its delicate stalk and velvety petals nodding and dancing slowly on the waves of warm air wafting up out of the steam grate where it grew.

It was as attractive as it was utterly inexplicable.

A black Mercedes screeched to a stop at the curb by the steam grate where the voracious flower bloomed. It was too bad that the street was completely empty of passing stockbrokers at that hour; the appearance of that sleek, expensive, state-of-the-art vehicle would have stirred up a lot more appreciation in their covetous corporate hearts than the sight of a thousand flowers.

The Mercedes's doors swung open and two men got out. One of them had the wholesome, clean-cut, corn-fed looks of a Big Ten linebacker, the kind whom college sports-journalists liked to tout as "all-American," whatever that means. The other man, an African American, was nowhere near as brawny, but the way he carried himself conveyed the feeling that there was plenty of strength in that slim, agile body. They wore identical black suits, simply styled, impeccably fitted, and black shoes buffed to a blinding shine.

The thin one got out of car on the driver's side. Maybe

he wasn't carrying the same amount of muscle as his partner, but he didn't need it any more than he needed a badge or a nameplate or any other outward sign to tell the world that he was in charge. His authority showed in the way he moved, the way he stood, the way he spoke, in everything about him, down to the slightest lift of an eyebrow.

His gleaming black shoes clicked out a crisp beat as he walked across the pavement to the steam grate, followed closely by his beefier partner.

"No fancy stuff," the first man said, laying down the law as he walked. "No heroics. Be cool. By the book this time, Tee. Okay?"

"So what you're saying, Jay, is—" his partner ventured.

The first man stopped. "Say 'okay,' Tee."

He said it in a way that left no room for argument.

The big guy could have picked him up and pitched him into the little fruit stand across the street, but that didn't happen. "Got it," he said, taking his orders like a good soldier. He walked past, right up to the flower. "Hey!" He prodded it smartly with his shoe. "What the hell do you think you're doing?" he demanded of the blossom.

The flower went rigid. Plenty of gardening gurus preach that if you want results, it's a good idea to talk to your plants, but this had to be the first time on record that a plant actually sat up and paid attention.

Without missing a beat, Jay stepped in, his words likewise aimed at the tensed-up posy. "Hey, Jeff," he said affably, doing a smooth segue into the classic good cop, bad cop *shpiel*. "How's it goin'? Why are you here?"

The flower didn't respond.

"C'mon, you know our arrangement," Jay coaxed. "You

don't travel outside the E, F, and RR subway lines and in return, you eat all the nonorganic garbage you want. *Nonorganic.* Okay?"

The flower still wasn't talking. It could've given *omerta* lessons to Don Corleone.

The second man stepped in, playing the bad cop for all he was worth. "Hey! The man's talking to you," he snarled.

"Tee . . ." Jay uttered his partner's name as a warning, a mild cautionary signal. Enthusiasm in the field was fine, in its place, but some situations called for the diplomatic touch. Just because you *had* the muscle didn't mean you always needed to *use* the muscle.

No use: The warning went right over Tee's head, if he heard it at all. The big guy reached down and grabbed the flower roughly by its dainty little stalk. "What the man *means* is—" He filled his broad chest with air and bellowed. *"—what the hell you doing here, wormboy?"*

He was a big man and he had a big voice, big enough to make windows rattle. Big enough to scatter pigeons twelve blocks away, big enough to make passersby look up and check the sky for thunderheads.

Not big enough to make the ground shake like it did at that moment.

Definitely not big enough to make the steam grate rattle and the pavement crack around it.

To do *that* took the flower.

The flower, and what was attached *to* the flower.

Jay had just a second to flash an *Oh, now you've done it!* look at Tee before the street cracked open like an eggshell, and a gigantic, wormlike creature erupted from underfoot, smashing its way through the steam grate and rearing skyward, taking Tee with it. Jay watched with astonishing tranquillity as his brawny partner dangled from the monster's head, still holding on to the stalk of the pathetically tiny flower.

Fool looks like some kind of weird mortarboard tassel hanging there, all set to spin, he thought. *And I just got the feeling that it's way past graduation day.*

Putting on a big buddy-buddy *we can talk this out* smile, he exclaimed, "Hey, you want to excuse my partner, Jeff! He's new, and—"

The worm-thing pulled his head all the way back and snapped it forward sharply, playing a one-sided game of crack-the-whip. With a scream of complete and utter helplessness, Tee went sailing off high into the night sky, like a pebble from a slingshot. The monster sank down to sidewalk level again, mission accomplished.

"—kind of stupid," Jay concluded, a little too late. He hunkered down, getting eye-to-eye with the monster. "Huh! Gotten big," he observed. "What the hell you been eating down there?"

Perhaps the creature forgot that Jay was an agent of the Men in Black, and thought he'd gone over to working for Weight Watchers instead. That, or the worm didn't want to listen to another free lecture about the virtues of a high-fiber diet. In either case, he wasn't in the mood to chat.

His spiked tail burst through the pavement behind Jay and whacked him clear across the street, using a slap-shot technique the New York Rangers might envy. Jay crashed into the fruit stand.

The worm-thing didn't stick around to check out the results of his no-hands handiwork. He popped back down the hole and out of sight, leaving an angry and juice-spattered Jay shouting after him.

"Jeffrey!"

For a gigantic, rat-choking-ugly worm, Jeffrey had a house cat's disposition, because he totally ignored Jay's summons, even when called by name. Jay sprang up, snorted disapproval over the creature's attitude, and jumped down the hole after him. He paused just long enough to flick on the Mercedes's alarm system.

Then he, too, was gone, leaving the street deserted once more.

TWO

In his natural habitat, Jeff barely had the time to draw a deep breath of the hot, fetid, summer-in-the-subway air before Jay dropped in, landing right on top of him.

"Out of line with that tail thing, man!" Jay said, shaking his head. "*Way* out of—whoa!"

Before you could say *watch the closing doors*, Jeffrey had taken off down the yawning subway tunnel at top speed, with Jay holding on to the worm-thing's back for dear life. They zoomed through the darkness on a wild ride that would have left amusement-park engineers drooling on their loafers. And through it all, Jay clung to Jeffrey's back while attempting to perform his official duties as a bona fide agent of the Men in Black, reading off a list of charges while the wormlike alien plunged on.

"*Failure* to file for movement authorization," he declared. "*Withholding* information from agents of MIB. *Appearing* as a worm before the populace at large."

Jeff chose that moment to do the hardball version of thumbing his nose at Jay's authority by slamming his head—and Jay's—against the roof of the tunnel. It was the best he could do, seeing as how he didn't have any thumbs or, for the matter, a nose.

The blow might have dislodged a lesser man, but the MIB didn't recruit lesser men. When the stakes were the peace and security of Earth, there was no room for quitters, whiners, or anyone who didn't look cool in a plain black suit. Jay grunted from the impact, then shook it off and got his game face on.

"Now you pissed me off," he informed the alien. Drawing a long, wicked-looking metal cylinder from his pocket, he leaned forward and thrust the injector delivery system deep into the flower-shaped lure atop Jeffrey's head. There was the sound of compressed air escaping as it shot home a payload of tranquilizer.

Jay grinned. "Sweet dreams, big boy. Just enjoy the pretty—"

With an ear-splitting screech, Jeffrey bolted down the subway tunnel as if the air-syringe had shot him full of amphetamines.

"—*colors!*" Jay shrieked as his otherworldly steed stampeded on.

It takes a lot to impress New Yorkers. This is doubly true of commuters on the New York City subway system. Unless something is actually on fire, it's not worth checking out. Do that and you might lose your place in the newspaper article you're reading. Even then, there are some straphangers who can't be bothered to look up unless the item that's on fire happens to be their own personal copy of the *Post*.

So when you're standing on the Prince Street Station platform, waiting for the local, you might glance up from your paper when you hear the sound of an oncoming train. Of course, nine times out of ten, it turns out to be the express, just passing through, so you go back to reading and thinking about how good it's going to feel when you get home at last and can take your shoes off.

But how about if you hear that distant roar and look up to see a gigantic wormlike monster come shrieking through your stop with some sharp-dressed guy in a black suit clinging to its back like it's the world's biggest, nastiest bucking bronco, and he's reading it its rights at the top of his lungs?

So okay, maybe you *do* look up a second time—trying to look like you're not *really* looking. This is New York—you gotta be cool, man—just one little follow-up glance and that's all.

There was light on the track ahead, the taillights of the subway car rumbling through the tunnel ahead of them, but Jay didn't notice. His mind was on more pressing business, like holding on to Jeff while simultaneously trying to get the worm to understand the full gravity of the situation. He had already gone through the MIB equivalent of reading Jeff his Miranda rights ("You have the right to remain ugly. You have the right to have your squirmy, extraterrestrial butt put in a sling for whiplashing me into that fruit stand and getting mashed banana all over my new shirt . . ."), and now he was down to the business at hand.

"With the full powers vested in me as an agent of MIB, I hereby place you under arrest," he declared. "Now pull your wiggly-ass self over!"

It was a valiant effort on Jay's part, but ultimately a futile one. Jeff hadn't obeyed a single order he'd been given so far; why should he start now?

As if to answer that unspoken question, the worm

snapped his head forward sharply, employing the same maneuver he'd used earlier to rid himself of Tee. You can't beat the classics: It still worked like a charm.

Jay was whip-cracked straight into the back of the last car of the fleeing subway train. The worm had a good eye—wherever the hell he was keeping it on a body like *that*—and launched the MIB agent right through the window panel on the rearmost car's back door. Tinkling, gemlike shards of glass cascaded down around Jay like hard-edged snow.

Picking himself up for the second time that night, Jay looked back down the tunnel to see that, rather than turning tail and making good his escape, Jeff had decided that the best defense was a good offense. Even though he lived down in the subway tunnels of the city, where you couldn't swing a cat without hitting a poster advertising— in English *and* Spanish—the services of this or that law office, Jeff must've figured that, having been placed under arrest by the MIB, screw the lawyers—his best course of action was to handle it himself. Hire a good attorney or de- vour your arresting officer? A real no-brainer, in Jeff's tiny mind. The worm was coming, and he looked mad.

Even worse, he looked hungry.

Oh, man, and he is not *a picky eater,* Jay thought. *This could be bad.*

Turning from the end door of the subway car, Jay drew himself up into his most official-looking pose and an- nounced, "Transit Authority. Everyone move to the front car. Bug in the electrical system."

There was no more than a handful of passengers in the car, most of them reading their evening papers. And though they were of a wide variety of ages, races, and social classes, they were united by that one ineffable skill that brings all citizens of the great metropolis together.

They knew bullshit when they saw it.

The man standing before them had come out of nowhere, appearing in their midst while the train was in the middle of a tunnel, dressed in clothing that looked nothing like any Transit Authority uniform they'd ever seen. And *he* was giving them orders?

They barely even looked up from their papers long enough to glance in Jay's direction before they wearily went back to reading the box scores and the gossip columns and sometimes, for a good laugh, the editorials.

"Yo! People!" Jay shouted.

This time they looked up and kept looking. They didn't say a word, but the car was heavy with *Yeah? What?* vibes.

"We got a *bug* in the electrical system," Jay repeated. He nodded toward the back door.

Which suddenly, noisily, disappeared. With a mighty *crunch!*, Jeffrey's massive jaws sheared right through the back end of the subway car, taking off a twenty-foot-long mouthful, his wormy version of snapping into a Slim Jim.

Finally the passengers screamed and dropped their newspapers. They didn't even wait for Jay to issue a third warning; they were way ahead of him, dashing into the next car forward just as Jeff's clashing jaws obliterated the rest of the car. Faced with this wave of bodies, Jay tried to keep things from getting even further out of hand.

"No, no. Sit down. It's only a six-hundred-foot worm!"

Nevertheless, chaos reigned, hysteria took over, and *rush hour* took on a whole new meaning as panicking passengers pushed, shoved, and clawed their way to what they hoped would be safety. Their screams of abject terror were loud enough to drown out the sound of the onrushing train and the *crunch-smash-gnash-crush* of the worm jaws snapping at their heels.

Looking back, Jay decided he agreed with them.

"Go! Go! Go! Just scream one more time!" he shouted.

They burst into the next car with Jay right behind them, about two steps ahead of the worm. "Move! Move! *Move!*" he shouted at the seated passengers.

This group didn't wait to ask questions; the frenzied stampede of their fellow New Yorkers proved a great persuader. *When in Rome, do as the Romans do,* especially if the Romans are all running the hell away from a monster. They all leapt up and made a dash for their lives, just as Jeffrey took his next bite out of their small slice of the Big Apple.

Car after car after car, it was the same story: An ever-growing horde of terrified passengers shot through one door and swept along everyone in their path. Old men remembered how to get the most out of their army basic-training days. Teenage girls called upon the same inner strength that had taken them through the mosh pits of a hundred rock concerts. Women grabbed their children, got in touch with their inner warrior princesses, and plowed through the crowd.

It was a miracle that no one fell; the trampling feet of the other commuters would have mashed any poor schmuck into a thin red paste before Jeffrey's jaws could snap him down along with the train car.

Bringing up the rear, riding herd on the mob, Jay cast another uneasy glance behind him, in time to see Jeff treating the subway cars like a string of sausages, munching each one down split seconds after it was abandoned.

He tightened his lips grimly. No casualties so far, besides the property of the New York City Transit Authority, but this couldn't go on forever.

Sooner or later they were going to run out of subway cars.

The crowd was about thirty strong when it came charging into the head car. In his little booth at the front of the car, the motorman sat at his post, hands on the controls, mind on how good it was going to feel when he could finally go home and take his shoes off.

He was just imagining the taste of that first ice-cold after-work beer sliding over his tongue when his reverie was interrupted by the screaming mob. He stuck his head out of the booth.

"*Hey!* Everyone out, before I start knocking heads together here," he told them. He sounded only mildly annoyed; the air-conditioning was down, and it was too hot to get really mad.

Jay drew his double-barrel shotgun and held it so that the motorman could get a nice, clear view of the nasty-looking weapon. On this baby, size *did* matter. Standard issue MIB weapons weren't known for honoring the concept that less is more. It was strictly a more-is-more-and-a-*lot*-more-is-even-better kind of weapon.

What Jay got from the motorman was reminiscent of how the passengers in the rearmost car had looked at him, just before Jeffrey made his munchy-crunchy entrance.

"Oh, *please*," the motorman said indifferently. "This is the C train. Know how many guns I've seen this week?"

Jay didn't have time to play games. "Put the hammer down on this thing," he commanded.

The motorman gave him a *you-and-what-army* look.

"I'm Captain Larry Bridgewater, and I decide what happens on this transit transport," he informed the MIB agent.

A screech and a crunch punctuated the noble captain's declaration. He looked past Jay, through the back door, to see Jeff chowing down with a vengeance on the last car behind them.

"Larry just made a decision," he told Jay, and threw the throttle down.

Jeff made a decision, too, somewhere in the twists and tangles of his wormy little brain, and Jeff's decision was that New York City Transit Authority property made for some mighty good eating. And he knew he was within his rights: He was allowed to eat all the nonorganic garbage he wanted. If a fully functional subway car couldn't honestly be called "garbage," especially in its present state, it came close enough for jazz. Jeff liked to think of this as cutting out the middleman.

His gaping jaws tore into the rear end of the last car standing, tearing a big chunk of metal off the back. The captive passengers screamed, at last knowing how it felt to be Today's Secret Ingredient on *Iron Chef*.

Jay ran back, gun in hand, to protect and prevent innocent bystanders from being served up as alien hors d'oeuvres. But just as he raised his weapon and took aim, Jeff paused in mid-lunge. His beady little eyes rolled back in his head, something very like a giggle escaped those awful jaws, and with a tunnel-rattling *thud*, the big monster hit the rails, out colder than an extraterrestrial mackerel.

Lurching and chuddering along the track, its wheels squealing in protest half on and half off the rails, the wounded subway car limped out of the tunnel and into the station.

It staggered to a halt and fell silent. For long moments the only sound to be heard in the station was the wild, hysterical weeping of the passengers and Captain Larry.

Jay glanced out the window, though he had a better view of things out the half-eaten rear of the car. "Eighty-first Street," he remarked. "Museum of Natural History."

He slipped on his Ray-Bans and held up what appeared to be a rather fat-barreled silver pen. It wasn't. The deceptively small, shiny tube clicked open to reveal a little red light at its tip.

"May I have your attention please," he asked the passengers. They turned their tear-wet faces upward just in time to get the full flash of a memory-wiping white light. "The city of New York would like to thank you for participating in our drill . . ."

He paused, and a strange look flitted across his face as the events of the evening caught up with him. Losing some of his hard-fought control, he said, "If this had been a real emergency, y'all woulda been eaten! 'Cuz you're hard-headed! That's the problem with all you New Yorkers!" Getting angrier, he continued, his voice rising, "Explain to me . . . I asked y'all *nicely* to move . . ."

Jay stopped himself, and regained his composure. He held up the neuralyzer again, and after another flash of white light, he continued. "We hope you enjoyed our new smaller, more energy-efficient subway cars. Watch your step. You will have a nice evening."

The doors slid open. One by one the passengers filed out onto the platform and passed through the turnstiles, placidly, as if everything were business as usual. Jay escorted them on their way, all the while talking into his communicator:

"Need cleanup crew at Eighty-first Street and Central Park West. Get Transpo to tow off what's left of the train." Even as he spoke, at his back he heard the silence broken by the quick, crisp, efficient scurrying of dozens of MIB agents swarming into the station, doing whatever needed to be done to return that little patch of New York to pre-Jeff normalcy.

"Revoke Jeff's movement privileges immediately," he continued. "Have a Transfer Team take him back to his place at the Chambers Street Station . . . and could somebody *please* check the damn expiration dates on all the worm tranquilizers?"

He emerged from the subway in time to dodge through a crew of MIB agents wearing Con Edison uniforms. They already had the station entrance roped off, and—this being New York—a crowd of peeved customers had gathered to raise a group grumble over having their access denied.

Eventually the dissatisfied New Yorkers shambled off, leaving Jay pretty much on his own. It had been what the old Chinese curse would call an interesting night, and he wouldn't mind getting off his feet. He found a bench in front of the glowing glass facade of the glorious Rose Planetarium and sat down. Then, as an afterthought, he moved over a little. He knew what was coming.

Tee walked up and sat down with a thud right where Jay had been sitting. The brawny MIB agent sat there, stunned, then pulled himself together and shakily, sheepishly said to his partner: "I know. By the book."

Jay looked up at the night sky. As far as any of the passengers he'd just rescued knew, it was full of stars and moons and planets and used-up space stations—and that was all. He knew otherwise—*really* knew it, and not just with the vague hopes of dreamers or poets or lifelong science-fiction fans.

It was nothing new to him; he'd known the truth for quite some time now, ever since he'd been recruited to join the Men in Black, but it was knowledge that still left him feeling . . . strange. Odd. Other.

The worst part was, he couldn't talk about how he felt, not to one single, solitary soul outside the MIB. Outside the MIB he didn't even exist. All evidence of his former life had been systematically erased as soon as he'd decided to sign on, from his birth certificate, to his Social Security card, right down to the very whorls and loops and traceries of his fingerprints.

As for talking about those strange feelings of his to anyone *inside* the agency . . . why bother? The only guy who might have listened and understood was gone, mustered out, retired with a nice, mundane life and all his memories of the MIB blanked from his mind courtesy of a neuralyzer flash. Jay knew that if he talked to any of the others, they'd only look at him as if he'd gone soft. You didn't go soft and keep on working for the Men in Black, and when your whole life had become the Men in Black, that didn't leave you with a lot of other options.

"Ever feel like you're alone in the universe, Tee?" Jay asked quietly.

Tee tensed up.

"This is a test, right? I can get this. Yes." He sounded hopeful. Then, quickly: "No." He sounded doubtful. And finally: "I'm not sure." He wilted. "I'm toast."

Jay stood up and did his best not to sigh. No sense upsetting the big guy needlessly. "Let me buy you a piece of pie," he said.

"Really?" Tee perked up immediately. "Thanks." As they walked off, he put one arm around Jay's shoulders and awkwardly offered: "Hey, you're not alone in the universe."

"Remove the arm," Jay directed.

THREE

Contrary to popular belief, Central Park is not a natural feature of the geography of Manhattan; it's a construct. This island of greenery, this bucolic shelter from the hustle, bustle, hum, and shriek of big-city living, began life as a wasteland coupled with a dream.

Sometime during the mid–nineteenth century, with the city growing at a fabulous rate and the signs of progress springing up everywhere, some visionary sage realized that it wasn't enough for people to live in the greatest city in the world: They would also need a place to *hide* from the greatest city in the world, sometimes.

Following a spirited competition for the rights to design and build the park, the winner's laurels went to Frederick Law Olmsted. His plan called for a varying terrain that included hills, meadows, thickets, lakes, formal gardens, places where the rich could see and be seen when they went out driving in their carriages, and places where the poor could breathe air that wasn't tainted by the stink of coal smoke and tenements. The completed project was opened to the public in 1859, shortly before the start of the Civil War.

Of course, it wasn't as simple as that. It never is, in New York City.

After upward of ten years' worth of heavy-duty politicking just to get approval and funding for the park, there was still the matter of transforming the designated territory. This was more than a matter of draining swamps, blasting boulders to smithereens, trucking out countless cartloads of rocks, and bringing in similarly numerous cartloads of topsoil—to say nothing of planting said topsoil with more than a quarter million trees and shrubs.

This was a matter of removing unwanted people. The wasteland that was to become Central Park was already home to almost two thousand squatters, the poorest of the poor, plus the pigs, goats, and miscellaneous livestock they had accumulated in the course of their hardscrabble lives.

Not for long, though. The park was conceived of as a pleasure ground for rich and poor alike, so the poor had better get out of the way. Progress *would* be made, juggernaut-style, and nothing would stand in its way without being crushed. The unwanted denizens were evicted with much efficiency and little fanfare. So were their goats.

And thus, artfully planned, beautifully planted, free of unwanted interlopers, Central Park was born.

Funny thing about unwanted interlopers . . .

The illuminated Gothic bulk of the Dakota loomed above the trees of Central Park West, reminding the late-night joggers and dog walkers passing beneath the canopy of the trees that civilization wasn't so far off as it seemed. This was an intrusive thought if you were trying to create the illusion of pastoral solitude, but rather a comforting one if you were the sort of person who wanted to feel not so completely alone. After all, solitude could be dangerous. As every good predator knows, the first thing you do to secure your prey is cut him out of the herd.

The peace of the park on that sweet summer night was abruptly broken by the clamor of a dog barking, loudly and insistently. In a grove of trees, a handsome golden retriever sat on his haunches, staring up into the night sky and yelping furiously. Whatever had grabbed his attention—bird or beast or bogeyman—the dog was treating it as a serious threat and doing all he could to attract the attention of someone who might be able to do something to neutralize the danger.

He attracted someone's attention, sure enough. The sound of labored breathing arose out of the darkness as a fat man carrying a leash came staggering up, angry and exhausted.

"Heel, Harvey!" he gasped, snapping the leash onto the golden retriever's collar. *"Heel!"* He took a little time to catch his breath, then tugged on the leash, wanting to get the hell out of this dark and secluded spot. He might not be in the best of physical shape, but he would have taken the gold medal if there were an Olympic contest for survival instincts.

The dog sat tight and barked on, indifferent to his master's voice.

"You're barking at the *moon*, moron," the fat man said, mistaking the dog's devotion to duty for sheer obstinacy. In Paleolithic times, this same man's ancestors had tamed and treasured dogs for just such steadfastness, knowing that the dog's bark was always the signal to grab their spears and stand on guard, ready to repel an approaching enemy that would be invariably bigger, meaner, and toothier than themselves. They paid attention to the loyal dog's bark in the night, and as a result they survived to pass along this wisdom to their children: *When the dog barks, listen up or be lunch!* This ongoing teamwork of dog and human became an inspiration to future generations, and a bond that had become sanctified by the passage of time.

The fat man cared less about inspiration than perspiration. He was dripping with it. He'd had to chase after his wayward pooch, fearing that he'd lost him, terrified that the beast had left the park and gotten flattened in traffic, only to find the mutt apparently barking at nothing. It left him steamed. Literally. Now all he wanted was to go home, get into the shower, and take a blood oath that his next pet was going to be a hamster.

"Come *on*, Harvey," he commanded, and when the dog still refused to obey, the man dragged him away by force. "Stupid dog," he muttered. "Barking at the freaking moon."

The dog gave one last raspy yelp as his collar cut into his throat, then went along with his master. If dogs could talk, no doubt Harvey would have said: *Okay, fool, have it your way. But remember: I tried to warn you.*

So he had. For no sooner were Harvey and his master out of sight than the night sky gleamed momentarily with the metallic shape of a swiftly descending spacecraft. It was shaped like a golden teardrop and moved with the grace and intensity of purpose of a great white shark in need of a meal. It came gliding in from precisely the direction that Harvey had been facing, unwitnessed and unheralded, and performed an unmolested landing in the lee of a grassy hillside in the park, settling itself on spindly legs, pointy end downward.

An opening appeared, and a ramp descended from the spacecraft's side. From the shadows within the belly of the starship, something small and gnarled and green and ugly slithered down the ramp and onto the grass. It looked very much like a root of some kind, one of the hairier, twistier varieties, the sort of thing that no sane gardener could nurture without falling prey to nightmares. Even though the creature bore no more resemblance to a human being than a frog to a wad of cotton candy, there was still something about the way that it set foot/root/whatever on Earth that was reminiscent of Cortés taking his first step onto the shores of Mexico. It was all very portentous, ominous, and significant.

An indignant shout from somewhere among the trees broke the moment as Harvey came barreling back to his abandoned guard post. Thousands of years of social conditioning refused to let him walk away from his responsibilities, no matter what the fat guy said.

He barked wildly at the creature, which, as it turned out, was about the size of his favorite rawhide bone. Harvey was ready to defend Earth against something small enough to fit comfortably inside a spacecraft that was, at most, one and a half to two feet long.

"Harvey!" The fat man's voice rang out through the night, but Harvey still wasn't heeding. Now that he saw the size of the danger, he knew he didn't need any help dealing with it. He'd chewed up shoes that were bigger than this pint-sized helping of nasty. He barked louder, baring his fangs, getting ready to close in for the kill.

The creature rose up suddenly and *hissed*. The horrible noise hit the dog right between the eyes with the force of a blow. Terror seized Harvey's brain, self-preservation evicting all thoughts of loyalty. Whimpering like a puppy, Harvey bolted back to his master, leaving the field to the foe. Somewhere among the trees the fat man said again, "Stupid dog."

Alone at last, the alien explored the turf around it. Leaves from earlier autumns blew past, tangled up with litter dropped from the hands of careless passersby. Newspaper pages skittered past, like urban tumbleweeds, along with discarded magazines and junk mail that had never quite managed to find its way into a designated trash receptacle. A copy of an abandoned *New York* magazine attracted the creature's attention. On the cover was New York City itself—a skyline shot emblazoned with the familiar I ❤ NY.

The creature reared up and launched a glob of blue spittle onto the center of the picture. It said a lot for the little alien's marksmanship, given the size of the target.

Then, with a gust of wind, the magazine fluttered open to an advertisement for Victoria's Secret. Suddenly the creature was all attention.

All at once, the root began to bloom. Wispy strands like tiny hairs began to multiply in the moonlight. Snaking out, extending, doubling back in on themselves, ever growing, growing, taking shape, taking form, thickening from filament to strand to tentacle. They grew larger, stronger, morphed themselves with a hideous grace into a torso that in turn sprouted legs, arms, feet, hands, head, hair . . .

The moon gazed down on the open newspaper magazine and the Victoria's Secret lingerie ad that had inspired such a wonderful, terrible transformation. On a fur-covered chaise lounge, a lovely model posed provocatively in black lace lingerie and high-heeled shoes, her seductive smile writing promises on the air.

A hand reached out and picked up the magazine. A face that was the manufactured twin of the model in the photograph smiled with deep satisfaction. The change was complete, and it was perfect. Where once there had been only a contorted knot of misshapen root-creature, there now stood a heartbreakingly gorgeous woman: thick, luxuriant hair the color of midnight, perfectly chiseled features for any camera on Earth to fall hopelessly in love with, a slender yet voluptuous body that radiated strength, and a penetrating gaze that took in her new surroundings, weighed them in the balance, and cynically decided that Earth and all who dwelled there would be a cinch to conquer, a piece of cake, a walk in the park—

A thin blade of cold steel flashed out of the shadows, and a knife licked suddenly across the woman's throat. "Hey, pretty lady," said a voice behind her. She turned her head just enough to see the chilling, uncanny eyes of a creepy urban park dweller clad in a long, black leather coat. She scarcely had time to register his image before he pulled her roughly behind some trees.

"Stay calm and I won't mess up your face," he rasped in her ear. Slowly, like a gourmet relishing the first taste of a banquet, he licked her neck and grinned. "Ummmm. You taste good."

Calmly and with a minimum of fuss, the woman reached back over her head, seized the would-be lady killer by the coat, peeled him like a grape, and swallowed him whole. Boa constrictors could have learned some valuable techniques.

"Ummmm," she said, licking her lips. "You do, too."

She looked down to see an unsightly bulge distorting the previously sleek contour of her belly. After repeatedly double-checking this unwanted beer belly against the image she'd adopted from the magazine ad, she shook her head in disapproval; it simply wouldn't do. She sashayed into the bushes, and moments later a monster belch sounded. A few moments of this set everything right. When she reemerged, her stomach was once more the perfectly flat surface she desired.

She smiled, picked up the discarded leather coat that her meal had been compelled to leave behind, and disappeared into the night.

Serleena had arrived.

FOUR

One of the best things about New York City is that no matter what the hour, early or late or so late it's early, you can always find someplace to sit down and get your hands on a cup of coffee and a piece of pie. The best place to find this sort of sustenance is, of course, a diner.

Diners do exist in New York City. Exist? Nay, thrive— though they aren't the lunch wagons of yore, those chrome-covered, detached structures you find by the roadside beyond the city limits and that bring to mind the old Airstream trailers. New York real estate constraints being what they are, diners are usually indistinguishable from other restaurants, except for the amount of neon used to proclaim names like "The Westway Diner," "The Metro Diner," and even an oddity like "The Malibu Diner" to the public.

The Empire Diner didn't cave in to this homogenizing architectural trend. Relatively neon-free, it maintained a proud air of having escaped from an Edward Hopper painting and refused to go back. Sitting comfortably in the neighborhood known as Chelsea, it positively reeked with retro charm, though without giving in to conscious kitschiness. It was what it was—which was a pretty Zen attitude for a building to have—from the Art Deco lettering on its facade to the 1950s clip art adorning its menus.

It also served some very good pie, the hallmark of a *real* diner, the thing that sets such places apart from the plastic poseurs and the diner-wannabes.

Diners are good for sitting down, too, taking a temporary load off your feet, staying warm in winter, cool in summer, and ending a relationship that just isn't working out. Because they're public places where, no matter what the hour, there are always some other customers present. Thus they exert a restraining influence on any ugly post-breakup scenes that might otherwise occur.

That's the theory, anyway.

Breaking up, like the song says, is hard to do. No matter how careful the party-of-the-first-part—aka the Dumper—is about trying to soften the blow for the party-of-the-second-part—aka the Dumpee—it's never easy. There's something about an impending breakup that announces itself long before the Dumper broaches the subject. It hangs on the air between both parties involved, like the presence of a very old egg on a very hot day. All attempts at gradually leading into the subject are in vain: Sometimes it's best to get it said and get it over with. Otherwise, the longer you wait, the more awkward it becomes.

Tee and Jay sat in a booth at the Empire Diner, feeling the weight of that awkward silence. Business was brisk, the place was crowded, and there was the customary clatter and hubbub of harried waitstaff and clamoring customers, but there was a dead zone for sound entrenched around the partners. Two cups of coffee and two servings of pie lay on the table between them. Tee was eating, trying to act as if everything were normal when he knew full well it was not.

"Good pie," he said, trying to kindle a little conversation.

"Yeah," Jay replied, and left it there.

"Crowded," Tee remarked, glancing around the diner as he made a second attempt at banishing the silence. He knew what it held, what was coming, and even if it was inevitable, he was bound and determined to do anything he could to put it off just a little longer.

"Yeah," Jay said. "They have good pie."

Tee burst into tears.

"What the hell are you doing?" Jay demanded. He looked around sharply, feeling his cheeks go hot with embarrassment. With his luck, this would be the one time and place in all of New York City history where everyone in the immediate vicinity of an Incident decided that yes, it *was* their business. "What's wrong with you?"

Tee sniffled and sobbed: "You're gonna neuralyze me."

"No, I'm not," Jay said, trying to placate him, desperate to get a lid on things.

"Yes, you are," Tee insisted, his voice dripping with despair. "You brought me to a public place so I wouldn't make a scene."

"You *are* making a scene." Annoyed by how well Tee had called his shot, Jay leaned in across the table and softly inquired, "Let me ask you something. Why did you join MIB?"

Tee shook off the weepies and straightened up, looking like his old, gung-ho self. "Six years in the marines," he said. "Like to serve. Like the action. Protect the planet."

"Like being a hero," Jay concluded.

Tee shrugged. It was the closest he dared to come to saying *Well, duh!* to his partner's face.

"Then you joined the wrong organization. You ever heard of James Edwards?" His own given name sounded unfamiliar to Jay's ears, even as he said it. He knew he was the last person on Earth who remembered it, or the man who'd once answered to it, and it left him with a weird, off-kilter feeling in the pit of his stomach. "He saved eighty-five people on the subway tonight and nobody even knows he exists. And if no one knows he exists, no one can ever love him." Another pang hit; it was all Jay could do to suppress it.

"No one," he repeated. "Think about that."

Tee nodded, apparently mollified, and composed himself once more. Then a rogue tear slipped out of the corner of his eye and he blurted out: "Who cares about love?"

That was too much, even for New Yorkers. Half the diners turned to look. Jay rolled his eyes. He knew what they were thinking: *Not that there's anything* wrong *with that.* This *was* Chelsea.

"Tee, how long have we been partners?" he asked, trying to move things along, get this ugly business over and done with.

"Since Feb. one, this year," the big man replied.

"So, five months and three days . . ." Under the table, Jay's hands were adjusting the settings on his neuralyzer, adjusting the force of the flash to cover the proper period of time, readying it for what had to come.

"You're thinking maybe I'm not cut out for this," Tee said, his voice beginning to rise. "Thinking maybe I'm too weak. Thinking maybe I'm—"

"—too human." Jay said it for him, not unkindly.

"Oh God!" Tee wailed. "You're getting rid of me! It's over!"

He blew his nose mightily into a napkin just as one of the waiters, no longer able to maintain his distance, came up to the table and told him, "Been there. Hated it. Survived. Three words: Work-it-out. Love the suits." Having done his part for the ranks of amateur Dear Abbys everywhere, he left just as Jay, no longer able to hang on to the tiniest hope of keeping this breakup low-key, pulled out his neuralyzer and gave Tee the full for-your-eyes-only flash.

Tee stared straight ahead in the afterdazzle, seeing nothing. Jay plucked a fresh paper napkin from the tabletop holder, wiped his mouth, and stood up.

"Get married," he told Tee. "Have a bunch of kids."

"Okay," Tee agreed happily.

As Jay was on his way out, he spotted a very pretty waitress. "My friend thinks you're really hot," he told her, nodding back to where Tee sat poleaxed. What the heck, it was just plausible enough to work; some people mistook that semistunned expression for the look of love. "He'll take the check."

Jay ducked out, leaving Tee to resume life in a world where the MIB meant nothing, not even as a rumor, not even as part of a really bad dream.

FIVE

Scrad's apartment was a dump. There was no other way to describe it. It wasn't just the fact that it was a total loss when held up to Gotham Realty's Holy Grail of *location, location, location,* or that all the self-respecting rats had moved out under protest because the cockroaches had organized themselves into gangs and muscled in on their territory, or that it was so scuzzy you couldn't even convince a performance artist to live there: It was quite literally a *dump*.

Trash, like the rest of the physical universe, obeys the laws of gravity. Like calls to like, and birds of a feather flock together. Only in the case of Scrad's apartment, the birds were piles and piles of pop-culture doodads, relics, talismans, and thingamabobs, plus the magazines and catalogs that sold them.

Toys from kid's meals cluttered the floor beside the computer, Chia Pets gathered dust on the windowsill, sets of commemorative plates were stacked under an avalanche of Beanie Babies that also concealed the controls for a brandnew video game system. Television sets of assorted sizes were everywhere, either as fail-safe measures for those occasions when the services of a VCR were insufficient, or to provide confirmation that there were indeed umpty-ump video channels available, and nothing good on any of them.

The old model Frigidaire refrigerator—which had a small television set on top of it, a larger one wall-mounted above it, and a third one standing by on the counter—was apparently held together with magnets and bumper stickers. The latter proclaimed love of New York, another car that was really a skateboard, and some unknown person's child being an Honor Student.

Some of the items were costly, many were cheap, all of them merged into a mind-numbing hymn to high tech and low taste. Lots of Americans could rightfully admit to having bought a Pet Rock or an eight-track tape player or a beer hat, once, back in their experimental days, perhaps in college. Then they had stopped. Scrad had not. The evidence was overwhelming.

It wasn't the sort of place to come home to, unless you found comfort in staring at wall and kitchen cabinetry the greenish yellow color of what a good cat that's had a bad meal does all over your carpet. But Scrad wasn't your typical New Yorker. Far from it.

Still, when the front door, that portal to the Lost Graveyard of Terminal Tackiness, opened to admit its lord and master carrying a large bag of Burger King delicacies, he did exhibit a behavior familiar to many of his fellow Manhattanites.

He started screaming—at no one.

"Shut up, Charlie!" Scrad railed, stomping across the floor to the refrigerator, his backpack jouncing with every step. "I'm tired of you constantly talking behind my back."

Ducking his scruffy head to peer into the mildew-scented depths, he announced, "Only one beer."

"What about me?" someone asked, though there was no one else to be seen in the cramped and cluttered apartment; no one at all.

"Shut up," Scrad replied, as if disembodied voices were old hat to him. "I'll share."

"Forget it," the voice said, sounding disgusted. "I know where your mouth's been."

"Fine. See if I care." Scrad shut the refrigerator door, beer bottle in hand. "Have it your wa—*hey!*" The beer bottle dropped from his hand and smashed to pieces on the floor.

Serleena met his eyes with a look that spoke volumes, none of them containing a happy ending for the seedy little lowlife.

She was wearing an outfit of her own devising, a sexy but sinister ensemble confected from the leather coat her would-be assailant from Central Park no longer needed.

"Who—who are you?" Scrad stammered, trembling to the roots of his five o'clock shadow. "How'd you get in here?"

The backpack behind him flew open and a second head, identical to his own, except smaller, popped up like a randy jack-in-the-box. "Hel-*lo*, nurse! Any interest in a ménage à trois?" Charlie asked with a big-toothed, lascivious leer.

Serleena wasn't in a mood to waste words. Her hands sprouted clusters of neural roots that whipped themselves around Scrad's and Charlie's necks, and *squeezed*.

"K-kinky," Charlie gasped. He didn't sound entirely displeased.

The light of recognition dawned in Scrad's eyes as the oxygen left his brain. "Y-you're Ser-leena!" he said, struggling to get the words out before everything went black. "Why . . . didn't . . . you say . . . it was you?"

The roots retracted without warning, letting Scrad and Charlie drop unceremoniously to the floor. Ignoring them, Serleena surveyed the apartment slowly, condescension giving way to scorn and finally to full-blown contempt for the accumulated Earth paraphernalia.

"High-definition TV . . . Internet . . . PlayStation Two," she said, enumerating Scrad and Charlie's most expensive investments. "*People* magazine . . ." She snatched up another magazine from the many scattered piles of slick-paged periodicals and thrust it at them like a dog owner might rub his pet's nose in its own housebreaking faux pas. *"Entertainment Weekly?"* she exclaimed, forcing them to gaze into the glossy faces of Brad Pitt and Ed Norton.

Scrad and Charlie hung their heads in shame.

"Is *this* how you do your job?" she continued. "I hired you for a mission and you go Earthling on me? You go *native*?"

"We *hate* Earth," Scrad said, trying to sound sincere.

Charlie's head bobbed up behind Scrad's, eager to be his backup and save both their necks. "We're just trying to fit in," he wheedled.

Serleena closed in on her unsatisfactory hirelings, towering over them. "You have the information?" she asked in a tone capable of turning the Sahara Desert into a winter wonderland.

"In-information?" Scrad knew enough of Earth culture to have heard of the Pearly Gates. At that moment, he could almost see them opening wide to greet him. No sense waiting until the last minute, after all. He was going to die; he knew it. He only hoped it wouldn't hurt too much. Then he did a reality check and resigned himself to the bitter truth: This was Serleena. His death would hurt. A lot.

"I sent you an interstellar fax," the lady said. She sounded astoundingly patient.

Charlie decided it was his turn to try to save their collective bacon. "Oh, a *fax*," he said, as if that explained it all. As if everything was just one great, big, silly misunderstanding, and they would all get together later and laugh about it over a couple of rounds of beer. "Well, *there* you go. *That's* it: Toner cartridge went bad. *You* try to find a replacement for a Kylothian Z-Eleven fax machine on a backwater world like—"

"Yes, or no?" she interrupted. Roots shot out of her fingers, burying themselves deep in their ears. Scrad and Charlie screamed in agony, singly and in chorus, until it was even money whether their heads would explode before one of them could blurt out the information Serleena was after.

"We couldn't find the Light!" Scrad howled as fast as he could get the words out of his mouth. "We couldn't find it, but we tracked it to a guy who might know where it is. Runs a pizza parlor on Spring Street. *Ahhhhhhhh!*"

As abruptly as they had invaded Scrad's and Charlie's ears, the neural roots retracted, just as the two-headed alien's shriek reached a crescendo. Serleena only spared a moment to examine her flawlessly manicured nails for possible chips before commanding, "Take me there." Then she strode out of the apartment, grabbing the Burger King bag as she went.

Moving with the clumsy wariness of beings who have just endured unspeakable pain, Scrad/Charlie got to their feet and drew a few tentative breaths.

The holiday was over.

Charlie cast a longing look at the television set. "We're gonna miss *Friends*," he lamented.

"Shut up," Scrad said, heading for the door. He knew better than to keep Serleena waiting, no matter how much he'd miss keeping up with the madcap antics of Ross, Rachel, and his particular favorite, Phoebe. She seemed like the kind of girl who'd be willing to overlook his little . . . dating handicap.

He was almost out the door when he stopped short, dashed back to the set, and hit a button. "TiVo!" he said in contented relief.

"Beauty, Scrad," said Charlie as they dashed out the door. "We da man."

It was a solemn occasion, as most unveilings tend to be, even if it was taking place inside a cozy little neighborhood pizza joint deep in the heart of Soho. It looked like many other such mom-and-pop enterprises: a big pass-through window from the kitchen to the dining area; rustic wooden signs boasting PIZZA and CALZONE; a touch of wood paneling here, a hint of fake brick veneer there; some framed photos of unknown significance to anyone but the person who'd first hung them. Utilitarian chairs and Formica-topped tables for the benefit of those patrons who opted to eat in rather than take out. A vintage pressed-tin ceiling and large black and white linoleum tiles in a checkerboard pattern on the floor.

The kitchen itself was a model of cleanliness, pans

gleaming, huge pots for cooking unimaginable quantities of pasta nicely scoured and ready for action. And wafting over everything, like a warm, thick, comforting blanket, was the rich, tomatoey, yeasty, mozzarella-Parmesan-sausage-oregano aroma of really, *really* good Italian food.

It was known as Ben's Famous Pizza, though *famous* was a relative term at best. It was famous enough to stay in business, and wasn't that all that really mattered? Ben thought so. He was a fairly nondescript, middle-aged man, going a little larger around the middle, a little thinner on top. He proudly wore a spanking-clean white apron over his slacks and a lime-green shirt that bore his eatery's logo. And why not? He *was* proud of his place, and proud of himself for being yet another New York immigrant who had come to the Big Apple and made good.

He beamed as he contemplated the dedicatory plaque on the wall, still covered with a piece of fabric, awaiting the big moment. It wasn't every pizzeria that could sponsor such an event. By rights there should have been a flourish of trumpets to herald the removal of the cloth, but these things cost money, and so . . .

"Ta-*daaaah!*" said Ben, whisking away the cloth. And there on the wall, in all its glory, hung the photograph of a very pretty young woman with the engraved plate beneath reading:

BEN'S FAMOUS PIZZA
EMPLOYE OF THE MONTH
LAURA VASQUEZ

At his elbow, the girl from the photograph smiled out of the simple pleasure of being appreciated by her boss.

She had large, luminous eyes almost as dark a brown as her hair, a full, expressive mouth, and a face whose soulful beauty had the power to make casual customers spontaneously remember whole pages out of that Shakespeare play—*Romeo and Juliet*—even though they'd slept through it in eighth-grade English class.

Of course, if anyone had tried telling her she was that lovely, she'd have laughed in a friendly way, taken his order, and forgotten all about it.

"Hey, people will look at the plaque for years to come and you know what they'll say?" Ben asked.

"That *employee* is spelled wrong?" Laura countered.

"They charge by the letter." Ben spread his hands. "Nah, they'll say, *Imagine that. A big shot like her used to work here.* That's what they'll say."

"Oh, Ben . . ." Laura gave him a quick peck on the cheek, truly touched by his pride.

He shrugged it away. "No biggie. You deserve it. Now bring up a case of Mountain Dew from the basement, would ya?" He went back to his work and left her to her own.

Laura gazed at the misspelled plaque a moment more and heaved a theatrical sigh. "Fame is fleeting," she declaimed, and went outside to get the soda.

The little storage elevator that they used to move the cases of soft drinks, the cans of crushed tomatoes, the sacks of flour, and all the other staples necessary to the running of Ben's Famous Pizza came up in the alley just behind the restaurant. Laura wrangled the two cases of Mountain Dew off the lift with the ease born of having done the same task countless times before. An unexpected noise behind her made her jump just a little—it was always kind of creepy, working alone in the alley—but when she turned to see what it was, she recognized one of the familiar cats that haunted the neighborhood.

"Hey, Bruno," she called to him softly, but he bounded away. A night seldom went by without her asking Ben for a plate of scraps to put out for Bruno and the other strays. Ben invariably found something to spare for the cats whenever Laura asked him—he claimed he never could refuse her anything—but just because he was so generous, she always made it a point to get his approval before putting out the dishes full of leftovers. To do otherwise would be taking advantage, and that wasn't her style.

She toted the sodas into the back of the pizzeria and was about to call out to Ben when she heard the sound of voices, arguing violently from the front of the store. Quietly she closed the alley door behind her and stole up to the kitchen door. Using extreme caution, she eased it open just a crack and peered through.

What she saw sent her heart plummeting into her stomach and left her mouth sour and dry. Two strangers— one a grungy, vile-looking man with a backpack, the other an impossibly beautiful woman—had Ben cornered and were holding him off the ground with one hand under his chin. They worked with the skill and efficiency of a pair of experienced strong-arm men.

"Where is it, 'Ben'?" the woman was saying, pronouncing the pizzeria owner's name with a sarcastic sneer.

"I don't know what you're talking about," Laura's boss replied as he dangled in the air. She squeezed his face in and lifted him higher. He groaned softly.

Part of Laura's mind rejected the whole picture—it was just too bizarre—but another part of her consciousness said *What difference does weird make? This is New York. Don't just stand there, you moron!* and propelled her hand straight for the wall phone to summon help.

Dialing 911, Laura spoke urgently, sotto voce: "Hello? I want to report a robbery at—"

A sudden metallic squeak behind her yanked her attention away from the phone. She turned in time to see the back door swinging open on its unoiled hinges, blown by a sudden gust of warm summer wind. It bounced hard against the wall with a *bang* loud enough to make her jump.

And if it was loud enough to do that . . .

Laura didn't need to peek back into the kitchen to know what was going on. Those two nasties who were beating up on Ben had heard the door—they must have. The little creep might have let it go, but that woman . . .

Laura shivered. No. No way that *she* would ever let anything slip past her. There was something cold about her, cold as a snake's eyes. She wasn't the sort to overlook anything, let alone dismiss a suspicious noise. Either she'd check it out herself or she'd send her accomplice to do it.

Laura didn't wait to find out which it was going to be. She hung up the phone fast, and dived for the safety of the storage cabinet under the sink just a heartbeat before the kitchen door opened and Scrad shuffled in.

He looked around the back room while Laura cowered in her hiding place. She'd left the cabinet open just a hair—there was no way she could endure being closeted in total darkness, not knowing what was happening outside. The tension would have driven her insane. So she spied on the repulsive little man through the barely open cabinet door, holding her breath and praying he was as stupid as he looked—that he wouldn't think to search for her once he saw the back door still swinging back and forth in the breeze on its creaky hinges.

Nobody here, she thought at him urgently, wishing she had the power to make her thoughts seep into his skull. It looked so easy when Mr. Spock did that Vulcan mind-meld thing on *Star Trek*! But that was TV; this was real. *Nothing to see, no one made that noise, it was only the wind. Now go away! Please, please, please, go away!*

She almost relaxed completely when she saw him go to the back door and close it. Then she heard the woman's voice calling from the kitchen:

"You idiots see anything?"

"The wind blew the door open!" the little man yelled back.

And then, with all the casual horror of the best nightmares, the backpack opened and another head popped out to add: "Nothing outta the ordinary."

Laura was gaping like a beached fish as the two-headed creature returned to the kitchen, first one head and then the other looking behind him to give the back room one last check for anything suspicious. As soon as they were gone, she forced herself to calm down, get a grip, and crawl out from under the sink. Peeking through the kitchen door once more, she heard them all talking.

"For twenty-five years I've traveled the universe looking for it," the beautiful woman was saying. "But it never left Earth, did it, 'Ben'?" Again she pronounced the pizzeria owner's name in a voice dripping with sarcasm. "You kept it here."

"What are you talking about?" Ben replied. There was only a little tremor in his voice.

"I'm running out of time. Where is it? Where is the Light of Zartha?"

"I—I swear I don't know what you're—"

The woman placed one finger on Ben's forehead. Even from so far away, glimpsing the whole scene through such a narrow opening, Laura could see that it wasn't a human finger. It looked . . . twisted. Like a miniature tree root, green as the moss on an ancient oak. No, not human at all.

"While you hid here like a coward, we've been preparing to invade your planet," the woman was telling Ben. Sarcasm had given place to gloating. "Once I have the Light, Zartha will be ours."

"You're too late." Despite the pain he must be feeling and the fate that no doubt awaited him, Ben was defiant. "Tomorrow the Light will leave the Third Planet and be back home . . . and you'll wish you'd never started any of this."

"I didn't come all this way to leave empty-handed," the woman snarled. As casually as if she were slitting an envelope, she yanked her rootlike finger straight down Ben's forehead, his face, the rest of him, ripping him open the way an angler guts a fish. She was, in her own sick, twisted, and casually sadistic way, an artist: She had bisected him perfectly.

The pizzeria owner's humanoid skin dropped in a heap at his feet, looking as if someone had taken a gigantic buzz saw or laser beam to one of the character balloons in the Macy's Thanksgiving Day parade. His forcibly discarded shell was reduced to a pair of deflated halves, slumped across the checkerboard tiles as Ben's true shape stood revealed for all the world to see.

Behind the kitchen door, Laura never even had the

chance to gasp as her transformed boss gave the woman one last, brave look and said, "Sorry you made the trip for nothing," before exploding into a thousand twinkling, phosphorescent pieces. The shards of his destruction fluttered down with the tranquil loveliness of a gentle snowfall.

The head sticking out of the backpack clicked its tongue. "Got nothing out of him," it said. "Too bad. Now we don't know if it's on Earth or not."

"Weren't you listening? He said *Third Planet*," the woman gritted. "It's here, you idiot!"

"Third Rock from the Sun," the backpack wearer whispered helpfully to his second head.

"Ohhh." The head in the backpack nodded, then whispered back: "I never got that till now."

"It's on Earth," the woman said, looking grim and determined. "It's on Earth, and I know who will tell me where it is." She stormed out of the pizzeria kitchen, grabbing a fresh pizza pie as she left. The two-headed creature tagged obediently after.

In the back room, Laura sat with her knees pulled up to her chest, too stunned and terror-stricken to do more than hug herself, and shake, and murmur, "Oh my God, oh my God, oh my God," while the tears streamed down her face.

Outside, in a world that was still sane, thunder boomed and it began to rain.

SIX

At the very foot of Manhattan Island, just at the point where the city dangles its big toe in the waters of the bay, sits a little patch of trees and grass called Battery Park. It was the site of a Dutch fort established in 1624, perhaps in case the Native Americans from whom they'd bought the island reconsidered the deal, and it derives its name from the battery of British cannons that occupied the site in the seventeenth century.

Subsequently known as Castle Clinton, its strategic defense location provided reason enough for the young United States of America to choose this place to build the West Battery Fort there in 1811, for the protection of New York Harbor. As it turned out, this was just in time for the site to serve as U.S. Army headquarters during the War of 1812, a fine example of Planning Ahead by Sheer Dumb Luck.

Today the big guns are ghosts, and the fort hasn't fulfilled a military function for ages. From here, you can no longer defend New York against British invasion, but you *can* catch a ferry to Staten Island, if that's your pleasure, or a different one that will take you out to see the Statue of Liberty. The guns are gone, but their heritage remains:

This is the place where it all began, the digit of land where the Dutch got their toehold and the English shoved their foot in the door.

It's a small piece of ground crammed full of a whole lot of history, with more being made on a daily basis. If you were to take a good-sized slingshot in your hands and you decided to stand on top of that austere, monolithic white building just across the road from the park—the one that's clearly marked INTERBOROUGH BRIDGE AND TUNNEL AUTHORITY—and if, from that vantage point, you started firing off stones in all directions, you could hit City Hall, the Financial District, the old Customs House, the Holocaust Museum, Fraunces Tavern, and Ellis Island, to say nothing of Lady Liberty herself.

Of course, it would have to be a damn *powerful* slingshot.

On the other hand, if you just let one of those stones drop from your hand to the roof of that monumental yet unimpressive building where you were standing, you'd hit something a lot more interesting than all of the above sites combined.

Not that it would ever be a good idea to attack the headquarters of the MIB, whether or not you had the stones to do it.

Its presence wasn't noted in any of the guidebooks. As far as the tourists knew, the big white building was exactly as advertised: home of the Interborough Bridge and Tunnel Authority, an establishment as necessary as it was boring.

That was the point. *Boring* doesn't attract snoops. *Boring* works like a charm for keeping people at a distance. In New York City, where nothing draws a crowd faster than

signs reading KEEP OUT, or POLICE LINE: DO NOT CROSS, or
NO ACCESS, it takes only a hint of PAPER PUSHERS AT WORK
to make folks head for the hills.

So the Interborough Bridge and Tunnel Authority building stood unremarked and unremarkable. Only those with
a need to know were privy to its secrets. The guns of Battery Park might be silent, but cross the road and you'd find
that this site was still a good place to ward off invasions,
after all.

The best thing about serving as a security guard at MIB
Headquarters was, well, *security.* Job security. Like any
efficiency-obsessed agency, the MIB wasn't all that keen
on making any more changes than needed to be made. If
you got rid of the old-timers, you lost valuable man-hours
training the incoming newbies. If it ain't broke, don't fix it.
Don't rock the boat. Don't make waves. Et cetera.

All of which left the old security guard sitting pretty. As
long as he did his job well enough to get by, no one was
going to take it away from him.

He liked knowing he was more or less a fixture, like the
stylized depiction of an atom with its circling electrons
that was embedded in the smooth stone floor, and the two
colossal ventilation fans flanking the entryway where he
manned his post. They gave him a certain sense of smug-
ness, entitlement, and none of these hotshot young whip-
persnappers in their fancy-dancy black suits was going to
ruffle his feathers.

So when Agent Jay marched past him, en route to the
elevator, the guard didn't even bother looking up from his
newspaper to ask, "Don't you ever go home?"

"You the hall monitor?" Jay countered a little testily.

The guard shook his paper a bit to straighten out the pages. "Wouldn't be so cranky if you got eight hours," he opined. Jay ignored him and got into the elevator.

The elevator, like everything else in MIB Headquarters, was running smoothly. It dropped below the surface of the city with barely a whisper of sound to indicate that it was moving at all. When it came to a stop, the stainless-steel doors opened onto a scene so familiar to Agent Jay that when he did close his eyes in sleep, it sometimes ghosted through his dreams.

The place was the size of an airplane hangar or a gigantic soundstage, huge, high-ceilinged, and cavernous. Honeycomb-patterned steel girders arched overhead, and towering white pillars rose up like the trunks of giant redwoods. Glass lined the walls, whether it was the vaulted curve of frosted panels letting in muted light from some undisclosed source, or the more prosaic, but no less impressive, straight-up-and-down windows opposite where he stood. They were at least two stories tall, and behind them lay the many offices, laboratories, armories, and other necessary rooms serving the Men in Black. A catwalk ran the length of the frosted-glass side and cut across the hall at several points. The ceiling was liberally pierced with huge, round openings holding recessed lighting. They looked for all the world like a fleet of flying saucers coming in for a landing.

One section of the big room was thronged with fresh off-world arrivals and the mostly human MIB personnel who had to process them before they could take up their new, discreet lives among unsuspecting Earthlings. Everything gleamed in shades of white and silver and gray; every piece of furniture was a tribute to that slick, streamlined,

"modern" school of interior design that had flourished in
the 1950s, come back with a vengeance in certain fast-
food restaurants, and lingered on in any number of airport
waiting areas. There were very few sharp edges, and absolutely no rough ones.

Chairs were of white plastic, molded to fit the con-
tours of most human bodies. It kind of made you stop
and wonder *what* in the name of heaven the MIB
purchasing-and-design group had been thinking when
they furnished the place: Those seats were definitely not
going to accommodate the anatomy of many of the incoming aliens with any degree of comfort. Come to think
of it, Jay mused, those chairs seldom accommodated Earthlings comfortably.

Maybe that was the whole point: This wasn't a destination but a way station, a place to pass through as quickly as
possible. No sense in furnishing it so anyone had a chance
to get comfortable or settle down. The best, most efficient
thing you could do with a transient population was *keep* it
transient.

Everyone moved with a purpose, their energy directed
to their individual tasks. Customs officials stood behind
long counters, checking passports, work permits, health
records, miscellaneous forms of identification, and all the
niggling paperwork any efficient organization demands.
They did their best to move things along quickly without
sacrificing vigilance or provoking some of the toothier,
more peevish species of incoming extraterrestrials.

On the other side of the hall, row after rectilinear row of
desk jockeys working in their impeccably white shirt-
sleeves did their bit to keep the problems of intergalactic
refugees to a minimum. Important-looking people made

important-sounding noises as they bustled into and out of the glass-walled rooms lining the whole area. Sometimes the presence of a white lab coat would stand out from the crowds of omnipresent black suits, but not too often.

The entire hall was dominated by the presence of the Egg Screen, a colossal white ovoid that looked as if it might have been laid by a *Tyrannosaurus rex*, but not without giving Mama some especially intense and vehement second thoughts about the Joys of Motherhood on the way out. Word in the ranks had it that the huge viewing and information display device had originally been the CRT from some incoming refugee alien's PC, only the previous owner had dumped it when he bought himself a shiny new PalmPilot. No one knew what had become of the mouse. There are some things that Humankind is better off not knowing.

There was a lot happening at Men in Black Headquarters; there always was, and no one was fool enough to suppose that the pace would ever slacken, or the demands of the job would ever let up. It was busy enough when things were going according to the rules, but that—to quote a favorite managerial catchphrase—was subject to change without notice.

Jay's route took him past several other MIB agents. "Bee, Dee," he said, addressing a pair who were standing next to one of the many aliens in the hall. "Next time you use a fission carbonizer, put a subatomic molecular de-atomizer on the barrel so it doesn't sound like a cannon going off."

Bee and Dee nodded, Dee from his place next to the alien, Bee from the ceiling, where he stood upside down. It wasn't street-normal, but inside headquarters it wasn't something worth even a passing comment.

Jay strode past another pair of agents. "Double-check his visa," he directed, nodding back at the alien with Bee and Dee. "Cephalopods have been making counterfeits at a Kinko's on Canal."

His route became momentarily blocked by a third team of agents pushing a gurney across the floor. It was laden with the gigantic body of a stone-cold dead alien. Whatever had brought the unlucky extraterrestrial to the shores of Earth, it was no longer important; dealing with the body was. Large and rubbery, the alien's corpse was one of those anatomical fusions that put some folks in mind of a squid, others of a spider, yet others of a wad of much-abused chewing gum. It was not only bigger than a breadbox, it was larger than most single-family homes.

Its tentacles sagged limply, and whatever purposes its many orifices had served in life, they were now sealed, still, and useless in death. The gurney must have had modified antigrav devices installed, or at least one hell of a suspension system, because the agents wrangling it weren't even breaking a sweat.

Jay gave the whole shebang the once-over and made a face.

"And could *somebody* please tell me who had the bright idea of bringing a dead Tricrainasloph through Passport Control?" he demanded in the same way another man might want to know why the hell there were never any doughnuts left in the coffee room, except those disgusting ones with the coconut?

More MIB agents came past, wheeling a high-tech light cage. Behind the glowing bars stood an old man. He didn't look dangerous, though he was about eight feet tall, and all experienced members of the Men in Black knew that looks didn't matter.

"Jarra," Jay greeted him. "Long time."

"Five years and forty-two days, thanks to you," the ancient hissed. "You count every one when you're locked away like a primate."

"Shouldn't have been siphoning off our ozone to sell on the black market," Jay reminded him.

"Tanning is silly anyway," Jarra countered. "Why does everyone want to be brown?" His eyes dwindled to slits of suspicion. Like most malefactors, he was convinced that the rest of the universe was as untrustworthy as himself. "Maybe I've said too much," he concluded.

"What's he doing here?" Jay asked one of Jarra's attendant agents.

"We're moving him to supermax," the man replied. He was young, a real rookie. "He hasn't been playing well with his fellow inmates. Killed two plasma beetles from Andromeda."

"*Killed* is such an ugly word," Jarra said, with a smile ugly enough to match it.

Jay ignored the prisoner. He made it to Zed's office without any further interruptions. Zed was at his desk when Jay came in. The older man looked up, his craggy, trimly bearded face revealing nothing. He looked to be pushing the far side of fifty, but was still in fighting shape. He was one of those men for whom *in the line of duty* wasn't just a catchphrase or a movie title. He had paid his dues, but saw no reason to demand a receipt.

"Good work in the subway, Jay," he said. "I remember

Jeff when he was only yea big." He held his hand out flat
about a foot above floor level.

"Sewage does a body good," Jay replied. "What else do
you have for me?" He looked ready and eager to take off
on his next assignment, like a runner at the starting blocks.

Zed studied the younger man and spoke slowly, forcing
Jay to rein himself in and pay attention. "Look out that
window," he said, indicating a fine view of the bustling
main hall through the glass walls of his office. "See all
the guys in black suits? They work here, too. We've got it
covered."

"Zed—" Jay began.

The head of the MIB cut him off. "Listen, friend, dedi-
cation's one thing, but if you let it, this job'll eat you up
whole and spit you out after. You wanna look like me when
you hit fifty—"

He caught Jay giving him a skeptical look, one that
forced Zed to recall that he had enough facial sags and
wrinkles to outfit an entire hunting pack of bloodhounds.
For him, fifty years old on the button was just a memory.

"—ish?" he conceded.

Jay's mouth tightened. "With all due respect, Zed, I
don't want a lecture; I want to do my job. You want to play
games with me about this, fine. You're the boss. Knock
yourself out. If you need me, I'll be in the gym." He turned
to go.

Zed had the look of a man who knew when he was
preaching to an empty church. He couldn't force a man to
slow down, grab some perspective, and take care of himself. He probably figured, if Jay was going to wear himself
out, drive himself past the limit, then the agency might as
well get some use out of him while there was still time. He

was one of the best agents the MIB had to offer, especially since Kay had left the service.

Zed sighed. Too bad it had to be like this. Too bad that the ones who burned the hottest and the brightest were also the ones who burned themselves right out.

"We had a killing earlier," Zed said. He didn't need to raise his voice; Jay stopped cold. "One-seventy-seven Spring. Alien on alien. Take Tee with you and file a report."

"Tee," Jay repeated. He bit his lip. "Uhhhh . . ." He knew it wasn't going to be a picnic telling his boss that he'd given Tee compulsory retirement, a free neuralyzer treatment, and an attractive waitress in lieu of a gold watch. Zed might not see it as a necessary downsizing for the good of the company. Zed might even get mad. When your job was all you had in your life, you didn't want to get the boss-man mad. Not *too* mad, anyway. He was still stalling when Frank came in.

Frank was one of MIB's alien employees. He was also a pug dog, or at least that was the form he'd adopted to make his stay on Earth more comfortable. He was cute as a button and had the manners of a dock walloper. His toenails clicked across the highly buffed floor of Zed's office as he trotted in, carrying a file folder in his mouth.

Dropping it into an empty chair, he said, "Passports. No rush." He looked up at Jay and gave him a big, tongue-lolling grin. "How they hangin', Jay?"

Jay didn't get a chance to answer. His stalling was all for nothing: Zed already knew. Zed *always* knew.

"You are not authorized to neuralyze MIB personnel," he told Jay. "Period."

"Aw, come *on*," Jay pleaded. "The man was crying in a *diner*!"

"I hate that," Frank put in, trying to bond. It was a good thing the pug's nose was already as brown as it was going to get.

"Anyway, I can handle this job alone," Jay continued. "I don't need a partner."

"You need a partner," Zed said.

"I'll be his partner!" Frank volunteered, his curly tail wagging.

Zed looked at Frank, then at Jay. Jay shook his head, denying the oncoming, unspeakable thing that Zed was about to do to him, trying to ward off the inevitable. This was exactly the sort of thing that happened to you when you pissed off the boss. For an instant Jay's eyes begged Zed, *No! Please, no! Aw,* c'mon, *man, don't* do *this to me!*

But he knew it was no use, and so he assumed the expression of a condemned man who had been told that yes, there *was* word from the governor. Unfortunately, that word was:

Bye-ee.

It wasn't a happy partnership from the get-go.

To start with, there was the way Frank chose to present himself for his new assignment, meeting up with Jay down in the MIB Impound. Jay tried to ignore it at first, fixing his gaze on the long row of black Ford LTDs, lined up and ready for action. The electronic device on his key chain summoned his ride, a gleaming midnight Mercedes-Benz E500. The car responded to the *chirp-chirp* of the key ring like a faithful dog.

The only problem was that Frank, disguised *as* a faithful dog, had shown up wearing his own miniature version of the full MIB uniform: jacket, shirt, and tie, pug-sized, though pants were out of the question. Jay had the sinking feeling that the little pug had also stashed a pair of teeny-tiny Ray-Bans somewhere on his person. A pug in Ray-Bans was right at the top of Jay's list of Mental Images I Do *Not* Need. It wasn't professional jealousy or prejudice against covert aliens: He thought those sad and sorry photographs of big dogs dressed up in people clothes were as twisted as a weasel's gut, too.

" 'Preciate the shot, man," Frank told Jay. "Never thought I was gonna get outta the mailroom."

Jay didn't even spare him a second glance. "Lose the suit," he said.

Frank did as he was told, but that wasn't the end of it. In the car, zooming through the streets of Soho with Jay at the wheel, the little alien rode with his head sticking out the passenger's-side window, tongue flapping in the breeze. To add insult to injury, he was singing "I Will Survive." If disco wasn't dead already, Frank was sure as hell going to kill it. Doggie spittle flew everywhere.

Everywhere included the lapel of Jay's jacket. He was *not* happy.

"Nice," he commented bitterly, hands on the wheel. "Slobber flying all over the— *Get* your damn head in!"

"Sure thing, partner," Frank said, affably. "But remember: You're the one who said you wanted me to act like a real dog."

"I'll 'real dog' you," Jay grumbled. He floored the Mercedes all the way to the scene of the crime.

By the time they came to a screeching halt in front of Ben's Famous Pizza, several agents were already there ahead of them, dusting for fingerprints, scanning the room with magnetic imaging devices, trying to dope out what had happened.

Jay and his new, unwanted partner went up to the one agent who was busy making notes. "What do we got?" Frank asked him, taking the lead.

Jay glared at the pug. Realizing he'd spoken out of turn, the eager-to-please alien made a zipping-it-and-throwing-away-the-key gesture with one paw, and backed off.

"What do we got?" Jay asked the agent.

The agent pointed to the spot where Ben had gone all to pieces. "There's a phosphorous residue on the wall and floor. We've sent samples back to Em for analysis."

"Hey, Jay," Frank called. He nodded to where the discarded skin lay puddled on the floor. "Someone notify the infomercial people: zero percent body fat."

The note-taking agent laughed. Jay gave him a tight little frown. The man shrugged. "Hey, I thought it was funny."

"Witness?" Jay demanded, keeping things on track.

"Girl," the agent replied. "Saw everything."

He handed Jay one of the paper napkins emblazoned with the restaurant's logo. It was a pretty snazzy design, for a little hole-in-the-wall place like this: Above the point of a triangular slice of pizza stood the distant prospect of the Statue of Liberty, her torch held high, while a single star shone just above the tip of that eternal flame. It was all very "I ❤ New York" as well as "I ❤ to Eat Pizza," heart-*burn* be hanged. Jay figured that the proprietor must've hired some art student from Cooper Union to create it for him. Impressive.

Impressive, yeah, but his fellow agent hadn't passed him this scrap of paper for an impromptu graphic arts critique. Jay turned the napkin over and saw that the man had scrawled down a name: VASQUEZ. Always nice to go in to a witness interview knowing as much as possible.

The agent who had handed Jay the napkin indicated the back room. "She's actually taking it pretty well," he concluded.

Jay's eyes followed where the agent had pointed and caught sight of Agent Cee interrogating a very pretty young woman. He didn't yet know who she was, but he had a feeling he'd like to correct that oversight as soon as possible. Even without being introduced, he could tell that he and she had a lot in common: She, too, was definitely not happy with the way things were going tonight.

"No, *you* listen to *me*," she told Cee in no uncertain terms. He was a stocky guy with a brush-cut hairstyle flat enough to land Harrier jets on, so the whole effect of the girl giving him a hard time was a lot like watching a Yorkshire terrier trying to take down a rottweiler. "I don't answer any more of your questions until you answer mine. I want someone to tell me what happened here."

Jay tucked the napkin away in his pocket, just in case it might come in handy for future reference, and sighed. This wasn't the first time that a witness had started asserting the right to know. It was astonishing how people would buy and eat a hot dog off a pushcart, never once thinking to ask what had gone into it, whether it had an expiration date registered in this century, or how it had been stored and cooked for future dining pleasure. Yet those same people hollered the loudest that by God, they were entitled to full and complete disclosure of everything else that touched their lives.

Hadn't they ever heard that ignorance was bliss? Not just when it came to hot dogs, either.

It was the way they all reacted once you gave them what they asked for—told them the truth about what they'd seen—that made him thank his lucky stars for the neuralyzer.

"I'd better handle this," he said. He made eye contact with Frank and added, "Alone. The whole talking-dog thing might not be good for her right now."

"Whaddaya want me to do?" the pug asked.

"Sniff around."

He went into the back room. The agent taking notes laughed. Frank scowled at him.

The agent shrugged again. "Funny."

In the back room, Cee was doing his best to get Ms. Vasquez calmed down, trying to make her see reason. It was working about as well as trying to extinguish a volcano by having a mouse pee into the crater.

"Try taking a deep breath, ma'am," Cee said. "Everything's all right."

"No," she said strongly, very sure of this. "All right? No. Everything is *not* all right."

"Ma'am—"

"One." She held up a finger. "Who were those creatures who killed Ben? Two." A second finger joined the first. "What the hell did Ben turn into just before he died?"

"Three," Jay said, stepping into the conversation and confronting Cee. "What part of this is she supposed to feel all right about?"

"Yeah, what he said," Vasquez chimed in, welcoming her unexpected champion.

Jay motioned for Agent Cee to leave, then turned to introduce himself. "I'm Agent Jay," he said. "You are—?"

"—not crazy," she concluded. "Your pals are pretending they don't believe me, but I know they know I know what I saw." She lifted her chin defiantly, every inch the feisty New Yorker ready to defend her point of view—to the death.

Jay took over Cee's attempts at smoothing things over. "Okay, why don't you just relax, Mrs.—"

"Miss," Laura corrected him brusquely. "Vasquez. Laura Vasquez."

"Pretty name," Jay said. *Pretty girl,* he thought.

"Another calm guy," Laura observed, just a hint of irony in her voice.

Jay could tell there would be no distracting this witness, even with his smoothest moves. He decided to take the straightforward approach. "Why don't you just tell me what you saw."

"If I answer your questions, you answer mine," she said. *Take it or leave it,* her eyes added. Jay nodded; she relaxed just a little. "Okay. I saw a two-headed guy. And a woman in leather."

"Caucasian?"

"Gray. With tentacles coming out of her hands. And she—"

Laura stopped short, in midsentence, suddenly aware that Jay had his eyes locked on to hers. She made the logical assumption, that this man was staring at her the way a lot of people might stare at a raving lunatic, wondering what new bit of random madness was going to pop into the conversation, wondering if things were going to escalate into the more dangerous realm of violence. Her hackles rose and she went on the defensive.

"You think I'm crazy!" she accused him. "Fine. Have it your way. I'm crazy, so I *didn't* really see her—"

"—rip the skin off his body," Jay said evenly.

"—rip the skin off his body," Laura said. Then she did a double take that said, *Hey, if I am crazy, I'm not the only lunatic here.*

"Actually, it's not skin," the MIB agent continued. "It's a proto-plasma polymer similar in chemical makeup to the gum you find in baseball cards."

Laura raised one eyebrow. "This is something you run into a lot?"

"Never south of Twenty-third."

The eyebrow went up just a little higher. "Who are you?" she asked, never taking her eyes from his face. *"Really."*

Jay didn't miss a beat. "You like pie?"

SEVEN

It really *was* good pie. Good enough to bring Jay back to the same diner where he'd gone through that ugly, messy, embarrassing scene with Tee only a few hours earlier.

Yeah, damn good pie to be had at the Empire Diner, and the coffee wasn't so bad either. He alternated sips with bites while he listened to Laura Vasquez as she told her story.

"—a light," she was saying. "They kept asking Ben about a light. Light of Zartha. Something like that." Unlike Jay, she wasn't enjoying her pie. That was kind of tough to do with a hand shaking so badly that manipulating a fork became impossible.

Jay noticed. "You okay?"

"An hour ago a man I've known my whole life vanished right in front of my eyes," Laura said, struggling bravely to keep her voice from shaking almost as badly as her hand. "He was killed by a woman who had things coming out of her fingers, and her accomplice was a two-headed guy. What I saw doesn't exist." She didn't need to add, *Would you be okay with that? Would anyone? Even in New York?*

"Laura—" Jay began.

"When we were kids—before we were taught how to

think and what to believe—our hearts told us that there was something else out there," she said, choking out the words that needed to be said. Her glance drifted wistfully to the nighttime sky outside the diner window. "We stop believing, because we stop listening *here*." She touched her heart. "I know in my heart what I saw. *You* tell me what I'm supposed to believe." Her eyes searched his, begging for answers.

Jay did the only thing he could: He gave them to her.

"I'm a member of a secret organization that polices and monitors alien activity here on Earth. Ben was an alien and so were the people who killed him. I don't know why they did it, but I promise you, I'm going to find out."

Laura took in all of this in silence. Then she said: "Okay."

"Okay?" Jay repeated, dubious. *That's it? That's all?*

"I believe my eyes," she told him frankly. "And I believe yours."

"Oh. I mean . . . okay." He looked into her eyes a little longer, feeling deep within himself—his heart? his soul?—that he could go on looking into her eyes forever, and never grow tired of all the marvelous things to be discovered in that steady, radiant gaze. He wondered what would happen if he were to say a single word to her about these unbidden, undeniable feelings. Would she smile? Would she laugh at him? Or would she simply say . . . okay?

Slowly, reluctantly, he dragged himself back to reality, back to the business at hand. It was like he'd told his ex-partner Tee, when you worked for the Men in Black, no one could know you, no one could love you; all you had to know and to love was the job.

He took out his neuralyzer and got ready to do what must be done.

"Listen, Laura, I'm sorry, but I'm gonna have to—"

"—kill me," she finished his sentence the way she assumed it would have to go. She didn't sound afraid, just resigned.

"No," Jay said. He couldn't tell why, but suddenly it mattered to him a great deal that he set her mind at ease. Immediately. "This'll help you to forget, that's all. Little flash and everything will be back the way it was."

She was still looking at him, never taking her eyes away from his, only now they looked sad. "After you . . . flash me," she said softly. "After that, if I see you again, will I know it's you?"

"No." Jay felt his own throat tighten as he clicked the activation button. The red-tipped silver wand began to whine, warming up. "I'll see you, but you won't see me."

"Oh." She lowered her eyes. "Must be hard."

"What?"

She looked up at him again. "What you do. Keeping secrets. Never knowing anyone. Must be very lonely."

There was still sorrow in her eyes, but now Jay saw that it was the kind of sorrow that comes from pity, from sympathy, from a heart that ached for another human being's pain.

He looked away, out the window, just in time to see a bicycle built for two go sailing past the diner window. The tandem riders moved as one, they and their bicycle twinkling through the night with myriad dancing lights. Before he could determine whether this was something he really had seen, or just an optical illusion, his communicator beeped.

"Excuse me," he said, and left Laura sitting at the table as he went to take the call. "Zed?" he said when he was out of earshot.

"Talk to me," his superior directed.

"The pizza guy was a Zarthan, the perp wasn't. Any unauthorized ship landings?"

"Central Park," Zed replied. "West Seventy-second off the drive. Four hours ago."

"On my way." Jay broke communication and went back to the table where Laura still sat toying with her pie. "I have to go," he told her.

"What about the 'flashy' thing?" she asked, not very eagerly.

He put the neuralyzer back in his pocket. "Flash you some other time," he said. He wheeled around to leave and bumped right into the same waiter who had witnessed his earlier "breakup" with Tee, and had *loved* the suits.

The man glanced from Jay to Laura and back again. The corner of his mouth quirked up. "Looks like someone can't make up his mind," he said.

Jay gave that remark all the attention it deserved.

Out in the street, Frank was sitting in the Mercedes, listening to the radio. Jay clicked it off as soon as he got inside.

"Whassamatter, you don't like 'Who Let the Dogs Out'?" the little pug inquired. When he got no response, he added, "Did you tell the girl you loved her?"

"She was a witness to a crime," Jay replied shortly. "That's it."

The pug wasn't buying any. "Yada, yada. Didn't see a neuralyzer flash. You're attracted. She's not even my species and *I'm* attracted."

"Great," Jay muttered. "I'm getting advice on love from someone who humps fire hydrants." He peeled the car out of its parking spot with a vengeance.

"That's canine profiling and I resent it," Frank maintained with wounded dignity. They didn't exchange another word all the way to Central Park.

There was a yellow tent on the site where Serleena's ship had landed, totally surrounded by trucks. MIB agents swarmed everywhere, like ants on a Twinkie. Jay and Frank got out of the Mercedes, and Frank decided it was about time he started throwing his newfound authority around.

"All right, all right, comin' through," he announced, trotting ahead of Jay. "MIB brass here, look sharp. I'm Agent Eff now, Agent Jay's new partner. Hey! Who you eyeballing?"

Jay stopped and tried to put a figurative leash on the belligerent pug. "Frank, *shhhh*."

Another agent laughed. Frank gave him a hard look. "Have children?" he asked.

"No," came the somewhat puzzled reply.

"Want 'em?" The pug bared his teeth and gave a little growl. The meaning was unmistakable.

As soon as Frank felt he'd established his rights to a little respect, he joined Jay inside the yellow tent. A number of other MIB agents were already there, standing around Serleena's spaceship. From nose to tail the little craft wasn't more than eighteen inches long, which meant that examining it up close and personal required special equipment. This was no problem: Special equipment and the MIB were old friends.

Jay pulled out his alien identifier. There was no need to talk about what needed to be accomplished: Everyone knew their job and they did it, period. Chitchat was for rookies. The fate of Earth itself might be on the line. It probably was—the alien who'd ditched this ship had killed once already. Once that they knew of. Perps like that didn't come to Earth to sell Girl Scout cookies.

Jay took the device and aimed it into an opening in the spacecraft, then plugged the endoscope into his communicator, establishing a direct audiovisual link for Zed. Once this was done, he motioned for the other agents to leave him and Frank alone with the spacecraft. They obeyed, no arguments.

"Okay, Zed, you're patched in," Jay reported as he looked into the eyepiece.

"Talk to me," Zed said. "Back in MIB Headquarters, he called the relayed image up on the Egg Screen in real-time transmission. What Jay saw, he saw.

The minuscule camera inside the identifier panned across the interior of Serleena's teardrop ship. You couldn't call it cozy interior decor, unless Martha Stewart had decided to start accessorizing with deadly weaponry. This was a ship built to carry a warrior. Size didn't matter, but lethal force did.

"Kylothian Class C battle cruiser," Jay reported, tallying the Barbie-doll-sized arsenal. "With enough antimatter torpedoes to turn this island into another Atlantis."

"Well, happy birthday to me," Zed replied dryly. "Who says only good things come in small packages?"

"The witness at the pizza place said the aliens who did in her boss were looking for some kind of light," Jay went on. "Light of—"

"—Zartha." Zed spoke like a man who knew.

"Yeah." Jay didn't sound surprised to find Zed on top of things that way. He was used to it. Being two steps ahead of the next guy was why Zed was the head of the MIB, and not just another agent. "What is it?"

"A kind of power source. Like the sun. More powerful. Different physics. In the wrong hands it's big bad mojo. But this was settled a long time ago."

Much as he hated to contradict the boss-man, Jay said: "Obviously not."

"Look," Zed said patiently. "Twenty-five years ago the Zarthans came to Earth asking us to hide the Light of Zartha from their enemies, the Kylothians."

"We don't do that," Jay said. Earth's neutrality in the scheme of interplanetary politics was sacrosanct, like Switzerland, only without so much emphasis on chocolate. It was why the Men in Black existed—to preserve Earth as a safe haven for refugees fleeing the turmoil on other worlds, to keep her out of diplomatic messes her people weren't yet ready to handle, to keep her and all who dwelled on her *alive*.

"Exactly," Zed replied. "That's why I ordered it off the planet. That was one war I did not want to be in the middle of."

You wanna tell me one war you would *want to be in the middle of?* Jay thought.

Aloud he asked: "So why is there a Kylothian Class C in my park? Are you *sure* the Light's not still here?" It was the only way for recent events to make sense. His old New York Police Department training came back, coupled with all the Sherlock Holmes stories he'd ever read: Things didn't "just happen"; there were always reasons. Usually the right one was the most obvious, except in old *Perry Mason* reruns.

"Positive," Zed affirmed. "I gave the order. My best agent carried it out. It's as if I gave the order to you."

Jay took the unspoken compliment and filed it away to enjoy more fully later. Right now, there was business to tend to.

"Then just ask the agent—"

"Can't." Zed cut that notion off cold.

"Dead?" Jay deduced.

"Sort of. He works at the post office."

Outside the yellow tent it was still night, but inside, dawn broke early for Jay.

"No," he said. It was denial and it was futile and he knew it.

My best agent carried it out. Who else could that be but Kay?

Kay, who had left the Men in Black and gone back to civilian life. Kay, who had been neuralyzed as thoroughly as Jay had ever neuralyzed anyone. Kay, who was finally freed to go back to the sweetheart he'd left behind on that fateful night when an unlucky combination of circumstances had put him on the very spot where Earth's first contact with alien visitors was taking place, virtually guaranteeing that he would have to become a part of the MIB and all it stood for.

Kay, whose last known place of employment was the post office in Truro, Massachusetts.

"Earth's very existence may rest on what Kay knows," Zed said solemnly. "Too bad you wiped out his entire memory of it."

Jay started to protest. Agents of the MIB who left the

service, for whatever reason, *had* to be neuralyzed. Not one glimmer of memory could remain of the sights they'd seen and the things they'd done in the name of protecting their homeworld from the scum of the universe. It wasn't the sort of thing you wanted a fellow blurting out by accident down at the Bowl-O-Rama or in the middle of a Kiwanis Club meeting.

Zed didn't wait to hear Jay's justification. "Bring him in," he said. "Now."

EIGHT

In Truro, Massachusetts, it was a lovely, fresh summer morning. Truro was a place that could boast at least as much history as New York City, but was nowhere near as in-your-face about it.

The streets radiated charm, grace, and peace. The people on the street exuded the New England virtues of duty, discretion, and decorum. The heritage of early America overlay the whole scene like a fine patina bringing out the golden highlights in an oil portrait of one of the Founding Fathers. The only circumstances under which a citizen of Truro would demand, "Are you talking to me? Are you talking to *me*?" would be if he were unsure whether or not the interlocutor in question really did wish to initiate a conversation.

It was all very serene and amiable. Narrow minds might dare to call it dull. Even the city post office gave the impression that its employees might be occasionally miffed or, at worst, peeved, but *disgruntled* was never an option.

The Mercedes pulled up right in front of the post office. Jay had been driving all night in order to get here, and he looked disgruntled enough for a whole battalion of postal employees.

The drive wasn't the only reason for his monumental bad mood.

"You're still mad." Frank's rueful voice came from out of sight, on the passenger's side.

"Shut up."

"I had to take a leak," the pug pleaded. "What's the big deal?"

"We're undercover," Jay shot back in an *I-can't-believe-I-have-to*-explain-*this-to-you* tone. "Undercover is *not* walking into a gas station and saying 'Who the hell's got the key to the little boys' room?'!"

"If they didn't keep it locked up, it never would've happened," Frank replied self-righteously. "And anyway, I think you *like* using that neuralyzer."

Jay got out of the car and pointed at his partner. "Stay."

The pug gave him the stink-eye. "I may look like a dog, but actually I only play one here on Earth," he commented in an offended tone.

The inside of the Truro post office was wholly unremarkable. It was quaint and picturesque, in its own utilitarian way. A number of service windows lined one wall, each designated by a large overhead sign bearing a letter of the alphabet. Customers milled around or stood waiting their turns, standing in line with the same stoic attitude that got them through wars, blizzards, and nights when the cable TV went out.

Under the big, square sign marking window C, former MIB agent Kay manned his post. His weathered face hadn't changed much, and neither had his take-charge manner.

"Good people of Truro, Mass., may I kindly have your attention," he called out. Jay looked up, along with everyone else, wondering what the hell this was all about.

"In order for us to expedite your shipping needs, I'd like to remind you that all packages must be properly wrapped," Kay continued.

He held up a package that not even the most charitable critic could call "wrapped." Its covering was loose in a dozen places, wadded down with layer upon layer of tape in a dozen more; the finished product was a testament to the fact that whoever had created that pathetic attempt was as bad as the federal government at making ends meet.

The woman at the head of the C window line squirmed, blushed, and kept her eyes fixed on the floor, but Kay was too dedicated a worker to let a little thing like one person's public humiliation prevent him from delivering a valuable lesson. If the many would benefit, the needs of the individual sometimes had to be sacrificed.

"Now *this*—" He made sure that the whole post office got a good look at the offending parcel. "—*this* would be an example of 'go home and do it again.' I think you know what I mean, Mrs. Vigushin," he said, turning his attention to the woman who had tried to mail that affront to hardworking United States Postal Service employees everywhere. "Brown paper and double-twist twine are the preferred media. Thank you for your time."

As Mrs. Vigushin grabbed back her pitiful-looking package and scurried away in search of a rock to crawl under, Jay stepped up to the window.

"Kay?" he said.

Kay looked up, then pointed at the sign above his window. "*C*," he corrected. "Express mail, two-day air."

His old MIB designation didn't register at all. Jay hadn't expected it to, though there was one tiny cell in the back of his brain that foolishly held on to the hope—the smallest spark of hope imaginable—that Kay would remember him.

Man recruits you, gets you into the organization, works with you, watches your back, risks his life with you, you'd think there'd be something *left behind*, he thought. *Damn, that neuralyzer's good.*

He sighed. *Damn.*

He looked at the name tag his former partner now wore: KEVIN.

"Kevin," he said, reading it out loud. "Kevin." He had to laugh. "Never thought of you as a—" He stopped. Kay was staring at him as if he were out of his mind. Jay snapped back to business. "You don't remember me, but we used to work together."

Kay studied Jay's plain black suit. "Never worked at a funeral home," he said. He glanced at the line that was beginning to form behind Jay. "Something I can do for you, slick?"

"Okay . . ." Jay leaned in, having decided that the direct approach was the best. "Straight to the point: You are a former agent of a top secret organization that monitors the activities of extraterrestrials on Earth. We are the Men in Black. We have a situation. We need your help."

Kay didn't even blink. "There's a free mental-health clinic on the corner of Lilac and East Valley." Craning his neck, he declared: *"Next!"*

Jay found himself being shoved aside by an eight-year-old girl.

"Twenty Rugrats stamps, please," she said.

"Elizabeth, while the United States Postal Service hasn't exactly kept up with the interests of today's youth, could I perhaps offer you something else?" Kay pulled open his drawer and paged through the block plates of postage stamps, offering Elizabeth such stamps as Berlin Airlift, Amish Quilts, Opera Legends; all of which she flatly rejected.

Before Kay could show Elizabeth more options, Jay muscled his way back to Kay's window. " 'Scuse me, sweetie, trying to save the planet here," he mumbled, physically lifting her up and replacing her firmly out of the way.

To Kay he said, "Where do you think you were before you came here? Anyone ever give an explanation for that? One that made sense?"

Kay turned over another page of stamps, offering no comment.

"They told you that you'd been in a coma for years, didn't they?" Jay pressed. "Only there wasn't any coma. Your coma was a cover."

Kay closed the stamp drawer and looked up, his expression betraying nothing. It was a look Jay had seen many times before, a look that said it was possible to keep your cool without becoming cold, that you could take care of business and still care about the lives you were touching. They hadn't worked together for years—far from that— but there was still a bond between them, part mutual respect, part admiration, and part true friendship.

Too bad it's all one-sided now, Jay thought.

Kay's eyes narrowed. "Who are you?" he demanded.

"Question is, who are *you*?" Jay countered.

"Postmaster of Truro, Massachusetts," Kay replied with military precision. "And as such I am ordering you to leave these premises. Break!" He closed his window and made a snappy about-face, leaving a disappointed Elizabeth Rugrat-less.

Kay headed straight for the mail-sorting area. Either he didn't know that Jay was right behind him, or he didn't care; he could handle it either way. He wore competence the way other men wore aftershave. As soon as he crossed the threshold he spotted one of his underlings, a young postal employee, fiddling with the coffee machine.

From his earliest days with the Men in Black, Kay had hated fidgeters.

"That decaf?" he snapped.

The pot slipped from the young man's trembling hands and smashed to the floor. Some people just weren't cut out for work in the armed forces, especially when they'd been expecting a career in the postal service.

"Sorry," he said, his voice shaking worse than his hands.

It's either the caffeine or Kay that's got that kid jumping half out of his skin, Jay thought. *And my money ain't on Mr. Coffee.*

You can take the man out of the MIB, but . . . man, Kay, you haven't changed a bit. Maybe this is gonna be easy. Maybe.

As if to prove to Jay just how right he was, Kay swung into action right before his former partner's eyes. "All right, people, we have a breach," Kay announced, indicating the smashed coffeepot. "Farrell, cordon off the area. Billings, full perimeter wipe-down—"

"Kay—" Jay said, trying to get the man's attention.

He did. Kay noted his presence, logged it, and decided what to do about it. "Farrell, please escort this nonessential civilian away from this site immediately!"

Jay easily shook off Farrell's attempt to obey orders and

rounded on Kay. "*Listen* to yourself!" he commanded.
"Who talks like that? About a damn smashed *coffeepot*?
What's it gonna take to—?"

Inspiration struck. He whipped out a compact device
and held it up to the assembled postal employees. Strings
of alien characters spilled down the screen, a crash-dump
of information telling Jay what planet they hailed from
and the language they spoke.

Jay looked up from his device and said, loud and clear:
"*Skalluch.*"

The workers stopped what they were doing; stopped
dead. Jay drew his MIB ID and held it up so that they could
all get a clear view of it.

"*Hytuu saee habbilmuu,*" he directed them in their own
tongue. It was a variation on the standard police command
Drop it.

They dropped it. Human disguises hit the floor faster
than the smashed coffeepot. The full complement of the
Truro, Massachusetts, post office workforce stood revealed in their true forms, complete with beaks, bug eyes,
scales, tentacles, and a wide assortment of other physical
characteristics that made Earth's resident alien populace
so . . . visually interesting.

Kay was still taking this in when Jay reached under the
machine that was sorting letters and hit a recessed keypad
panel with the proper code sequence. A door on the machine swung open, revealing neither a tangle of wires, a
pack of closely stacked circuit boards, nor a medley of
flanges, doohickeys, and electronic whatzits. Rather, there
was a multilimbed extraterrestrial perched inside, using
those limbs to distribute letters into their proper slots at a
phenomenal, eye-blurring rate. One free limb held a ciga-

rette, another a latte grande from Starbucks. The critter didn't slow down for a microsecond, even on being discovered. It was a double-shot latte.

"Why do you think you ended up working in the post office?" Jay said to Kay. "They're all aliens. You're *used* to working with aliens; that's why you feel comfortable here."

Kay behaved as though Jay were a bad TV program with the sound track muted. He looked at his newly revealed coworkers, letting it all sink in, then went right for the multilimbed creature inside the mail-sorting machine.

"No smoking," he said roughly, confiscating the cigarette. Then he turned on his heel and marched out of the building.

Jay raced after him and caught up with his former partner just as Kay was getting into a mail delivery jeep. He was expecting the usual questions and protests, the same ones that MIB agents always got from civilians who were confronted by the impossible knowledge that We Are Not Alone. Even though Kay had once had all the answers, since he'd been neuralyzed he was in the same boat with the rest of the uninitiated population. So Jay figured he'd be wanting to know the full story—like Who, What, When, Where, and Why am I losing my mind?

Jay was wrong.

"Wife and I been to Vegas," Kay said, deadpan. "Saw Siegfried and Roy make a white tiger fly around the room. Your routine's nothing special, slick." He made as if to start the jeep.

Jay held on to the rearview mirror and the door frame. Before he'd come up here from New York, he'd been given a standard briefing, bringing him up to speed on everything that had happened in Kay's life since he'd left the MIB. Parts of it were painful. He didn't like to open up an old friend's wounds, but this was business. A man did what it took to get the job done. Kay had taught him that himself.

"You look up at the sky at night and think you know more about what's going on out there than you do down here," Jay said urgently. "You got a feeling in your gut like you don't know who you are, and it eats at you every day of your life. It's why she left you, Kay. It's why your wife left."

He didn't see Kay's fist coming at him until it connected with his chin, knocking him back a few steps. He shook it off and with a touch of pride observed, "Stayed in pretty good shape." Then, more earnestly, he told him, "Look, if you want to know who you *really* are, come take a ride with me. If not, people are waiting for their *TV Guides*."

He left it at that and walked away. Sometimes no more words could be said to tilt the balance. Some things a man had to decide for himself. He went back to the Mercedes and got in behind the wheel.

Moments later, Kay opened the passenger door and slid in beside him.

"Just going for a ride," he stated. "Things don't add up, *hasta luego*. Hear what I'm saying, Junior?"

"I hear you." Jay did his best not to smile, but it was hard. Hearing Kay call him "Junior" like that made it seem like old times. He started the car.

A faint noise from the backseat made Kay turn around. All tongue-lolling doggie smiles, Frank the Pug wagged his fat little tail.

"Hey, Kay," he said. "Long time no see."

"Your replacement," Jay explained, privately enjoying every minute of it. "So who you calling Junior?"

He floored the gas pedal and the Mercedes took off in reverse, spewing smoke and fishtailing wildly before it sped at a roar around the corner.

NINE

For as long as Jay had known him, Kay had been a man of few words, but this was ridiculous. Even driving the Mercedes at top speed, it was a long trip from Truro back to MIB Headquarters, but for all the conversation inside the car, Jay might as well have been bringing home a gravestone.

Maybe I am, he thought. *Here lies Agent Kay, survived by his ex-wife and some postmaster dude from Truro named Kevin.*

Kevin! If that don't beat all . . .

Worse than Kay's silence, though, were Frank's irrepressible attempts to keep the nonexistent conversation going all by himself. By the time the Mercedes pulled into its parking space, Jay was ready to have the pug neutered.

Several times, just to make sure.

Kay's expression didn't give up a single iota of recognition as they entered the building where he'd served so loyally, for so many years. The roar of the twin exhaust fans in the entry hall barely made him blink.

"Good to see ya, Kay," the guard said, still not bothering to look up from his newspaper.

"Good to see you, too," Kay replied, but the twinge of

encouragement Jay felt was quickly quashed as they stepped onto the elevator and Kay muttered, "Whoever the hell you are."

He turned to a crestfallen Jay and said, "Okay, let's see what you got here, sport." He didn't need to add: *And it had better be worth the trip.*

Jay couldn't help grinning just a little as he looked at his old friend's impassive face. Then he looked down at the Bermuda shorts Kay was wearing as part of the official summer uniform for the United States Postal Service, got an eyeful of his former partner's knees, and grinned a little more.

"God, I missed you," he said, shaking his head.

Kay's stony expression didn't change a hair when the elevator doors opened, revealing the main hall of MIB Headquarters. Nothing seemed to startle him, scare him, or even impress him enough for it to register to where another person could read it.

What's this dude got running through his veins? Jay wondered. *Ice water?*

It was as good a guess as any. Kay walked through the midst of the huddled alien masses yearning to respire freely, as if he saw this kind of thing on a daily basis. Back in Truro he'd rubbed elbows with aliens—the ones who *had* elbows—but since he'd never actually seen them in their alien forms until today, that didn't count.

Blue-skinned blobs with warts, tentacled critters half wombat and half vending machine, slime-sloughing multipedes that looked like trampled Easter bonnets whose ever-changing flesh tones would never match the drapes in anyone's home, all these and more slid and slopped and sashayed across Kay's field of vision with about as much impact as a gnat bite on a hippopotamus.

The guy's a natural, Jay thought. *Lucky thing, him stumbling across that whole first-contact scene, way back when. There's just so much training can do. Man wants to be MIB, man's got to have natural-born talent.*

He straightened his necktie, preening, remembering how this was the same man who'd tapped him to join the ranks of the Men in Black. Jay smiled. *Man's got talent, man knows enough to* recognize *talent when he sees it.*

Then his smile winked out. *Too damn bad he's not recognizing anything else right now.*

It was true, and painful for Jay to watch. Though Kay was taking everything in, it was obvious that none of it was ringing any mental bells. Not so a man could tell by looking at him.

On the other hand, if the sight of MIB Headquarters wasn't having any effect on Kay, Kay's reappearance sure as hell was having a big effect on MIB Headquarters.

The first thing Jay noticed were the whispers. They welled up all around as he and Kay crossed the floor, little ripples of sound as the agents on duty stood witness to the return of a legend.

"Kay . . ."

"Hey, look, isn't that—?"

"—seen pictures. Before my time, but . . ."

"—thought he wasn't—"

"—*sure* he's not dead! What kind of dumb-ass rumors have you been listening to?"

"That's him, I tell you!"

"—clone?"

"I swear to God, if I ever get my hands on the jackass who started that stupid clone story, I'm gonna—"

"Yeah, that's Kay."

"Kay? For real?"

"Son-of-a-gun, what's he doing back here?"

"—think he'll remember me?"

"Welcome back."

"Good to see you."

"Agent Kay . . ."

Some acknowledged his return with a nod, some with a discreet salute, some with a thumbs-up so quickly there and gone that its very appearance was debatable. The whispers and the murmured greetings and the gestures followed the two former partners down the main hall.

An eager young rookie, still showing that just-out-of-the-training-box shine, ran after them. His given name was gone, all traces of his former existence had been erased as surely as his fingerprints, but he was new enough to the agency so that none of that mattered to him. For the moment, it was all about proving that he could do this job, showing the world that Agent Gee really was the best of the best.

He focused on the task of the moment with laser-beam concentration, often to the exclusion of everything outside his field of vision. The result was that he spent an awful lot of time doing delayed reactions and double takes.

Right now he had urgent business with Agent Jay. Sighting his target, he rushed up behind him and pounced.

"Don't mean to bother you, Agent Jay," he began, crisp as the neatly starched points of his shirt collar. "But if you—"

That was when he saw Kay. Picture the kid you knew in

algebra class, the one who taped all the episodes of every single science-fiction show, and memorized all the dialogue. Now *double* that and you might have some faint idea of the transformation that overtook Agent Gee. All of his slick professionalism fell away, leaving behind a core of pure, unadulterated, gushing fanboy. It wasn't pretty.

"Oh . . . my . . . *God*. You're Agent Kay!"

"So they tell me," Kay replied evenly.

"This—this is an *honor*." He edged Jay out of the way without so much as a *May-I-cut-in?* and insinuated himself up close and personal with Kay.

"Gee," he said. It could have been an expression of wonder, but really it was only an introduction. "Agent Gee." He turned to Jay as if imparting the secret combination that would unlock the way to King Solomon's Mines and needlessly explained: "Kay: The legend. Most respected agent in the history of MIB. The most feared human in the universe. In the flesh."

Jay adopted his best *Do tell, do tell . . . fool* expression. It went unnoticed. Agent Gee was in full-blown gonzo hero-worship mode. There were beagle puppies with less enthusiasm and better drool control.

Gee looked back at Kay and struggled to find the right words to express his total fulfillment as a human being, now that he had met the man himself.

"Oh, man, I can't—I just can't—" Clearly he couldn't, so he switched tacks, trying to buddy up to his idol. "Maybe I could buy you a cup of coffee sometime," he suggested, trying to make it sound as if they were very nearly equals. "Hear some of the old war stories."

Kay raised one eyebrow. "Black, two sugars, if you're going," he said.

"An honor." Gee came perilously close to giving Kay a Prussian heel-click before he scampered away.

"I'll have a—*Hey!* My man!" Jay tried, but he was too late. *Damn,* he thought. *One hour ago—shoot, one* minute *before that boy saw Kay, he'd've been all over himself running to bring* me *a coffee, going on about how* that *was an honor. Nasty little brown-nosing . . .*

Ah, hell, who'm I kidding? I'm back in the Number Two slot. And it feels a lot *like Number Two, uh-huh.*

Their route brought them right up against the massive dead alien. It was still dead, still on the same gurney as before, only now the MIB agents surrounding it were all wearing lab suits, up to their elbows in an autopsy. Assorted lumps and gnarls and spongy bits and lengths of interior tubing presented themselves wetly in a gut-churning array that would have sent a bevy of tabloid editors into ecstasies.

One of the suited agents looked up from the corpse and saw Jay. "Freight elevator's down," he said. "We have to do the autopsy here. This guy's not getting any less—" When he caught sight of Kay, his reaction was much less intrusive than Gee's, but that was the sort of thing that separated the rookies from the seasoned personnel. "Hey, Kay! You're back," he said with a grin.

"Yup," Kay replied.

A second agent on autopsy duty asked, "Any idea what might've done him in?" After all, it wasn't every day they had one of the founding fathers on hand. This was a far greater tribute to Agent Kay than a thousand gosh-wow rookies fetching him his coffee. Often the best *welcome back* of all was having people expect you to slip right back into the old routine without fuss or fanfare, just as if you'd never been gone.

Kay looked at the body and pursed his lips. "Had a cousin about that size choked on a peanut," he opined. Without another word, he walked off.

"Choked . . ." the first agent mused. "Possibility." He considered which of the deceased creature's orifices might contain the guilty nut. To Jay he said, "Good to have him back."

"I'm throwing a party later," the thoroughly upstaged Jay replied without cracking a smile.

In his office, Zed was taking care of business via the Egg Screen communicator when Jay came in. The vista on the screen was a wasteland of snow and ice, a frigid nightmare torn from somewhere in the wilds of Antarctica. A man in an MIB suit stood in the midst of this frozen desolation, addressing Zed via his communicator. That must have been some suit, Jay thought, to grant its wearer such obvious immunity to the bone-chilling cold.

Of course, the suit wasn't exactly the most startling thing about the scene on the Egg Screen. That would be the identity of the man *in* the suit. Either Agent Zed had developed a fondness for music videos, or the King of Pop had decided it was time to become the King of Popsicles.

Then again, given the celebrity's true identity and planet of origin, a stint in Antarctica was like a stroll on the beach for real Earthlings.

"How'd it go?" Zed asked the alien known to the public as Michael Jackson—his real name was definitely *not* meant for a human tongue to pronounce.

Michael looked pleased with himself as he reported, "Zed, the Drolacks are gone and the treaty is signed."

"Good work," Zed replied. In truth, he was only half listening. It was hard to concentrate on run-of-the-mill status reports when the fate of the entire planet was moonwalking on a high wire above a pit of crocodiles.

Michael didn't know this, though. He had his own agenda. "Zed, what about that position you promised me in MIB?" he asked.

"Still working on the Alien Affirmative Action Program," he told him. "I'll keep you posted."

"Wait a minute!" Michael objected. "That's not what you promised me!"

Zed turned his back on the screen and started to walk away.

"You're breaking up. Can't hear you," he said smoothly.

"Zed! Hello? Zed?" Michael called frantically into his communicator.

"I'll call you back."

"I could be Agent Em!"

The last of his protests were cut off dead by a click and the return of the dial tone as Zed turned to greet Agent Jay.

Then he realized who else had walked into his office. "Kay!" he cried, giving the returned former MIB agent a friendly slap on the back. But his initial gladness at seeing his old comrade in arms dimmed quickly under the oppressive urgency of the matter at hand. "Friend," he said. "Think Earth might be in a bad way and you may be the only one who can save it."

Kay wasn't conspicuously impressed. "Well, you know, neither rain nor snow," he said with a dismissive gesture.

"Good man," Zed said, not picking up on the fact that

he'd just been handed part of the postal worker's creed. He looked at Jay. "Get him armed and up to speed," he directed. "Then over to Deneuralyzation."

Jay didn't even bother to acknowledge Zed's orders: He didn't need to. He just moved to comply with the same speed and efficiency that could get a worm-crunched subway car out of sight, and the whole ugly incident out of eighty-five-odd minds. He moved to gather up his old partner.

Frank the Pug was trotting along after them when a word from Zed yanked him back with the power of a choke chain. "Uhhh, Frank, I'm gonna need them together on this one," he said. *Only them* was implied. Zed had the kindness to sound almost apologetic about it. It didn't take much of the edge off. The little alien hung his head, obviously disappointed.

Zed didn't have a reputation as a softie. He was the head of the MIB and had a no-nonsense, all-business attitude that made Kay's own brusque style look as mushy as a three-week-old peach. Nonetheless . . .

"Frank," he said softly. "I'm looking for a new assistant."

The pug looked up.

"It's not fieldwork," Zed continued, "but you do get better dental."

The worst set of teeth in the whole agency—yellow and irregular, with a thin layer of something brown and sticky near the roots—showed themselves off in all their atrocious glory as a satisfied and happy Frank smiled broadly.

TEN

Within the agency, its official name was the Tech Unit, one of the many glass-walled rooms off the main hall of Men in Black Headquarters. It was the land where dreams came true for every overgrown kid who'd ever enjoyed a fireworks display, or ownership of an air rifle, or the results you got when you lit a cherry bomb and flushed it down the toilet at school.

Yes, this was the MIB's storehouse for all kinds of exciting alien technologies, strange machines, bizarre devices, and, of course, weapons whose outrageous firepower couldn't even begin to be determined just by looking at them.

Jay called it the Toy Store. This was the place to come when you had to save the planet, and you needed some heavy-duty persuasion to use on anyone who might . . . *disagree* with you. When you were dealing with creatures who could laugh off Mr. Smith and Mr. Wesson as easily as if they were Mr. Laurel and Mr. Hardy, this was the place to get whatever it might take to swing the winning argument over to your side.

Jay still remembered the first time he'd seen alien weapons, back in Jeebs's pawnshop. Initially he'd been dazzled, but that didn't last. His amazement faded quickly, as did the little voice in his head that kept insisting what he saw was impossible. Both reactions had been extinguished by an intense desire to get his hands on the goods, and see what those babies could *do*.

Later, Kay took him to the next level when he brought him into Men in Black Headquarters and showed him what the Tech Unit had to offer. Jeebs's Pawnshop simply couldn't compete. It was like the difference between a poor kid peering through the toy maker's window, and that same kid being let loose with an American Express gold card inside F.A.O. Schwarz.

Now the Toy Store wasn't even so much as a memory for Kay; it was Jay's job to bring him up to speed. The tables were turned, and those tables were loaded down with some mighty fascinating stuff. It was the first time Jay had seen the light of interest in Kay's eyes since they'd left Truro.

"Tech Unit," Jay said, introducing Kay to his surroundings. "The most advanced technologies from all over the universe are kept in this room." Even though he still went all kid-at-Christmastime whenever he came into this place, he felt constrained to act as if the wonders surrounding them were strictly ho-hum. For some reason he didn't fully understand, more than anything else he wanted Kay to think he was . . . cool.

Kay wandered over to a machine that displayed a glowing holographic globe in its center. "What's this?" he asked, casually poking a finger at it. His fingertip penetrated the holographic ocean, making one tiny little ripple.

Jay glanced over, not really paying attention, still playing it cool. "Don't touch that," he said automatically.

It was good advice. A shame it came too late for Jarithia 5, a nice little world some fifty million light-years away from Earth. On that fateful day, life there was going on pretty much as usual. The populace was coming and going, having their little squabbles and their great conflicts, their loves and their hates, their equivalent of the boxers-versus-briefs debate.

Suddenly, without a single sign of warning, the heavens seemed to open up before their startled eyes and a huge, pinkish . . . *thing* emerged from the dome of the sky. The Jarithians had no words in their own language to describe such an apparition, although "Yikes!" came close. Later, witnesses did attempt to describe it as "—almost like a fish stick, only much more evil."

Time slowed, the way it always seems to do in times of unfathomable crisis, as the Unidentified Fish-Stick-Like Object slowly descended and plunged into the waters of their ocean. Its impact caused a gigantic tidal wave to rear up out of the depths and advance with unstoppable force onto the coast.

Panic-stricken Jarithians stood shocked and dumb-struck, staring as the oncoming deadly waters cast the shadow of doom over the glowing spires, lush parks, and bustling streets of their entire city. Then the full horror of their situation hit them and they stampeded, shrieking piti-fully in their own tongue, "All is lost! All is lost!"

Back on Earth, Jay inspected the holographic globe critically.

"Nothing happened," Kay said. For once he sounded less like a hard-boiled hero and more like a little boy caught playing with Daddy's belt sander and Mom's best china teapot.

"Hands in your pockets," Jay directed, looking severe. Inside he was grinning like a fool, recalling the damage he himself had wrought the first time Kay brought him in here. He'd done more or less the same dumb thing, touching stuff he shouldn't have been touching, sending what looked like a harmless little toy ball on a high-speed ricochet course of destruction through headquarters.

Bet I don't look like such a big chump now, *huh?* he gloated. *Now we're even.*

He opened a metal cabinet, reached in, and grabbed one of the largest, most complex, most intimidating bits of weaponry ever seen on the planet Earth. "Series Four De-Atomizer," he told Kay.

Almost instinctively, Kay reached for the gun, only to have Jay hand him something smaller. *Much* smaller, and about as ominous to the eye as a forty-nine-cent water pistol. It didn't even have a recognizable barrel, as such, but instead threatened the world at large with what looked like an overgrown mosquito's snout. Placed side by side with this dinky implement of destruction, the dainty pearl-handled derringer that had once been the defensive weapon of choice for discerning dance-hall gals would have acquired delusions of grandeur.

It was called something unpronounceable by the extraterrestrials who had built it, so it was known around the agency as a Noisy Cricket. *Cricket* was accurate, if all you focused on was the size of the thing, but given the kick it could dish out, *Noisy* was one hell of an understatement.

"Your signature weapon," Jay said, handing it to Kay. Kay accepted it, only to hold the petite weapon disdainfully between thumb and forefinger, as if it were a kitten that had done naughties on the Aubusson carpet.

"Isn't the size that counts." Jay tried to mollify him. "It's what you can do with it."

"Signature weapon," Kay repeated, not convinced.

Jay turned on the charm. "Would your superior officer lie to you?"

"I took orders from you?" Kay sounded doubtful, cynical, and incredulous, all in equal proportions.

"Taught you everything you know, sport." Jay flashed him a smile. So it wasn't the truth; big deal. It was private payback for the way Kay's return had turned Jay invisible out there in the main hall. It was petty, sure, but it was harmless and *damn*, it felt good!

"Could we get on with this?" Kay said testily.

"Not in that Cub Scout uniform," Jay replied, giving Kay's postal service garb another once-over.

Be good to see you back in the suit, Kay, he thought as he looked at Kay's knees. *Be even better once we get you deneuralyzed.*

Aloud he said, "Come on."

A large share of the main hall at Men in Black Headquarters is devoted to the Immigration Center. It's not all that much different from its administrative sisters, those customs areas found at all major international airports, border crossings, or nautical ports of call. Here all incoming aliens went through the same rigmarole as any Earthling, whether traveling for business, on a pleasure trip, seeking political asylum, or simply desiring to better their lot in the Land or World of Opportunity.

The arrivals area was by no means a bleak, echoing warehouse for the mass-processing of immigrants, along

the lines of Ellis Island. Times change, even if bureau-
cracy doesn't.

The needs of Earth's newest arrivals weren't to be ignored, be those needs food, clothing, or a snazzy new cell
phone. The side of the hall opposite the actual processing
stations sported a Burger King, a Sprint store, a duty-free
store, and an "I ♥ NY" shop. What the hell, they figured,
might as well get the newcomers accustomed to the wonderful world of consumerism. Besides, some of the incoming aliens were traveling with children in tow. It's a
universally acknowledged truth that you can best persuade
a whiny youngster to shut up and sit still if you give him
something to eat or play with.

Whether visiting Earth for the most casual of reasons or
the highest of ideals, one thing was a constant: Pick a line,
stand there quietly, and wait your turn.

Oh, and pray that who-or-whatever's standing in line behind you isn't (a) a predator, (b) impatient, and/or (c) getting hungry.

Of course if possibility (c) seemed both probable and
imminent, it was best to have the critter *ahead* of you in
line hold your place, while you went off to buy everyone a
round of Whoppers, extra cheese.

The agents who staffed the Customs Area were the
unsung grunts of the Men in Black, the dutiful, diligent
data crunchers of the team. If they were lucky, things
went more or less according to Standard Operating Procedure: Call for the next creature in line, ask him/her/it/them
a few questions, check the accompanying documents—
passport, work visa, the whole nine yards—and process them.

These agents listened to creatures who looked like the

love child of David Bowie and a giant parakeet complain that their ID pictures made them look positively *feline*. They assured the distraught immigrant that even though the ATM machine had eaten her card, it could've been worse: The guy who repairs the machine could've eaten *her*. They mended fences and put out brushfires.

In time they collected their retirement benefits. They didn't worry about the fact that they didn't have any thrilling tales to bring home to the spouse and kids, because they didn't have any spouse or kids. And if they did manage to scrape together a family after they were mustered out of the agency, no problem. Neuralyzed retirees didn't need stories to tell.

On this particular day, the line of immigrants and tourists was moving along nicely when a sultry female in black leather reached the head of the queue and was waved up to the counter. She looked Earth-normal, though a nitpicker would insist on categorizing her as Earth-normal-gorgeous. She even looked fetching with her mouth full of hamburger. The longer the customs lines got, the better the business at Burger King.

She was accompanied by a scruffy person-or-persons who might also be categorized as humanoid, though Earth-normal was out of the question until he managed to pick one head and stick with it.

The agent behind the counter hardly bothered to look up when the little group presented itself before him. He had gone through this same routine a hundred times already today and he'd go through it a hundred times more, at the outside, before it was quitting time. He was supposed to have a coffee break, and a lunch break, but someone had screwed up and forgotten to send in his relief. He supposed it was just as well, because the same administrative screwup had also neglected to send him off on a bathroom break.

"Name and planet of origin?" he asked mechanically.

The lady swallowed a mouthful of sandwich and fixed him with a penetrating stare. "Serleena Xath," she said, her voice smokier than one of those legendary back rooms on the sixth day of a weeklong political convention. "Planet Jorn. Kylothian system."

The agent duly entered this information on his computer terminal. Serleena's seductive tones were having no more effect on him than her smoldering eyes. Regulations for the Men in Black specifically forbade fraternization with offworlders, so either this immigration agent was loyal and true to his company training, or else his job in the bureaucratic netherworld had wrung all natural human reactions out of him.

"Any fruits or vegetables?" he asked.

"Yes," Serleena replied, enjoying herself despite her inability to ensnare the agent with her feminine wiles. "Two heads of cabbage." She indicated Scrad and Charlie.

The joke didn't register on the overworked agent. He'd heard a million of them. What the hell was it with some aliens that the minute they set foot on Earth, they decided they were Jerry Seinfeld?

"Reason for visit?"

"Education," Serleena purred, turning the heat up a notch. "I want to learn how to become an underwear model."

The agent looked up at last. Now *this* sounded interesting.

"I'm told I have raw talent," Serleena went on. And she flashed her jacket open wide.

And lo, there was black lace. And behold, there was much cleavage.

Clearly the immigration agent hadn't surrendered all his basic urges during MIB training and indoctrination, after all. Oh, he knew the rules, he'd been schooled in the regulations, he understood perfectly that he was supposed to comport himself like a professional at all times because he was, after all, the best-of-the-best. But he was also human.

His eyes popped, his jaw dropped, and he went into a full deer-in-the-headlights stunned stare before the splendor of Serleena's bared assets.

He wasn't alone. The Men in Black prided themselves on being team players, and this occasion was no exception. The sight of Serleena's perfect body, arrayed in Victoria's Secret's finest and flimsiest lingerie, along with her handmade leather additions, nabbed the undivided attention of every individual customs agent along the line. Her bosom exerted a black-hole-like gravitational pull on all the available male eyeballs in the area, and there was the clear sound of vertebrae cracking like bullwhips and jaws hitting the floor like sacks of flour.

That was when Scrad and Charlie launched Phase Two.

The two-headed alien collapsed with a loud thud. Charlie's eyes rolled back in his head dramatically, as a wildly distraught Scrad hollered, "Help! Help! Heart attack!" He snaked his head around in an attempt to blow the breath of life into Charlie's mouth, meanwhile pounding rhythmically on his own chest, administering a bizarrely repellent version of CPR.

"Don't die on me, man!" he cried. "Come on, you

no-good son-of-a-bitch, don't do it! Hang in there! Damn it, can we get some *help* here?" he appealed to the room.

Those few MIB agents not yet in thrall to Serleena's formidable bosom came running over to render first aid. It was just what she had been waiting for.

Like the hedge of magically sprouting thorns in *Sleeping Beauty*, neural roots sprang from Serleena's hands, growing at a fabulous rate, leaping out, doubling back on themselves, forming scores of green, snaky cables that swiftly wound themselves around every MIB agent in the vicinity. The roots became a series of unbreakable bonds, then an inescapable mass of brambles, immobilizing Earth's best-of-the-best like flies in a spider's web.

Serleena threw her head back and laughed. It was a hokey, melodramatic, overdone supervillain's laugh of evil triumph, but by God, she'd *earned* it.

Meanwhile, in a room whose curving glass sides conjured up images of the World's Biggest Goldfish Bowl, Jay was introducing Kay to a handy-dandy modern appliance no household should be without:

"The deneuralyzer," he said, indicating the outlandish machine taking up most of the space inside the giant fishbowl.

Kay regarded it neutrally. He had been relieved of his U.S. Postal Service uniform and was back in the black, wearing the same classic outfit as his former partner. All that was missing was a pair of Ray-Bans.

Not that Kay needed shades to look cool. He came by it naturally. Jay knew this, and it bugged him. Sure, he was happy to have his friend back, and as soon as he ran him through the deneuralyzer he was pretty certain that Kay would be happy to be back, too. But what was it about this guy's *attitude*—! Did *nothing* impress him? Could one man be so hardcore so . . . effortlessly?

If anyone was going to have coolness laid down, paid for, monogrammed, and gift-wrapped, Jay thought he was the man for the job. He also knew that if he wanted to lay an honest claim to all that cool, he'd have to make Kay get het up about *something*, or that was it, game, set, and match. The old guy took all the marbles.

Jay didn't even know how you played marbles, but he figured he could dazzle Kay with this fresh chunk of alien tech that was literally at his fingertips.

"In a few moments, transverse magneto energy will surge through your brain, unlocking information hidden deep and dormant, that might hold in the balance the key to Earth's very survival." He sounded like one of those mad scientists from a 1950s sci-fi flick, explaining the workings of his atomic-powered mulligan, but apparently over-the-top was the way to go: Kay was running his fore-finger around the itchy inside of his shirt collar.

"Oh . . . ," he said, obviously not paying attention.

"Okay. What's that thing?" Kay asked, pointing at the deneuralyzer.

In the main hall, Serleena's victory was complete. She had every last agent hog-tied and powerless in the massive tangle of neural root brambles. As Scrad/Charlie gazed ad-miringly at their leader and her handiwork, she regarded the few pitiably protruding hands and feet of her captives.

"Silly planet," she stated with thick disdain. "Could rule the place, with the right set of mammary glands."

Charlie nodded, and remarked to Scrad: "Britney Spears." He didn't get any arguments on that one.

Serleena walked out, filing her nails to repair any damage the massive neural root outpouring might have done to her manicure. Scrad/Charlie followed her as closely as Mary's two-headed little lamb.

Silence flowed in to fill the hall in their wake. No one else was going anywhere. The dead alien, still stranded in midautopsy, had more of a chance of moving than any of the agents Serleena had entangled.

Then the alien moved.

It was only a small stirring, but it was there. It came from underneath the rubbery body.

It was Frank. As soon as he knew the coast was clear, the little pug stuck his head out from under his stone-dead shelter, surveyed the hall, and with a look that could only be called *hangdog* said: "Ah *jeez*."

Which just about said it all.

Unaware of the takeover, Jay had Kay hooked up to the workings of the deneuralyzer. Once he had his man in place, he went over to a nearby computer keyboard and punched in the preliminary information necessary for the restoration of Kay's memories.

"Ready?" he asked when he was done.

"Sure this contraption is going to get me my memories back?" Kay asked in a tone that implied he'd believe it when he saw it, and even then he'd be wanting to get a few affidavits.

"Yeah, if your advanced years haven't killed them already," Jay shot back. Kay got his mouth open, ready to fire off a fresh reply, but before he could utter a word Jay grabbed the opportunity to shove a mouthpiece between the man's lips.

Jay enabled his communicator and reported, "Zed, we're ready to go." There was no reply. "Zed?"

Silence.

Unexplained silence from Zed was *not* a good sign.

There *was* an explanation for Zed's silence, though Jay wasn't yet aware of it. Kay wasn't the only one having trouble getting a word in edgewise at the moment. In his office, Zed was in a similar fix, though his problem wasn't a deneuralyzer mouthpiece. Zed was having the breath half choked out of his body at the hands of one very beautiful, very peeved alien.

Even with his feet dangling just off the floor and Serleena's hand clutching his throat like a vise, Zed showed the stuff he was made of by managing to rasp out: "Serleena, please . . ."

She flung him to the floor like a used tissue. "Twenty-five years, Zed," she said, looking down her perfectly sculpted nose at his sprawled body. "Glad you remembered me."

"Never forget a pretty—whatever you are," Zed replied wryly. He reached up under his desk, as if groping for support to help him get back on his feet. What he was really reaching for was one of about fifty bright red panic buttons. He didn't even have to double-check his choice with a sideways glance: His finger zeroed in on the one marked DENEURALYZER ROOM.

A place for everything and everything in its place, even emergency alert buttons; that was Zed's way.

*   *   *

The loud, unignorable blast of a klaxon sounded through the Deneuralyzer Room, followed by the wail of a siren. Jay's head jerked around just as the room's glass door slammed shut, sealing him and Kay inside the transparent, bowl-shaped chamber.

"Breach," Jay snapped, looking grim. He got Kay out of the deneuralyzer in a hurry, saying, "We're being firewalled and flushed."

"Flushed?" his former partner repeated, his voice suspicious.

"Flushed," Jay confirmed.

"*Clarify!*" Kay commanded.

"Ever been to a water park?" Jay crossed his arms over his chest, and shot Kay a look that indicated he should follow suit.

The other man instinctively mimicked Jay's action, but still insisted: "Clari—"

It was a *very* bad day for trying to fit a word in edgewise. Before Kay could get the last syllable out, the floor beneath their feet opened wide, becoming the mouth of a colossal drain as torrents of bright blue water came pouring into the glass room from above, gallons upon gallons, sweeping them off their feet. The irresistible force struck Jay and Kay with all the power of a battering ram, hurling them around the curved sides of the room twice before . . .

When Jay said they were going to be flushed, he meant it.

They shot down the drain at fantastic speed, the floor shutting tight behind them. Screaming, they barreled through glass tubes on a wild, waterborne ride. As they picked up momentum, their bodies became human torpedoes, the emergency evacuation system sending them banking, turning, and corkscrewing down the pipes.

Kay's face was pulled back into a grotesquely warped version of itself, and still he managed to finish the last thing he'd been trying to say back in the Deneuralyzer Room, namely:

"—fyyyyyyyyy!"

Jay didn't know whether he wanted to admire the man for his perseverance in the face of adversity, or smack him a good one for being stubborn as a mule.

Mentally, he voted for mule. Then he screamed some more.

Times Square is the heart of the Great White Way, the hub of the Theater District, the crossroads of the city. Here you can still follow the news of the world as it's spelled out on the electronic crawl that circles the famous building where the ball drops every New Year's Eve, or get the latest word on how your investments are doing by casting a glance at the bigger-than-big LED display on the Nasdaq MarketSite tower.

The buildings surrounding Times Square form walls of flashing, glittering, scintillating neon, all advertising products for sale. This is the area famous for those big "gimmick" billboards where, in decades past, smoke rings puffed forth from the mouths of giants who were enjoying that cool, refreshing cigarette, back in the days before the Surgeon General's Warning. You can't look anywhere here without getting slapped right across the eyes by a hard sell. Even the sidewalk beneath your feet carries stenciled messages urging you to go here, go there, and fork over the cash once you arrive.

It's also the place where, if you hang around long enough, the whole world will pass you by at a brisk trot, all those people distracted by their own affairs, or simply bedazzled by all the pretty flashing lights. They probably won't even notice you standing there.

But the police will. It wasn't all that long ago that *Times Square* was synonymous with *sleaze*. The lovable lowlifes of quaint Damon Runyon stories gave way to far less picturesque riffraff, while the diners and Horn & Hardart Automats gave way to peep shows and movie theaters offering "adult" entertainment.

And then, just when it looked as if there wasn't a bottle of bleach big enough to get all the stains out of the Great White Way, Times Square was cleaned up. Transformed into a tourist-friendly theme park. And the police are there at all hours of the day and night to see that you don't scuff it up again, at least not *too* much.

At the corner of West Forty-fourth Street and Broadway stood two large, metal tanks. They were both marked NITROGEN, and they had any number of duplicates scattered on other street corners all around the city. Just another part of the urban scenery, the visual equivalent of background noise or Muzak. Thousands of people passed by them thousands of times a day, and no one would bother to remark on their presence, any more than they would notice a curb every time they crossed the street.

If anyone *did* happen to notice the tanks, they wouldn't give them a second thought. Nitrogen? What the heck does the man on the street know from nitrogen? Especially the New York man on the street.

These nitrogen tanks, however . . . these tanks were *special*.

*   *   *

Dusk was falling over the city, including the corner of Forty-fourth and Broadway, as a pair of matching doors set seamlessly into the bodies of two particular tanks swung open. There stood Jay and Kay, soaking wet. Even the wildest water-park ride has to stop somewhere, and this was it, the end of the line.

They stepped onto the sidewalk where pedestrians went dashing past with places to go, people to see, and after-work drinks to drink. The crowd just swerved around them. No one paused, no one even glanced up.

New York . . . gotta love it.

It's said that during the worst days of the Spanish Inquisition, a great scholar came under suspicion of heresy. The agents of the Inquisition found him giving a lecture to one of his classes and carried him off for "questioning." He was imprisoned in the Inquisition dungeons, but despite their best efforts, his interrogators were unable to trump up a conviction and so, after some three years, he was set free.

Whereupon he went back to the university, stood up in front of his students, and announced (in Latin): "As we were saying the other day . . ." as if nothing worth mentioning had transpired.

When Jay stepped out of his tank, he turned to Kay and said, "Flushed." If he'd known any Latin himself, he might have added "Q.E.D."—*quod erat demonstrandum*—which is how, when asked to explain the obvious, the ancient Romans used to say, "Well, *duh!*"

But it didn't take a Latin scholar to see from Kay's dripping face that the man was ready to check out departure times for the next bus back to Truro. Jay thought fast, then slapped on a big grin and launched into a stream of rapid-fire chatter:

"Flushed!" he exclaimed cheerfully. "Man, back when you were an agent, you *loved* getting flushed." A quick glance told Jay that Kay wasn't buying this, so he cranked it up a notch: "Yeah, every Saturday night you'd be like, 'Flush me, Jay! Flush me!' and I'd be like, 'No . . .' "

He stopped the hard sell—it just wasn't working worth a damn. Getting serious again, he spoke to his former partner with all the sincerity in his heart.

"You can't quit on me now, Kay."

Still standing motionless in his tank, Kay calmly replied, "I save the world, you tell me why I stare at the stars." He straightened his dripping tie and stepped out onto the curb.

"Cool," Jay said, relieved that he wasn't about to lose Kay as easily as he'd feared. "Hop in." He pulled out his key chain and hit a button on the car alarm control dangling from it.

"Hop in what?" Kay asked.

The sleek, black Mercedes that was Jay's pride and joy came screaming around the corner and squealed to a dead-on-a-dime stop in front of them. An MIB autopilot dummy, dressed in full MIB uniform, was sitting behind the wheel. Jay hit another button on his key chain and the agent collapsed. The onboard mechanism sucked the PVC mannequin back into its compartment.

"That come standard?" Kay asked as they got into the car and slammed the doors.

"Used to be a black dude," Jay answered wryly as they got into the car, "but he got pulled over too often."

The Mercedes drove like a dream. At the wheel, Jay

tried to contact someone to determine what had caused the breach, and to get some idea of the status back at headquarters. He tapped a button on the steering wheel and commanded, "Computer. Surveillance. MIB."

Immediately a video display pivoted up in front of them and began to scroll through a rotating series of images, each one showing a different perspective of Men in Black Headquarters.

Things looked grim. Serleena's all-imprisoning neural root bundle dominated the great hall. The aliens who had been passing through customs were gone, either scattered and fled or caught up in Serleena's takeover. No moving MIB agents could be seen anywhere.

But some of us got out, Jay thought to himself. *Some of us* had *to get out. Whoever did this, they may be good, but they're not as good as we are. No way.*

Round Two's gonna come before they know it and then it's payback time, baby.

His grip on the steering wheel tightened. "MIB's locked down" was all he said.

Suddenly, something in the midst of the images caught his eye. "Computer," he said, eagerness glinting through his veneer of cool professional detachment. "Zoom in. Camera Six."

The computer obeyed, filling the small screen with a close-up shot of the gurney where the dead alien lay. It wasn't saying much, even if it was spilling its guts.

Realization hit home, and Jay pressed a button that opened up a communication channel. From somewhere inside the unlucky extraterrestrial, a tone sounded, soft but clear, and definitely *not* gas.

Frank the Pug popped out of the alien's guts, looking

like a demented prairie dog. He was wearing a comm headset.

"Jay?" he murmured urgently. "Where are you, partner?"

"Flushed," Jay shot back.

"MIB's Code One-Oh-One," Frank reported.

"Who did it?"

Frank raised himself a little higher out of the corpse, allowing him to peer at Serleena. She was far enough away from the gurney that there was small danger of their conversation being overheard. "Some chick in leather," the pug answered. "I think I've seen her in a Victoria's Secret catalog."

"Stay where you are," Jay ordered. "I'll be in touch." He cut the comm link.

Frank sank back into the guts of the dead alien, muttering, "Stay where you are. I'll be in touch." He sounded disgusted but resigned.

In the car, Kay was studying a shiny piece of paper. "What do you make of this?" he asked Jay. "I found it in the pocket of my suit."

It was a photograph. For a moment, Jay wondered how it had gotten there. Then he realized that, when a legend like Kay left the agency, his suit would have been archived, never to be issued to another agent. It was like retiring a ballplayer's jersey, only jerseys didn't have pockets.

They'd preserved Kay's suit just as it was when he took it off for what everyone thought was the last time. In the natural order of things, no one expected him to come back and reclaim it.

When he'd shown up back at headquarters, and Jay had put in the order for him to be issued a uniform, the agent in charge of such things had simply *re*issued him his old one.

The photo was of a much younger Kay. He was smiling and pointing at something, though it was impossible to see what that something might be. The background, a blue sky with white clouds, was slightly off.

"Weird," Kay remarked.

"Yeah," said Jay. "You're smiling."

Kay changed the subject. "That deneuralyzer," he said. "Only one?"

"Only official one," Jay amended. "Couple of years ago plans leaked out onto the Internet. Zed always said odds were pretty good some kid built one in his bedroom."

"So?"

"Computer," Jay said. "Internet."

The familiar America Online start page came up on the Mercedes's video display screen, and a voice whose mellow, cordial tones were recognized by millions of citizens nationwide announced: "Welcome . . ."

Jay punched another button. He didn't care if he had mail. Not at the moment. The eBay Web site popped up. His fingers flew, keying in the word DENEURALYZER.

Kay watched all this with a skeptical eye. "You really think you're gonna find—" he began.

"Just found it," Jay said.

He had. No question about that. The eBay page offered the following information:

1 ITEM FOUND FOR "DENEURALYZER."

Jay clicked on it and saw: NEVER USED. BIDS START AT $200,000. WOULD CONSIDER TRADE FOR MERCEDES G WAGON.

Jay scrolled farther down the page to view the name of the vendor they'd be dealing with. When he saw it, he smiled.

"Perfect," he said. "An old friend."

The eBay page's glow lit up the interior of the Mercedes with the SELLER data:

JACKJEEBS@AOL.COM

Perfect.

ELEVEN

All of history's most successful conquerors agree: Getting your hooks into a chunk of territory is relatively easy. It's consolidating your conquest—that is, holding on to it and using it for your own purposes—that's the hard part.

The Macedonian Greeks under Alexander the Great subjugated a vast empire that slipped through their fingers in short order. The Romans under Julius Caesar overran an even greater empire that they were able to keep under their direct control for centuries—millennia, if you count how many helpless schoolchildren have been forced to study Latin over the years. This demonstrates three points:

One: That everyone should be grateful for the way history turned out, because things like *Q.E.D.*, *sub rosa, nova,* and *E Pluribus Unum* are much easier to say in Latin than in Greek.

Two: That anyone can win a battle, but it's the man with the plan who wins the war. Thus the Alexander Salad never made it onto menus at the finer restaurants everywhere, with or without anchovies.

Three: That when it came to knowing how to confirm your conquests, Alexander and Julius both could have taken notes from Serleena.

Serleena had a purpose, Serleena had a plan, and Serleena had MIB Headquarters sewn up tighter than a duck's
caboose. As soon as she was sure of her mastery of the
situation, she dispatched her henchman/men to locate and
restrain the one individual who possessed the intelligence
she required.

In other words: Find Kay.

As she strode through the corridors, she was seething
with frustration. Her own search attempts had proved to be
fruitless. That made her mad.

She hoped Scrad/Charlie were enjoying better success,
hunting the elusive Kay through their assigned part of the
building, because if they weren't . . .

The thought of what she could and would do to them
warmed the cockles of her heart-analog with an evil anticipation that nearly cheered her up. She picked up her
pace, rushing ahead to meet either success or the opportunity to inflict a whole lot of highly creative pain.

She rounded a corner and nearly collided with Scrad/
Charlie as he/they were hurrying to meet her at about the
same pace.

"Alien prisoners released and armed," Scrad reported.

To Serleena, this was small potatoes.

"Have you found Kay?" she demanded.

"Neuralyzed," Scrad replied.

"Not active," Charlie added. "Civilian."

"What?" Serleena was taken aback. She did *not* look
pleased. Scrad/Charlie knew that when Serleena wasn't
happy, she made damn sure no one else in her general
vicinity was happy. Or breathing.

Rapidly the two heads Ping-Ponged out more information in a desperate, wild stab at keeping on her good side:

"But he was—"

"—here."

"To get—"

"—deneuralyzed."

"Deneuralyzed?" Serleena repeated. It was tough to tell how she was taking the news.

"Memory's shot," Scrad said, frantic to mollify her. "Erased. We'll find him."

"Don't put anything in our ears," Charlie implored, ever the believer in getting to the bottom line.

Scrad took over, determined to compel Serleena to focus on what he/they had managed to accomplish, as opposed to what they had thus far failed to do. Buy some time. So he directed her attention to the line of alien prisoners who were awaiting her inspection.

The Men in Black motto—official or not—had always been *Saving the Earth from the Scum of the Universe*. That was what the Internet claimed, anyhow. These aliens were scum personified.

Serleena walked down the line of newly freed prisoners, like General George S. Patton reviewing his troops or, more accurately, like Lee Marvin checking out his crew of assorted sadists, criminals, and wackos in *The Dirty Dozen*.

She liked what she saw.

"Prisoners of MIB," she said slowly, reflectively, savoring the moment. "The scum of the universe. Well, now it's the scum's turn. I'm running out of time, so I'll make it simple: Whoever brings Kay to me gets Earth."

It was a simple deal, all right; straightforward, and extremely popular with the freshly mustered troops. They were the motliest of crews. Some of them looked definitely humanoid—enough so to pass amid the throngs of ordinary Earthlings without raising so much as an eyebrow. Others looked only a little less ordinary—here was one with a mouth so small it was a wonder he could eat anything but noodles; there stood another who looked as if he'd been practicing hideous grimaces and his face had become stuck.

Still others had nothing humanoid about them at all, save for the fact that they walked on legs and had upper limbs. When—and if—these creatures had been free to wander at large among the populace of Earth, they wouldn't have been able to do so without first donning full disguises.

One thing united the prisoners: Evil. And they liked it. They more than liked Serleena, for evil recognizes its own. Besides which, Serleena was freeing them to do once more what they did best, namely, their worst.

Those who could, smiled with nasty anticipation. Their teeth were as ugly as their moral characters. Those physically incapable of smiling showed their eagerness to serve Serleena—and their own interests—in other ways, some of them nauseating.

Serleena turned away from the lineup, back to Scrad/Charlie. "Start by finding a deneuralyzer," she instructed him/them. "They'll be trying to get his memory back. Find the deneuralyzer and you'll find Kay."

One of the erstwhile alien prisoners spoke up just as Scrad/Charlie were heading off to do Serleena's bidding: "I know a slimy creep who might have one of those."

"Take them," Serleena directed her two-headed minion, indicating the line of ex-cons. "If you fail—" She let Scrad/Charlie squirm for just a little while on the pointy end of that *If* . . . "—I'm going to kill you and let you watch."

"The first 'you,' " Charlie said to Scrad as they hurried out, followed by the aliens Serleena had tapped to give them backup. "Was that *you* or was that—?" Not that it would make a whole lot of difference, when push came to shove, but Charlie liked to keep the details straight in his head.

Not all of the freed prisoners went with Scrad/Charlie. Serleena zeroed in on the last alien in the lineup and motioned for him to attend her. He turned slowly, all eight feet of him swathed in a long black cape. His wrinkled, aged face looked even more malevolent without the bars of an energy cage blocking the view.

"Jarra," Serleena said, welcoming an old comrade. "Good to see you. It's a disgrace they've kept a genius like you locked away in this sewer."

"Their Eagle Scout, Agent Jay, caught me siphoning Earth's ozone to sell on the black market," the old one growled. "They're very touchy about this whole global warming thing."

That was enough of the social niceties to satisfy Serleena. In truth, she cared no more about Jarra's recent imprisonment than she cared about whether the polar icecaps of Earth melted, stayed frozen, or evolved little propellers. First, last, and always, Serleena cared about making the world a better place for Serleena.

She got right down to business: "I need a spacecraft," she said. "Something that can travel three hundred times the speed of light. More powerful than anything they have here."

Jarra shrugged. This was not a tall order for a creature of his genius.

"Do it and I'll give you whatever you want."

"Give me Jay," Jarra said, his eyes alight with malice. "We'll call it even."

Serleena nodded. Haggling was for chumps. Besides, what was one MIB agent's life to her?

Her consent was all Jarra had been waiting for. He left without further ado. Serleena was content: She could depend on him. That was what she liked about Jarra, the way he didn't dance around a deal, the way he put his cards on the table, kept it simple, told you his price up front, take it or leave it.

Well, that and his utter contempt for Earthlings. She liked that about him, too.

Now there was only one more thing to do.

She walked over to a small, alien robot and said, "Gatbot, come with me. I have something special for you." The little robot followed her obediently.

Serleena always liked to have something special for everyone she met, even if "something" was a particularly painful death.

Some people just live to give.

TWELVE

Jack Jeebs's pawnshop was a crummy place on a crummy corner in one of the crummier parts of the city. If the whole package were any crummier, it would've been a Krispy Kreme Doughnuts franchise after Godzilla stomped the place flat.

For a crummy place, though, it had one mighty fancy car parked outside. The Bentley sitting at the curb gleamed like a dark pearl, even by night. Jay and Kay gave it the once-over before going into the shop. Jay couldn't quite hide his admiration for the sharp automobile.

Kay could hide anything.

Jeebs was behind the counter when the Men in Black crossed his threshold. There was nothing extraordinary about his pawnshop per se—shelves and display cases exhibiting a broad selection of jewelry and valuables that had been hocked when their former owners fell on hard times. But the proprietor thereof was another story. He was a lowlife, a plug-ugly creep with frizzy black hair, pendulous lips, pop eyes like a cartoon frog sucking on an air hose, ears that could pick up radio broadcasts from Arizona, a nose that was on every anteater's wish list for

Christmas, and a five o'clock shadow like a smear of shoe polish spread over his sagging cheeks and jowls.

His style of dress was tastelessness personified—his gold neck chains and bracelets might be pricey, but on him they looked cheap. And those who knew him well had learned that he made up for his lack of physical appeal by being a whiny, cowardly, self-centered, opportunistic jerk.

When he saw Jay, he smiled. His teeth were as rotten as his personality.

"Hey, Jay!" he exclaimed. "Haven't seen you in a while. Check out my wheels?" He nodded toward the door, laying prideful claim to the Bentley waiting outside. "Business is booming from the Internet, I—"

That was when Kay came in. Ebenezer Scrooge reacted to the black-shrouded ghost of Christmas Yet-to-Come with more aplomb.

"Uh-oh," said Jeebs.

Like many of Earth's resident aliens who chose to slink along in the shadowy borderlands between honest society and the underworld, he'd had plenty of run-ins with Kay in the past. None of them had turned out in the way he would have liked.

Jeebs ducked out of sight behind the counter. Only his nasal voice rose up to protest: "He's retired! He—he—"

"Jeebs, we need the deneuralyzer," Jay said. He didn't feel like putting up with a whole lot of Jeebs's jive. Not with MIB Headquarters in lockdown, Zed not answering any calls, Earth's future on the everything-go-boom line. He didn't even like dealing with Jeebs *without* any of that messy stuff going down. The guy was like a garden slug; he left a trail of slime over everything in his general vicinity. Too bad you couldn't rid yourself of the obnoxious varmint by sprinkling him with salt.

Jeebs's head popped up from behind the counter. He looked at Kay, who regarded the pawnshop owner with unfeigned indifference. There was nothing in the former MIB agent's eyes to indicate that he recognized Jeebs, but that might not mean a thing.

"You're kidding," Jeebs said warily.

"Meter's running, Jeebs," Jay said, with just a hint of *move-it-or-lose-it*.

Jeebs came out from behind the counter and walked right up to Kay. "Know me?" he challenged.

"Can't say I do," Kay replied. "Pretty good with faces. Think I'd remember that," sticking his finger in Jeebs's face.

Jeebs threw his head back and let loose a loud, gloating guffaw. "*Ha!* The great Kay's a neutral. *Love it!* Just love—"

Kay thrust his face right into Jeebs's ugly mug so abruptly that the pawnshop owner could count the hairs of his eyelashes. "Friend, you're standin' between me and my memories," Kay told him, and this time there was an unmistakable note in his voice. "You got this thing or not?"

"No," said Jeebs. Jay gave him a look. The little slug started talking fast.

"Even if I did . . . if it doesn't work, he dies, you kill me. If it does work, I've brought back Kay, who'll hound me to my dying day. What's my incentive, here?"

Jay aimed his weapon right between Jeebs's bulbous, goggling eyes. "Doesn't friendship count for anything, Jeebs-ee?" he crooned.

Now *that* was incentive like Mama used to make.

Jeebs swallowed hard and appeared to give in. He headed for the door to the cellar, opened it, and started down.

"I keep it down here, next to the snowblowers, homey." His voice echoed back up the stairs as Jay and Kay descended after him, taking care never to let the slippery customer get too far out of range. Slime has a way of oozing away between the cracks if you give it half a chance.

Jeebs's version of the deneuralyzer was a far cry from the classy, top-of-the-line model now lost in the firewall-and-flush of MIB Headquarters. It looked a lot like what would happen if all the good old 1950s B-movie mad scientists' la-BOH-ratories threw up at once. The chair where the victim—er, *subject*—sat had been scavenged from a dentist's office, and was set up within a mostly open spherical metal framework. Some of the wiring was exposed. Gaffer's tape was everywhere. A few plumbing pipes stuck out here and there. Bits and pieces of a cannibalized iMac computer were hitched up to the God-knows-what of every professional electrician's worst nightmares.

The weird thing was, the whole Rube Goldberg contraption came close to resembling an electric chair, and Kay was the candidate for the hot seat. Nonetheless, he sat down.

"Ever use this thing?" he inquired, his fingers curling over the ends of the armrests.

"I used the exhaust fan once to make some hot-air popcorn, but that's about it," Jeebs replied. He shoved a mouthpiece between Kay's lips. It was nasty.

"Have you removed all your jewelry?" Jeebs asked.

Kay nodded.

"Are you allergic to shellfish?"

Kay gave him a death stare. The pawnbroker shrugged. He'd been on Earth long enough to know the value of covering his butt from even the remotest possibility of a negligence lawsuit. He feared the Men in Black, but he absolutely dreaded lawyers.

"Okay," Jeebs said, his preparations complete. He hit a switch.

The machine lurched to life.

Electricity flowed through unknown channels. The exhaust fan whizzed and spun madly. In the chair, Kay's eyes dilated to almost complete blackness.

Outside the pawnshop, all over Manhattan, the lights in streets and homes and offices leapt and died and leapt back on again as huge power surges ravaged the city. Sparks flew, arcs crackled, computers coughed once, twice, pathetically, then rolled over and played dead. And lo, there was much wailing and gnashing of teeth and frantic calling of Tech Support.

It took only an instant.

"That's it," said Jeebs, flicking the switch off.

As soon as the juice stopped flowing, Kay launched backward out of the chair and hit the floor behind it. His whole body was shaking uncontrollably. Smoke poured out of his ears while a horrified Jay watched, helpless.

Then it was all over. He lay still.

Dead still.

Jay and Jeebs leaned in over the limp body. "Kay?" Jay said, trying not to think the unthinkable.

Jeebs was less affected. "Dead," he pronounced cavalierly. "Oh, well."

His head exploded.

Jay didn't even flinch when the blast hit. He knew there was only one thing that could have wiped that devil-may-care smirk off Jeebs's face, along with the rest of his repulsive head. He glanced down to where Kay was sitting up, holding the Noisy Cricket that had just done its part for urban beautification.

"Kay, you back?" he asked. He meant memorywise, of course. Dead men don't pack heat.

"No," Kay replied.

"Then how'd you know his head would grow back?" Jay asked. It was true: Jeebs was vulnerable to many things, just not to having his head blown off. It was painful and it was messy, but he always grew himself a new one in jig time.

"It grows back?" Kay asked in unmasked disappointment.

As they spoke, Jeebs's head was already regenerating. First it budded up out of the ravaged neck, re-forming as a slightly gooey miniature of its former self, with some of the facial features grossly out of proportion to others. Next it began to inflate like a hideous balloon, until it reached its proper size.

"Nice," Jeebs muttered sarcastically throughout the process. "Real nice."

"Kay, you sure you don't remember—" Jay pressed.

Kay got up, brushed himself off, and simply said, "Take care," before heading for the cellar stairs.

"Kay—!" Jay's cry went unheeded.

"Kay, wait!" Jeebs called after him. "I never got the up-dated software. I'm still working off of six-point-oh. Your brain needs to reboot!

"Give it a minute, for crying out loud!"

It was no good. Kay climbed up the steps and was gone.

Jeebs turned to Jay, his eyes damp with regret and sincerity. "Bottom of my heart, Jay," he said. "Really sorry. I hope this doesn't affect our friendship, which is based on years of loyalty, trust, and respect for one another."

He might have had more to say, he might not, he might have had to pause in order to find a bigger shovel, but whatever the case, he didn't get to say any more because just then there was a deafening *crack*-boom-clatter-clatter, as the back wall of the pawnshop basement was kicked in and four vicious-looking aliens, armed to the teeth/gills/tendrils, stormed in.

Jay took one look at these uninvited guests and did a quick tuck-and-tumble behind the deneuralyzer.

"Where is he?" the first alien growled at Jeebs.

"Over there," Jeebs said, pointing toward the deneuralyzer and the hidden Jay without a second's hesitation. Some would call this a betrayal, but if you asked Jeebs, he would insist that it was a betrayal that came out of a friendship based on years of loyalty, trust, respect . . .

The alien took aim at the deneuralyzer and fired. Jeebs's cobbled-up piece of technojunk disintegrated with a thunderous *boom*, revealing Jay, his own formidable weapon out and ready, trained on the aliens . . .

. . . who had their weapons trained on *him*.

They circled each other slowly, in that classic no-win situation that the Men in Black liked to call a Gurkhoozian Standoff.

"Where is he?" the first alien demanded. "Where is Kay?"

Jay wasn't about to say, but Jeebs didn't suffer from fear of public speaking. He opened his mouth to be helpful to his newfound buddies, but his urge to be chatty vanished suddenly, along with his head, in a moist and sticky explosion. He staggered out of the room, complaining through rapidly regrowing lips. "Right in the *mouth*. Nothing's gonna taste right."

"No idea," Jay said without taking his eyes or his attention off his four circling adversaries.

He recognized them from the MIB lockup: not merely the scum of the universe, but the scumsuckers, and ugly. They were the living proof that the saying *Handsome is as handsome does* held true in the inverse, too. He mentally reviewed everything he knew about them, from their planets of origin to their criminal records to the length of time they ought to be serving in the slammer, if someone hadn't set them free and sicced them on his tail.

His and Kay's.

These guys were ruthless killers who couldn't find *compassion* in the dictionary, mainly because they'd devour the librarian who tried to show them how to use the book. And if these were the underlings, he couldn't wait to meet the boss.

He studied the row of faces glowering at him. *Some of these boys make old Jeebs look like Brad Pitt,* he thought. He made a careful, strategic retreat, placing one of the cellar's unbreached walls at his back.

"Give up," one of the aliens hissed.

Jay showed his teeth. "I like my odds."

Never play dice with the universe.

Two un-Earthly arms burst through the wall behind Jay. One wrapped itself around his throat, the other jerked the weapon out of his hand, but not before he managed to fire off one devastating shot, blasting away the bottom half of the first alien.

Unlike Jeebs, this creep wasn't going to be making any kind of a comeback.

"Where's Kay?" one of the remaining creatures demanded.

Jay said nothing, putting on the same stone face he'd seen Kay wear in similar situations many times before. His stoic silence didn't please his inquisitor. The alien picked him up and hurled him across the room, where a second one intercepted him in midflight with a hard forearm block to the throat.

Jay went down, sprawling.

He opened his eyes slowly to see a fresh face in the crowd. A fresh *pair* of faces, that is. Scrad/Charlie regarded him from a short distance away, with a patient, pitying gaze that was as genuine as a politician's promise to cut taxes and increase government funding.

"We really need Kay." Scrad spoke as if explaining the situation to Jay in this way would be enough to get results.

"He's a neutral." Jay forced the words out of a bruised throat. "He was neuralyzed."

"Tell us something we don't know," Scrad said.

"Yeah!" Charlie popped up to add his two cents' worth. "Tell us something we don't—" His contribution to the interrogation was interrupted by a big, wet sneeze that sprayed all over the back of Scrad's head. Scrad stiffened, staring straight ahead, mortified.

"I am sooooo sorry," Charlie offered.

Scrad froze him out, gave him the cold shoulder. He walked over to where Jay lay, surrounded by the extraterrestrial ex-cons. "I'm not much for violence—" he began.

He motioned to one of the aliens, who gleefully gave Jay a solid kick to the stomach. The MIB agent grunted and curled up into a ball. "—but if I don't bring Kay back, a certain squiggly somebody is gonna kick *my* ass. So where is he?"

"Don't . . . know," Jay said, panting for breath.

The alien that had kicked him leaned in close, leering. "You don't look too good," he observed smugly.

"*You* look like a can of creamed corn somebody threw up," Jay countered. It was a pretty accurate assessment. The alien in question had a pebbly yellow complexion, though the spiky protuberances framing his face actually made him look more like a horned toad that had been sculpted out of creamed corn.

Not that Jay had the time or opportunity to work out a more precise description. He landed a good punch, good enough to lay open the creature's grisly face. Another one of the remaining aliens laughed, which caused Jay to look at him and add: "And *you* look like what came outta the dog that ate him."

This was not only deserved, but accurate; disgustingly so. Back on his home turf, this alien had been counted as one of the most physically attractive of his kind. In fact, he'd been well on his way to becoming a supermodel before he fell in with a bad crowd, turned to a life of crime, and had to flee to the sanctuary of Earth. It was a source of great bitterness to him to realize that *here* his looks were only one step away from the contents of every pooper-scooper in the greater metropolitan area.

Enraged, the butt of Jay's jibe struck him with the butt of his weapon.

Can't take a joke unless it's on someone else . . . lousy

out-of-towner . . . The words reeled through Jay's mind, distracting him a little from the pain.

"Bend him," Scrad directed.

Such a simple command. The alien with the corn kernel complexion picked Jay up, held him high over his head, and began to bend his spine backward the way the strongman at the circus might show off by bending an iron bar.

But iron bars don't feel a thing.

"Where's Kay?" Scrad demanded again, as Jay's spine was pulled back, back, back, until it was a miracle that it didn't snap in two.

"Where's Kay?" Scrad repeated loudly enough to make himself heard over the sound of Jay's agonized scream.

The answer to Scrad's question was standing on the sidewalk just outside of Jeebs's pawnshop, trying to get across the street.

The traffic in New York was just a wee bit more . . . hectic than in Truro. His first attempt at crossing had nearly ended on the bumper of a speeding taxicab. Kay stepped back onto the curb just in time.

As he waited for an opening in the flow of vehicles, he couldn't help looking around, taking in his surroundings. Funny, how some things were just a part of the passing scene while others—

—others leapt out and caught your eye.

A postman walked by. Kay followed him with his eyes, and noticed that he hardly broke stride as he tucked a long, scaly tail back into his shorts.

A tandem bicycle flew past, surrounded by blinking lights, a boom box thumping on the handlebars.

A street person wandered past, pushing a grocery cart

filled with all sorts of junk, the gleanings of other people's rubbish. Kay stared into the cart as it passed. Two glowing red eyes stared back. A pair of little alien hands hooked their fingers over the wire lip of the cart.

Kay shook his head. This was worse than that incident back in the Truro Post Office. Why was he *seeing* things? Why *these* kinds of things? It was no good. He had to get out of this place. Somehow he was convinced that all this—this *craziness*—was somehow New York City's fault. He needed to get back to Truro, then everything would be okay. A man could hold on to his sanity in Truro.

If he could only get back to Truro.

If he could only get across this goddamn New York street!

He saw a gap in the traffic and got ready to step off the curb. Glancing down at his feet, he noticed a cockroach, one of those big, muscular, steroid-enriched cockroaches that could whip its weight in sewer lizards. Instinctively he lifted his shoe to squash the disgusting bug like . . . well, a bug.

He stopped, his shoe hovering above the doomed insect.

Something was happening inside his head. A series of little flashes, like a string of exploding lightbulbs, was going off. Strobing through his memory, illuminating an ever-growing swarm of moments from his lost past.

A picture zapped in and out of sight, the image of another bug, another bug that he knew *wasn't* just another bug. He knew this bug's name.

Edgar?

All at once he knew that not every bug you saw on the streets of New York was what it seemed to be. No more than every postman, or every street person, or . . .

Kay lowered his shoe gently, setting it down just beside the cockroach. The insect looked up.

"Damn decent of you," it remarked, and scuttled away.

Kay wasn't listening. He was gazing up into the night sky. Little by little, the glimmer of a smile crossed his face, like a distant shooting star.

Back in the basement of Jeebs's pawnshop, Jay wasn't smiling.

Scrad/Charlie and the other intergalactic scumsuckers watched, fascinated, as their accomplice continued to bend the MIB agent's spine backward like a plastic straw. Sweat drenched Jay's entire body, which shook violently as he tried desperately to fight the pain, to will it away.

Jay's torment was having an effect on at least one of the spectators. Charlie lowered his head, looking a little green. "I think I'm gonna be sick," he choked.

"You *really* don't wanna do that," Scrad cautioned him, still remembering the colossal sneeze.

And then, just when it looked as if the basement were about to echo with the sound of snapping vertebrae, Jay went limp as a leaf of boiled lettuce. The alien holding him overhead flung his slack body to the floor with a sneer. The MIB agent had undergone torture intense enough to wring information out of solid marble, and he hadn't said a word. There was only one conclusion to draw.

"I think he's telling the truth," Scrad said.

"Then he's no good to us," Jay's extraterrestrial torturer said. He smiled, showing off a mouth full of teeth like a great white shark's, then pulled out a particularly nasty-looking gun and took dead aim on the helpless man at his

feet. There was a loud report, and the air was filled with
tiny particles of a formerly living thing.

Jay was still there.

Shark-mouth wasn't. The cellar air shimmered with the
particles of one totally vaporized offworld tough guy.

Kay looked down at his partner, holding the Noisy
Cricket that had blown Shark-mouth to Kingdom Come,
and said, "Didn't I teach you anything, slick?"

No doubt about it this time: Kay was back. *Really* back.

The remaining aliens rushed him, thirsting for blood,
avid to be the one to put an end to a legend.

Scrad/Charlie cowered into a corner where Jeebs had
amassed a pile of pawnable junk. For a moment the two-
headed henchman wondered if it would be a good idea to
remind these guys that Serleena wanted Kay taken *alive*. It
didn't look like any of them was thinking along those
lines. Scrad opened his mouth to speak, only to have
Charlie snake his head around in front of him and shake it
sagely in the universal symbol for "nuh-uh" that as good
as said: *What, am I the only sane one here?*

Scrad recognized the wisdom in this and dived under
the junk pile. Maybe Kay would be alive when this was
over, maybe not. If not, he'd worry about what to tell Serleena later. After all, later was another day. Or something.

From the floor, a battered Jay played armchair quarter-
back while Kay took on the last three aliens singlehanded.
One of them had a face that looked like a child's early ex-
periments with Silly Putty. He pulled a knife and thrust it
at Kay.

"Gayroon, Kay!" Jay shouted. "Go for the mosh tendrils!"

Kay grabbed the squirming cluster of vinelike shoots
sprouting from the knife-wielding alien's chin, and tore

them off. The alien dropped the knife and collapsed, writhing in agony.

A human-looking alien wearing a cap low on his forehead leapt in to take his fallen partner's place.

"Pineal eye," Jay called out.

Without an instant's hesitation, Kay grabbed the cap off the oncoming alien's head, revealing the bulbous third eye. He nailed it with his fist, and the creature went down.

"On your left!" Jay warned him.

Kay wheeled around and saw the third alien. He wore a turtleneck sweater high, so high it almost covered the lower half of his face, and for a very good reason: Some evolutionary practical joke had caused this particular species to evolve two large, dangling globes of flesh that hung down heavily beneath his chin.

"Go for the—" Jay began.

"Self-explanatory," Kay concluded, and gave the balls a mighty roundhouse punch that sent the alien reeling, out of commission and singing soprano.

"Looks like you were in a tight spot here, sport," Kay remarked, helping Jay to his feet.

Jay brushed this off with a carefree: "I had it handled."

That was the instant the Gayroon picked to pop up behind him, out of tendrils and out of temper, ready to do some impromptu rend-and-shred.

Kay pointed the Noisy Cricket right at Jay, who jumped straight up, doing a split in midair. Kay fired right between Jay's legs, and the Noisy Cricket blew the Gayroon to smithereens before Jay hit the ground.

Securing his weapon, Kay said, "You need a partner."

"Had one," Jay replied. "Job got too rough for him.

Now he's delivering Hallmark cards." He looked at Kay meaningfully.

"I'm back," Kay said tersely. "Tuck in your shirt."

"Your memory's totally back?" Jay probed. He wanted to believe, wanted it more than anything.

"That's right."

"Light of Zartha," Jay said, and waited for the explanation, the big revelation, the answer to the mystery.

"Never heard of it," Kay said. "Let's go." He started back up the basement steps.

Jay took one look back over his shoulder, checking out the devastation in the basement. Everything was quiet, that ominous, haunting silence that comes after all great battles. Jeebs's cellar was strewn with the bodies and particulate matter of dead aliens. It was hard to get a body count on the ones that Kay had vaporized, but Jay was pretty sure he'd managed to keep track of how many there had been.

It didn't add up.

"See a two-headed freak on your way in?" he asked Kay.

"No," Kay replied, almost to the top of the steps. "I saw Jeebs with no head, running down the alley."

Jay frowned, then put it temporarily out of mind. *Damn,* it was good to be working with Kay again!

They left the basement. As soon as the sound of their footsteps faded out, the junk pile in the corner stirred and Scrad/Charlie emerged.

"We got problems," Scrad said.

"From the day we were born," Charlie agreed.

THIRTEEN

The black Mercedes was still waiting for them when they emerged from the pawnshop. Now, your ordinary New Yorker—if there is such a thing as an *ordinary* New Yorker—might be somewhat startled by this. Not that a classy car like that might not be safe on the city streets. Nuh-uh.

But New York is a *magical* city, and some classy cars do a fast disappearing act when left by themselves in certain sections of the Big Apple. That or they grow legs and walk away, which is another kind of magic. Whaddayagonnado?

But not the Mercedes. Even in Jeebs's neighborhood, a primo car like that one was as safe as a house. In fact, many houses were a lot less secure than the Mercedes. Any punk who thought he was man enough to take this Mercedes for a joyride would come out of the experience unable to feel anything resembling joy ever again.

If he came out of it at all.

"If your memory's back, how come you don't know about the Light of Zartha?" Jay asked Kay as they headed for the car.

"Must've neuralyzed myself," Kay said. "To keep the

information from me." He spoke as though it all made perfect sense. On some level, it probably did, though not to his partner.

"Good plan," Jay replied with a sardonic twist of his lips.

There was a brief moment of conflict when both of them reached for the driver's-side door at the same time.

"I drive," said Kay, reasserting his old authority as senior partner of the team.

"Yeah, a little blue van that says U.S. MAIL," Jay shot back.

He was glad to have Kay back—no mistake about that—but he was *damned* if he was going to relinquish his right to drive. Back in Kay's day, the MIB still drove the old Ford LTDs. Now, who did he think he was, expecting to shoot right back to the top of the pecking order?

Back less than ten minutes and already it's the same old crap, Jay fumed as he tried to stand his ground and hold on to his right to the driver's seat.

Kay paid him no attention, muscling him aside and getting behind the wheel. He looked uncomfortable.

"Doesn't feel right," he said.

"It's not the side you open the mailbox from," Jay told him.

"I meant you pretending you're in charge," Kay clarified. "Scene of the crime," he said, declaring their next destination.

Or was he asking for directions?

Jay just stood there.

Kay gave him a hard look.

Jay shrugged. "Forgot where it is. Must've neuralyzed

myself before." Game, set, and match. He motioned for Kay to get out of the car.

Kay did so, grudgingly, and Jay took his place behind the wheel. Kay got into the passenger's side.

"You've become a real wise-ass," he informed Jay.

"Taught me everything I know, slick," Jay replied with a grin, as the Mercedes peeled away from the curb, heading for Soho.

On the way there, Jay briefed Kay on everything he knew about the case so far. He was still doing so when the Mercedes pulled up in front of Ben's Famous Pizza.

"He was Zarthan and she was Kylothian, no doubt about that," he said, describing the victim and the perp. "Laura—the witness—saw the whole thing."

"If you completed her interrogation, why didn't you neuralyze her?" Kay wanted to know.

Jay dodged the question, opening his door and getting out. "Scene of the crime," he announced and headed for the pizzeria door before Kay could say another word.

It wasn't that easy to shake the restored Agent Kay when he scented a violation of the MIB regs. As they walked into the dark, empty pizzeria, he was in full dress-down lecture mode:

"—MIB Procedural Code number seven-seven-three-slash-I-one clearly states all civilian witnesses must be neuralyzed within—"

He ducked in mid-discourse, just in time to avoid being whacked in the face by a large pizza tray that came swinging out of the darkness.

Kay's old reflexes were back, too.

Jay wasn't so quick. The pizza tray hit him full in the face, making a lovely, reverberating *clang*. He went down.

It would have been a pure Bugs Bunny moment if not for the fact that it wasn't a rabbit holding the tray, but Laura.

Kay whipped out his Noisy Cricket in an eyeblink and pointed it at her.

"No!" Jay shouted through the ringing in his ears, yanking Kay's arm down.

"Jay!" Laura cried, dropping to her knees, hugging the tray to her chest. "I heard a noise out here and—I'm sorry."

"It's okay. I'm cool," Jay said as she helped him to his feet. To Kay he said: "The witness. Laura, this is Kay, my old partner."

"Pleasure," Kay said, as graciously as he could muster.

Laura wasn't paying attention to him. She only had eyes for Jay. "Thanks for sending those agents over to keep an eye on me last night," she said with a smile. "It was very sweet."

It might have been a sweet gesture on Jay's part, but it sent Kay right back into the saddle of his high horse. "MIB Procedural Code number five-nine-four-B clearly states MIB personnel shall never be used—"

"The Zarthan," Jay put in, cutting the lecture short. "Ben. He was vaporized right around here."

At the mention of the Zarthan's Earth-name, a change came over Kay. He became distracted, staring off into space as if more of those little neural flashbulbs were popping through his memory.

"What?" Jay asked, trying to bring him back to the here and now.

"Ben about five-nine?" Kay inquired, still with that distant look in his eyes. "Portly fella? Thinning hair?"

"You knew him?" Laura stared at Kay in wonderment.

The restored MIB agent crossed to a framed photograph hanging on the wall of the pizzeria. It was a very old photo, taken in the days before digital, before instant. The image showed Ben standing on a pier that looked like it was somewhere out on the Island—Montauk, maybe. It was the standard pose for a man who has just caught himself the great-granddaddy of all gigantic bass and wants the world to remember his prowess. The fish dangled by its tail from a wooden gallows while Ben stood there with his arm around it, beaming proudly. There was nothing too re-markable about that trophy photograph, except that the background . . .

. . . the background—blue sky and white clouds—didn't exactly seem to belong in the shot. That was odd, and because it was so odd, Kay was certain to notice it. More than that, he was bound to remark on it, to want to investigate the photographic phenomenon further—he usually had an eagle eye for oddities.

Only he didn't. This time he just studied the photo for a bit, then said:

"Never saw him before in my life. Helluva fish."

And that was the oddest thing of all.

He walked away from the picture. Jay was about to follow him when a nagging wisp of insight tickled his mind. He glanced back at the photograph of the happy fisherman, then went right up to it and studied it at close range. It reminded him of something, something he'd seen somewhere else, sometime not too long ago.

"Kay . . ." he summoned his partner. When Kay joined him, Jay produced the other old photograph, the one Kay had found in the pocket of his retired MIB suit.

Jay placed the picture of Kay over the picture of the

dead bass and slid it up and down until the two back-
grounds aligned with one another—perfectly. Now the
image in the frame showed Ben with his arm around Kay,
who was pointing and laughing.

The question was: What was he pointing *at*?

"Helluva fish," Jay muttered.

He considered the joined image from several angles,
trying to figure out what the oh-so-much-younger Kay
was pointing at.

Nothing in the picture. It wasn't a natural pose, either; it
was done with deliberation, purpose. But as for *why* it had
been done . . .

"So you left yourself clues?" Jay asked.

"Yeah," Kay said dryly. "In case I had to be deneuralyzed, because my replacement couldn't handle the
situation."

"Maybe the person who got deneuralyzed shouldn't
have *created* the situation in the first place," Jay countered.

"Boys . . ." Laura stepped in before the two reunited
partners could get bogged down in a bickering match.
They both caught her *I-don't-have-time-for-dealing-with-
children* tone, looked at each another long and hard,
dropped the quarrel, and returned to business.

"Looks like you're pointing in this direction," Jay said,
indicating the trajectory of Kay's telltale finger. "Pointing
at something . . ." He looked across the room to where Ben
had hung a photograph of an astronaut. A real American
hero—the sort who decorated pizzerias throughout the
five boroughs.

"Pointing—excuse me—" Jay stepped around his
partner, the better to follow the invisible trail. "—pointing
at the astronaut—"

"Jay—" Kay began, trying to get a word or two in edgewise.

He might as well have saved his breath. Jay was gathering momentum. He studied the second photograph only an instant before declaring:

"Okay, now the *astronaut* is pointing to those pizza boxes." He stepped over to the stack of the pizza boxes, and gave them a close scrutiny, particularly the logo. It was the same as the one decorating the paper napkins: a slice, a statue, and a star. "Now, to the layman, these are just stacked pizza boxes," he said in his best Sherlock Holmes voice, and pointing at the boxes in question, "but to the trained eye, this is a *clue*."

Jay was clearly pleased with himself as he continued: "This isn't a slice of pizza, but an arrow! And it's aimed directly at—"

"Jay—" Kay tried again. "Wait a minute, slick."

But by now, Jay was a veritable juggernaut of deductive logic, and woe betide anyone rash enough to get in his way.

"Slowing me down, slick," he told Kay. "Whatever we're looking for is in this cabinet." He could feel the spirit of Holmes hovering over him as he crossed to the cabinet indicated by the pizza slice/arrow.

Was he brilliant or what?

"Jay—!" You had to award Kay points for persistence.

Jay wasn't listening. Great detectives don't need to listen to their sidekicks. Sidekicks are only there to add their admiring voices to the rest of the chorus, once the great detective has solved the mystery. That was *exactly* what was about to happen, and as much as he wanted to bask in Laura's hero-worshiping gaze, once he produced proof that he was strong, brave, handsome, and *smart*, too, he wanted Kay's admiration even more.

He could almost hear Kay's inevitable gasp of awe as he got down and flung open the cabinet doors with a ceremonious flourish, thrusting one hand inside as he announced: "*Here* we go."

He grabbed the prize and held it out, displaying a small, flat, brightly colored can of distinctive shape for Kay's inspection.

"Anchovy fillets in virgin olive oil!" he declared victoriously. He wasn't sure what the heck the can would reveal when it was opened, besides the promised anchovies, but by *God* he was proud of himself for having found it.

"Anchovies—" The wheels of deduction were turning again. "—anchovies . . . fish . . . we need a boat . . ."

"*Jay,*" Kay said, bringing his partner crashing down to Earth. He pointed to a key that was hanging in plain sight on the wall next to the original photograph and took it from its nail. "Hope I'm not slowing you down, slick."

"Why didn't you just paint a sign on the wall that said KAY'S SECRET KEY?" the deflated Agent Jay wanted to know, putting aside the can of anchovies along with his shattered dreams of glory and adulation. He watched closely as Kay turned the key over in his fingers. On one side of it were the figures C-18, on the other side the letters G.C.T. "Now we just have to figure out—"

"I know where it goes," Kay said. Before he uttered another word on the subject, he looked at Laura, then donned his Ray-Bans and took out his neuralyzer. Her eyes widened, but she didn't say a word as she stared at the red light.

Jay's hand shot out and he pulled Kay's hand down before he could flash Laura's memories away. "No," he said. "Not yet."

"MIB Procedural Code number seven-seven-three—" Kay started up the Rulebook Recitation subroutine, one of the more annoying items the deneuralyzer had restored to his memory.

"I know!" Jay interrupted him. "I have a feeling she might be able to help me. *Us,*" he corrected himself quickly. "Help *us.*"

Kay regarded his partner impassively, then said, "Well, she can't stay here. They'll be back." With that, he turned and left the premises. His expression said it clearly. He'd cited Standard MIB Operating Procedure. If Junior chose to ignore it, for whatever reason, the ball was in his court, now.

Jay looked at Laura, and flashed her an encouraging smile. He took her by the hand. Her hand felt good in his, as if it belonged there, as if he'd spent his whole life building up to this moment, reaching out for it, and now . . .

She was looking at him in a way that told him she felt the same way he did, that their hands belonged clasped together that way, that she was as eager as he to put this whole weird business of aliens and secret keys behind them, so that they could stop making silly small talk and say the words they both knew needed to be said.

Unfortunately, that time had not yet arrived.

"You can stay with some friends of mine," he said.

"People like you?" she asked.

Jay didn't answer. He decided to let it be a surprise.

There's a stereotype of the swinging bachelor pad, seen in all the buddy movies, though most folks probably haven't actually seen one in real life. And those folks can count themselves among the fortunate.

Laura Vasquez needed a safe place to stay, and as far as Jay knew, this was her best bet. As for the bachelors themselves, the proprietors of the pad per se, he figured that if she could handle the type of traffic you got in a pizza joint, she could handle these guys just fine.

He just hoped she wasn't prejudiced. Too many women these days thought that the swinging bachelor was a cultural fossil, at best, and at worst some sort of miserable, sexist worm.

In this particular instance . . .

"Jay!"

Antennae aquiver, spindly digits raised in greeting, buggy black eyes alight with camaraderie, the whole caffeine-addicted pack of Worm Guys welcomed Jay and Laura into their humble home.

It was small, but sufficient to their needs. And since *they* were small—or rather, short—there was a bit less height clearance than in a normal apartment. It was the only way they could pull in a government salary and still own a swinging bachelor pad in New York City: low overhead.

At first sight, when looking over the apartment itself, the term that sprang to mind most readily was *retro chic*. Only not too much emphasis on the *chic*.

Whoever had done the interior decorating for this slithery crew of womanizers had been clobbered over the head by the boxed video set of every Rat Pack movie ever made. The spirit of *Sinatra, the Hollywood Years* stalked the linoleum floors, while the great Dean Martin would have felt right at home lounging on the praying-mantis-green sectional sofa that serpentined its way through the living area.

A fireplace stood to one side like a giant, circular hibachi with its funnel-shaped top, warming this surreal home-sweet-home. This was a good thing, because there was also a sunken hot tub, smack-dab in the middle of the living room floor, and the glittering panoramic picture windows were bound to allow drafts to seep through.

One of the wormy denizens of this hymn to a bygone-thank-you-dear-Lord lifestyle stretched out on the sofa, reading an issue of *Travel and Leisure*. Another was lifting weights, working on buffing up and bulking out the gangly ol' multisegmented bod'. A third was paying close attention to Miss Fitness USA on the tube, while a fourth was chilling out in the aforementioned sunken hot tub.

Jay didn't have time for the social amenities. "MIB's gone Code One-Oh-One," he informed them brusquely.

Immediately the worms broke into a manic, babbling, twanging, nasal gibbering.

"One-Oh-One!"

"Taken over."

"Bad."

"Very bad."

It didn't much matter which one of them said what. Curiously enough, they didn't talk that way because they belonged to a hive-mind or a collective consciousness or any other cliché from the annals of pop sci-fi. They just had no manners.

What mattered to Jay was getting them to clam up and pay attention.

"Guys, I need your help," Jay announced. He grabbed

Laura, who had been standing behind him, and presented
her to the group. "This is Laura."

"Lau-ra."

"Hey, Laura."

"Yeah, baby." This last was said a tad salaciously. The
worm in question might have been leering, though with a
face like that, it was hard to tell.

Well, they *were* swinging bachelors.

Laura looked at them, taking it all in with relative calm.
After having seen Scrad/Charlie, and Serleena, and Ben's
true shape beneath his fake human skin, she wasn't so easily
shocked anymore. Still, she felt compelled to remark:

"They're worms."

This pronouncement met with general approval and ju-
bilation in the ranks.

"Worms!"

"Yeah!"

"Once you go worm, that's what you'll yearn."

The Worm Guys gave way to berserk self-congratulatory
displays, high-fiving each other madly just as Kay stepped
into the room.

"They're all talk," he told Laura. "Pretty much."

Laura shrugged. "I've dated worse." This wasn't just a
witty response, or an attempt to keep her spirits up in the
face of a crisis beyond anything she had yet experienced. It
was the plain, unvarnished truth. Anyone who says different should try being a single, attractive woman in New
York for a while. Don't say you weren't warned, though.

Kay's appearance was perhaps the only thing that could
have excited the Worm Guys any more than their own
smooth repartee.

"Kay! You're back," they chorused.

One of their number, a worm with the euphonious name of Sleeble, said, "Somebody said you were dead. You look good!" It was unclear whether he meant *for a dead guy* or not.

"They're on suspension," Jay explained to his partner. "Caught stealing office supplies."

Another worm who went by the name of Geeble casually shoved a huge case of cigarettes behind him with his foot, and protested, "We were framed!"

"Zed's wormaphobic!" His comrade/sibling/roommate Sleeble backed him up.

Kay didn't care. "We're double-parked," he commented. He turned to go.

Jay knew Kay was right—they didn't have much time. But before he left Laura behind, he wanted to do everything he could to make sure she'd be all right. He spoke earnestly and intently to the worms: "Look, Laura is very important to me—"

In the doorway, Kay paused for a moment and glanced back over his shoulder, giving him a probing look. Jay quickly added: "—to *us*, to *MIB*, as a witness and all—so I want you to keep an eye on her."

The worms were more than happy to accept this awesome responsibility.

"Definitely."

"Noooo problem."

"Keep both of them on her." How could he tell when a worm was leering? With *those* mouths? Worms were *born* leering.

The worm watching TV motioned to Laura. "Why don't

you sit over here?" he offered, patting the seat beside him invitingly.

"Yeah, *you* got a shot," the weight-lifting worm sneered.

"Shut up."

"Make me."

Jay and Laura ignored the macho squabbling.

"My communicator," he said softly, handing it to her. If Kay had still been within earshot, he probably would have rattled out the MIB Procedural Code number that strictly prohibited agents from loaning their equipment to civilians. But if Kay was anywhere near enough to overhear, he didn't bother.

It was just as well; if he had spoken up, Jay would have told him to back off. No matter what Kay thought, Jay knew that now, maybe for the first time in his life, there was at least one thing in the world more important than MIB rules and regulations.

To him, anyway.

Laura took the device and gave Jay a kiss as if it were the most natural thing to do. It was impulsive, and her expression said it surprised her almost as much as it did him, but it was one of those nice surprises that came too seldom in life. Clearly she thought the world needed more of them.

Startled, blindsided by a bewildering storm of emotions, wishes, duties, and desires, Jay did the only thing he could do: He warned her to stay away from the lecherous Neeble and told her not to fall asleep. Then he ran. He had a world to save, didn't he? Not every man was lucky enough to have an excuse so big for getting himself out of an emotionally awkward situation.

Laura watched him go, dazed by her own feelings, then turned from the door.

A colorful spinner met her eyes. One of the worms was holding it up eagerly, looking hopeful.

"*Twister!*" they all clamored.

Laura did a mental shrug this time. What the hell. She really *had* dated worse.

FOURTEEN

Grand Central Station is one of the two great railroad termini that serve the Big Apple. There's an enchanting kind of old-fashioned charm to the place, a romantic aura that conjures up the ghosts of ages past. When you walk across the polished stone floors and your eyes meet one glowing face of the rounded, four-sided clock atop the central information booth, you can almost imagine turning the corner and running into William Powell waiting to meet Myrna Loy and sweep her away for drinks and torch songs at the Algonquin. Sometimes it feels as if the next train will discharge a swarm of 1940s GIs, home on leave, ready to paint the town red, or a bevy of 1950s ladies-who-lunch, resplendent in white gloves, chic hats with dainty nose veils, high-heeled leather pumps, and seamed stockings.

Unlike Pennsylvania Station, you can actually see daylight when you're in Grand Central. The high, cathedral-like windows that open on to Vanderbilt Avenue let in slanting beams of sunshine that remind incoming commuters, headed down into the subways, that there really *is* an outside world, and that they're not trapped in a bad remake of *The Mole People*.

In one of the better moves of recent history, the Powers That Be decided to put the *grand* back into Grand Central Station. Accordingly, a massive cleanup, spruce-up, gentrify-the-living-daylights-out-of-it action was initiated. Financing was secured. Contractors were hired. The cavernous ceiling was scoured with care, the *schmutz* of ages removed—to reveal a radiant painted turquoise sky that was gemmed with gold-flecked representations of the constellations, wired to light up at dusk.

This came as a surprise—nay, a shock—to everyone from the workers who made the discovery all the way up to the administrators who'd had the gentrification idea in the first place. One fellow compared the find to the prehistoric cave paintings of Altamira, and the opening of King Tut's tomb.

That's one of the beauties of New York City: No one really knows what they're going to find until they start looking.

On the lower concourse of the station, a food court was installed, served by individual retail outlets purveying a multitude of cuisines and comestibles—Japanese and Indian, caviar and cookies, cheesecake and chimichangas—with a clean, comfortable dining area where the plastic-covered tables displayed a faux collage of tickets and travel memorabilia from the station's original heyday.

A European-style grocery market provided a place where locals and commuters alike could purchase the makings for meals of their own cooking—offering the freshest cheeses, meats, fish, produce, and pastries and cakes so luscious that diet-conscious New Yorkers walked briskly past them with their eyes averted. Still other stores displayed everything from paper goods to potpourri to pea coats. Step inside Grand Central Station these days and you can get a train from Poughkeepsie, a magazine from Paris, olive oil from Tuscany, a necktie from Milan, and corned beef from Brooklyn.

What you can't get is a locker to store your luggage. Not any more, and everyone knows why. Too bad, but the world changes. So patrons are forced to schlepp those heavy suitcases, wrestle themselves into a hernia with all those shopping bags. Look all you want, you won't find a locker, not even if your life depends on it.

Not unless you really know *where* to look.

Not unless you also happen to know that another name for Grand Central *Station* is Grand Central *Terminal*. G.C.T., Q.E.D.

Kay knew all of this. That was why he was able to lead Jay straight to locker C-18, somewhere inside Grand Central but off the beaten path.

Way off.

"Why are we—?" Jay tried to ask.

Kay just held up the key and showed him the side with the three letters etched on it.

"You're not gonna slow me down now, are ya, rookie?" he jibed.

"Slow you down?" Jay's hackles rose. "Whose brain's working on outdated software?"

Kay ignored Jay as if he hadn't said a thing. He took out some money and handed it to him, along with the suggestion: "Why don't you go grab us some coffee while I do this?"

Visions of how Kay had used the exact same ploy to rid himself of the fawning presence of rookie Agent Gee sizzled in Jay's mind. He made a nice bit of business out of looking behind him casually and replying: "Oh, *I'm* sorry, I thought you were talking to Hop Sing."

So Kay dropped the condescending senior-agent act. "Look," he said, eyes like flint. "I don't know what's in there. I don't want you to get hurt. So move back."

Jay didn't like being sheltered any more than he liked being talked down to. Before he'd become an MIB agent, he'd been a New York City policeman. His motto then had been *To Protect and Serve*, not *To Be Coddled and Protected*. That hadn't changed.

"How far back?" he demanded. "Back around the coffee shop? Open the damn locker." He locked eyes with Kay.

Kay had known Jay long enough to recognize when the younger agent had made his stand and wasn't about to back down from it. You couldn't outstubborn a mule. No sense wasting time trying.

Not that he'd really expected Jay to go gentle into that coffee shop. Kay's reinstated memories told him that Jay was one of the best partners he'd ever had, loyal, smart, and true, not the kind to leave you without anyone to watch your back.

Good to know the memories hadn't lied.

He opened the locker.

A typical train or bus station locker will comfortably hold a duffel bag, an attaché case, a small valise, even a clutch of shopping bags. Lockers have also been used for more nefarious purposes, to hold more dangerous objects, which accounts for the present dearth of lockers in Grand Central Station. Jay was well aware of this. Whatever this locker held, the chances were just about fifty-fifty that it would either end the mystery of the Light of Zartha, or simply end the lives of Agents Jay and Kay. He knew the job was dangerous when he took it. He braced himself for the worst, while hoping that all he'd see was a Big Brown Bag from Bloomingdale's.

The locker door swung open. It didn't hold a Bloomie's shopping bag.

It held a world.

From where he stood, Jay could see an incredibly small, utterly perfect miniature land, peopled with minuscule aliens who were even now blinking and squinting up into the dazzling light that the opening of the locker door had sent pouring into their lives. The aliens were a furry, fuzzy, friendly-looking breed, their golden eyes large and saucer-shaped, seeming almost to glow with an inner light. They would have to, to allow the little creatures to dwell in the darkness of a closed luggage locker and find their way around without constantly bumping into everything. Maybe the delicate antennae atop their heads also served to help them navigate the darkness of their world. Maybe not.

With aliens, Jay had learned that often there wasn't a good reason behind each and every weird aspect of their appearance. It was the same conclusion he'd reached back in the days when he'd still been willing to go out on blind dates.

These locker-dwelling aliens most reminded him of something he'd seen once, up at the Bronx Zoo: lemurs. Yeah, lemurs, that was what they looked like, but only their faces. Their bodies were another story. These creatures stood upright. Memories of an old issue of *National Geographic* flashed through his mind, a photo spread of a meerkat family, the whole colony of weasel-like creatures standing tall on their hind legs, keeping a vigilant watch for predators approaching across the African desert.

The locker-dwellers didn't have any worries on that score. This was *not* the African desert, not by any means. A large, prosperous, bustling town occupied the foreground, but beyond it Jay could see a whole landscape stretching back, back, all the way back into the depths of the locker. Fascinated, he wanted to elbow Kay aside ever-so-gently—or not so gently; that bit about being sent for coffee still rankled—and get a better look.

He didn't get the chance; not right away. Kay stepped directly in front of the open locker, letting the tiny aliens behold him, encircled by the golden light of Grand Central Station.

And lo, a great shout went up from the multitude: "*Kay! He's back! The Life Giver! All hail, Kay! All hail, Kay!*"

Jay's lip curled. "You the Man Who Would Be King of the Train Locker?" he asked his partner.

Kay didn't answer him right away. The Life Giver was harking unto the petitions of his most devout adherents.

"Did you bring us food, merciful Kay?" they clamored, albeit respectfully.

Kay frowned momentarily, then winged it, retrieving a partially eaten Reese's peanut butter cup from a nearby trash can. He placed it in the center of the alien city, in the middle of their "Main Street," so to speak. Joyous and grateful, the aliens danced and cavorted around the divine gift, making a gladsome noise.

"Merciful Kay who brings abundance. All hail, Kay!"

"They think you're some kind of god," Jay observed. He didn't know whether to be amazed, amused, or disturbed by this revelation. On the one hand, there were plenty of worse gods the aliens could choose. At least he was sure Kay would never ask them to go kill all the inhabitants of Locker C-*19* in his name.

On the other hand . . . Kay, a *god*? In *those* shoes?

"Nahhhh," Kay demurred, dismissing Jay's notions of his divinity out of hand, while the little aliens continued to chant praises to his name. "More like the pope."

Having set Jay's mind at rest, Kay summoned the attention of the faithful.

"Good and gentle townfolk of Locker C-Eighteen," he said. The chanting stopped; they harked unto the words of his voice. "Did I leave something with you for safekeeping?"

One alien stepped forward, to act as spokesman for the rest. "Yes. The Time Keeper. You left it to illuminate our streets and our hearts."

He gestured to a clock tower that dominated the town. At the top there rested an old watch, a Pulsar model straight out of the 1970s, complete with glowing digital display.

"Ahhhhh . . ." The massed aliens breathed in reverent wonder as they gazed upward, for the shining miracle in their midst did not grow old, nor did the marvel of its presence become commonplace with the passage of years. Plainly their love for the Time Keeper was nearly as profound as their love for the Giver of the Time Keeper.

The Giver gaveth, and now the Giver tooketh away. It's been known to happen.

"Been looking everywhere for that watch," Kay said, reaching into the locker and removing it from its resting place atop the tower.

A chorus of horrified protests rose up from uncounted

alien throats. "But Merciful One! The clock tower! No, no—!"

"Here," Jay said. He took off his own watch and installed it in the clock tower in place of Kay's old Pulsar.

"Now you've got something with a little *style*," he told them, satisfied. "Titanium case. Alarm. Waterproof to three hundred meters. Like Miami in there now."

The spokes-alien dared to raise his eyes to this new Merciful One and ask, "Who are you, stranger?"

"Jay."

At once the jubilant cry went up: "All hail, Jay!

"All hail, Jay!

"All hail, Jay!"

Jay smiled. He could get used to this. He gave the aliens a little wave, the kind Queen Elizabeth II of England had made famous. Feeling pleased with himself, he began to close the locker.

"Wait!" came a sonorous voice from the depths. *"The commandments."*

Jay stopped. Impossible. No way they could have Charlton Heston in there.

Then again . . .

"The tablet!" the spokes-alien cried, and his words were taken up by the multitude, who echoed:

"The tablet! The tablet! The tablet!"

The same resonant voice that had bid Jay cease and desist now spoke again, making all things clear: "We have lived by its words, and peace has reigned throughout our world . . ."

Jay and Kay peered into the innermost recesses of the locker, seeking the source of those stirring tones. They gazed beyond the center of the town, beyond the town itself, past the outlying districts, over fields and roads until their eyes beheld a great mountain. Upon the peak thereof stood an elder of that same diminuitive alien race. He was garbed in dignity, piety, and a long, flowing robe. Upon his face was wisdom, plus a generous beard of blinding whiteness, and in his hand he held . . . *the tablet!*

Holding it out before him, he offered it to Kay. "Pass it on to others," he said, "that they, too, may be enlightened."

Carefully Kay extended his arm into the locker, reaching for the outstretched tablet. When his finger touched the revered object, the crowd of aliens raised a mighty cheer. Extracting his hand, Kay studied what the elder alien had given him, with Jay leaning in at his shoulder. What was this awesome artifact, this focus of worship? What deep moral truths might it contain, to have succeeded in bringing peace and prosperity to an entire world, no matter what that world's size might be, relative to our own? What was this sacred relic that the aliens' most honored elder had vouchsafed unto Kay?

A rental card from Tapeworm Video?

Jay was speechless.

So was Kay, but that was because he was examining both sides of the alien elder's bequest. It was indeed a rental card from Tapeworm Video, and one with his name on it. In addition, it was printed with the store's policies, special offers, and rules for proper stewardship of all rented tapes.

These the aliens began reciting piously, in unison, while from his mountaintop the robed and bearded elder elucidated the teachings so all might grasp their meaning to the fullest:

"Be kind, rewind!"

"Go back and reconcile your past in order to move tranquilly into the future."

2 *"Two for one every Wednesday!"*

"Give twice as much as ye receive on the most sacred of days—every Wednesday."

3 *"Large adult entertainment section in the back!"*

At this point the elder whipped out his arm and pointed dramatically to the shadowed regions of the locker, even farther back than his mountain. The congregation of tiny aliens burst into deafening—for them—cheers, and began to march whither the hand of their elder directed. They seemed in a hurry to follow the bidding of the tablet. It made a man stop and think.

What do *they have back there?* Jay wondered. Then: *No. Never mind. There are some things humankind wasn't meant to know.*

"Close the door," he told Kay. "They're headed for the back."

As they left the secured locker behind and emerged into one of the more popularly traveled parts of Grand Central, Jay asked, "So what's up with the video card?"

"Don't know," Kay said, still eyeing it.

"Why did you leave the watch with them?"

"To remind me."

"Of what?" Jay persisted. Getting information out of Kay was like milking a turtle.

"Don't remember."

"Take a wild guess," Jay snapped.

"Okay." Jay might be a little out of temper, but Kay was still the indisputable master of cool. He held out the digital watch he'd retrieved from the clock tower so that his partner could see the winking display:

59:37

And as they watched, the seconds were counting down.

36, 35, 34 . . .

"I'm guessing that's how long we've got to figure it out," Kay said. It wasn't a whole helluva long time, but he didn't say a word about that. No need to state the obvious. If it had him worried, he didn't show it. That was Kay, all the way through.

Lowering the watch, he gave the card from Tapeworm Video another look.

"Let's see if they're still open for business."

FIFTEEN

Most video rental outlets in New York City fall into one of two general categories: large and small.

The larger ones are usually the Big Brand Name franchise outlets. Seen one, seen 'em all. They offer multiple copies of the newest, hottest releases and a wide selection of popular comedies, action/adventure flicks, sci-fi epics, family fare, dramas, cartoons, and you-know-who-the-purple-dinosaur tapes for the kiddies, and so on. The clerks wear uniforms, smile included. It's a nice place to take the children. The "adult" section, if it's there at all, is kept discreetly out of the way, in the back.

The smaller video rental spots are more on the lines of a mom-and-pop store, found tucked away into parts of the city that have more of a neighborhood feel. Each is unique, many bearing cutesy, clever, or irritating names. In these places, you have to move fast if you want to snag one of the precious few copies of the hottest new releases before they become tepid oldies, or see if you can get your name on the prerelease waiting list, or set up a friendly arrangement with one of the clerks who, by the way, don't wear uniforms and only smile if they feel like it.

Here you can still rent comedies, action/adventure flicks,

sci-fi epics, et cetera, but your additional viewing options will be more eclectic, the offerings weighted between the proprietor's whims of taste and his rueful knowledge that a store that doesn't stock Barney videos might as well declare Chapter 11 from the get-go. There are more foreign films, and even animé for the neighborhood Japanophile or the viewer who feels one can never have enough big-eyed, small-mouthed, large-breasted, half-naked teenage schoolgirls with superpowers. And the tentacled monsters are *cool*.

The "adult" section—and there most definitely *is* one here, make no mistake about it—is almost always kept out of sight, in a curtained-off back room.

Places that offer the viewer nothing *but* "adult" fare don't figure into this equation, since they don't allow their rental tapes to be taken off the premises.

So that's what there is to choose from in New York: video outlet size Large and video outlet size Small. That's it, that's all she wrote. Pick one out of two options, no waiting. Simple, yeah?

And then, there's *Tapeworm* . . .

Tapeworm Video was open late. Tapeworm Video was *always* open late. As soon as Jay stepped over the threshold, he was seized by the inescapable feeling that it wasn't open any other time *but* late, because the regular customers feared the Great Yellow Orb-That-Blinds-and-Burns. That and the ubiquitous eyes of The Government.

Instead of the expected sections found in other video stores, Tapeworm offered its clients their films sorted into very specific categories, their names prominently displayed above the racks holding the cassettes:

Sci-Fact and Oliver Stone Films
The Occult and Oliver Stone Films
The Bizarre and Oliver Stone Films
Conspiracy and Oliver Stone Films

Jay didn't want to say anything, but he believed he could detect something like a *pattern* here.

When he and Kay first entered the creepy little store, a number of patrons were browsing those racks, most of them wearing hooded sweatshirts and trench coats with the collars pulled up. All of them were behaving in a furtive manner that positively begged: *Look at me! Look at me!* As soon as they scented outlanders in their midst, they pulled their heads deeper into those same hoods and collars and averted their eyes.

That was just fine with Jay. Just because he saw bizarre, sometimes hideous aliens on a daily basis didn't mean he was a man without limits, capable of seeing *any* damn freaky thing and still holding on to his sanity and his lunch. He suspected that if he were to get a good look at some of these people, he'd know what made Marilyn Manson wake up screaming.

He was also more than a little afraid that these were People With Theories. Somehow, in the course of their upbringing, their parents and/or guardians had neglected to teach them the niceties of social interaction. As a result, they'd been ostracized from the pleasant give-and-take of childhood, unless it involved some bully giving them regular beatings and them lying there and taking it. Such a life leaves a person prone to bookishness, and if not carefully monitored and controlled, bookishness leads—oh, the horror!—to independent thought, and lots of time to engage in it.

Unfortunately, too much time and too much independent thought leads a person to contract Mad Scientist Syndrome, a condition documented in *Scientific American*, or *Reader's Digest*, or *Cosmopolitan*. Jay couldn't remember which. The chief symptom is the tendency for the afflicted to mutter to himself, "Only *I* know the Truth! Someday, when it's Too Late, they will learn. When the aliens invade Earth in their neutronium-powered warships, only I will be able to communicate with them and then—! Then maybe I can actually get a date for Saturday night."

But it wasn't enough for sufferers of M.S.S. to gloat privately over their eventual vindication. No, they had formed certain Theories, mostly involving cover-ups and conspiracies of assorted stripes. For all their furtiveness and suspicion, they couldn't keep these Theories to themselves. Not even if you begged them to do so. At the least sign of interest, real or imagined, they would launch into a lengthy lecture on their favorite Theory. People had been known to chew off their own limbs gladly in an attempt to escape such "conversations."

It's not a very pretty syndrome. Just thinking about it gave Jay the shivers.

He avoided eye contact and stuck close to Kay.

The checkout counter was manned by a cute kid in her twenties, liberally pierced and tattooed. She would have been a whole lot cuter if her thick, dark hair had had more than a passing acquaintance with a brush and comb, or if her complexion were just a shade less waxy, or if some kindly soul had told her that the last time anyone had successfully pulled off that much eyeliner was sometime during the reign of Cleopatra. Anyone who wasn't a raccoon by birth, that is.

She was staring vacantly at the computer screen—which, for all Jay knew, was equally vacant—when Kay handed her his card. Coming back to life, she called up his account record.

"This card hasn't been used in a really long time," the girl said, as if accusing Kay of some crime against humankind, or at least against Western civilization. "Before I was born."

"Been traveling on business," Kay replied.

"Millions of frequent flier miles," Jay put in.

"Try and use 'em." The girl sniffed derisively. "I always wanted to go to Cambodia. You can get a lobster dinner there for, like, a *dollar*. And then the airlines told me they black out holidays, you have to stay over a weekend. It's a conspiracy—"

"Can you tell us anything else about the account?" Jay broke in preemptively.

"Only that you never checked out a tape," the girl told Kay, handing him back his card.

Kay's mouth turned down a fraction of an inch at the corners. Dead end. Dead planet.

Jay felt his gut tighten. The clock was running, the seconds were blinking away. If they were going to save the Earth, they'd have to hustle up a new lead, and fast. But where—?

Certainly not here. Don't beat a dead horse. He and Kay started to leave. The girl's voice brought them up short.

"You reserved one once, but you never picked it up." She turned her head and hollered into the back, "Newton!"

Newton emerged from the cloaked and mysterious regions of the Tapeworm's innards, a thirty-something man who wore weirdness as a badge of honor. Stereotypes are unfair, to be sure, but stereotypes don't just leap into existence spontaneously. They have to come from somewhere. Newton was the one true source and template for Geek/Dork/Nerd stereotypes everywhere. He was balding, beady-eyed behind his thick, black-framed glasses, and he was dressed in a style that screamed to the heavens: *I not only still live with my mother, I let her pick out all my clothes!* When he caught sight of Jay and Kay standing there in their snappy suits, with their *We're-from-The-Government-we're-here-to*-help-*you posture,* he went on guard faster than a Doberman scenting a burglar's backside.

"Still think I'm paranoid, Hailey?" he demanded of the clerk.

"Yeah," Hailey replied. Like, Q.E.D.

Warily he turned his attention to his too-well-groomed-for-comfort visitors. "I'm Newton," he said. "I run the place." He leaned across the counter and in a low, confidential voice asked, "Seen any aliens lately?"

"You need professional help, son," Kay told him.

"He's getting it," Hailey volunteered. "It's not working."

"You don't remember me," Newton went on. "Nineteen ninety-seven? The morgue? I was the guy slimed on the ceiling?" To blank stares, Newton continued, "The tape you reserved—" He consulted the display that Hailey had called up on the computer. When he looked up, it was as if he were seeing them through different eyes. "Episode twenty-seven—the one about the Light of Zartha, right? I've got it upstairs."

It was Jay and Kay's turn to go on point.

"Keep talking," Jay said.

Back in Zed's office, deep within the headquarters of the subjugated Men in Black, Serleena was just wrapping up an unsatisfying Employee Work Performance Review session. She hadn't read any of the myriad self-help books on the market for Upper Management, and she didn't quite grasp the point of *Dilbert*, but lacking outside guidance she had nonetheless managed to formulate a few of her own Rules for Highly Effective Neural Root Creatures.

Now she stood by Zed's desk, looking down on her two-headed henchman, Scrad/Charlie, while an unconscious Zed lay slumped nearby. Scrad/Charlie had returned and made a report, detailing the events that had taken place in the basement of Jeebs's pawnshop earlier that night. He had done his best to cast the whole thing in an optimistic light, but his skills as a spin doctor weren't up to the task.

Charlie's head was averted, perhaps out of shame for having fallen so heinously short of his lovely commander's expectations, so it remained Scrad's lot to say, "Thank you for taking mercy, Serleena."

"You really are proof that two heads aren't better than one," she said with equal parts malice and scorn.

"Good one, good one." No one could kiss butt like Scrad, especially when his own was on the line. "We'll find Kay again," he promised.

"You have less than an hour. Go."

Scrad nodded and turned to obey. Behind him, Charlie finally lifted his head, revealing the true reason for his display of demureness: His face had been beaten to a bloody pulp. It would be unfair to speak of the damage Serleena had inflicted in comparison to a plate of raw hamburger. Raw hamburger was still potentially appetizing. Charlie's face was not.

"That wasn't so bad," Scrad whispered back at his battered half.

"Wasn't pretty behind you," Charlie mumbled through broken teeth and swollen lips.

"Never is."

Having dealt with the hired help, Serleena tried a different route to getting what she wanted. She picked up the unconscious Zed by the throat, held him over her head, and shook him like a dusting rag.

"Zed!" she shouted, demanding his attention. He gasped, shuddered, and choked, but he came to his senses. She lowered him and brought him closer.

"Look at you," she purred. "Twenty-five years. Still so handsome."

"Cut out meat and dairy," he replied. "And look at you. Still a pile of squirmy crap in a different wrapper."

"So feisty." The insult didn't even touch her, water off a duck's back. She sounded amused. "Zed, we both need the same thing." She tossed him into his chair, hard, and handed him his communicator. "Bring him in."

"Don't think so," said Zed.

Still keeping her tone amiable, Serleena said, "You'll do what I tell you. Or have you forgotten the little secret of the Light?"

The inside story at MIB was that Kay had learned his facial expressions from Zed, who was the one true master of emotional control. So when a flicker of concern crossed Zed's face, it was clear that he did remember the little secret of the Light, and that it was what the experts call a "doozy."

"The fail-safe device," he said, his throat abruptly dry.

"If it isn't back on Zartha when it's supposed to be, Earth goes *pfft*," Serleena said. She was still smiling her most persuasive smile. "I lose, you lose. I win, everything keeps spinning."

Zed maintained his stoic front for just an instant longer, then let it crumble. He looked like a man whose last hope of deliverance had run out. "All right, Serleena," he said. "You win." He punched up a series of numbers on his communicator and handed it to her.

She was grinning in triumph as she heard the telltale ringing, the sound of the call going through, and then . . .

"*The Waverly Cinema is proud to present the one thousandth showing of the* Rocky Horror Picture Sh—"

She was just starting to lose that grin when Zed reached back, grabbed the lamp off his desk, and whacked her upside the head. Jumping up, he delivered a series of lethal-looking roundhouse kicks to Serleena's head as a follow-up to the blow from the lamp. As he hit the ground, he reflected that it really *did* help to cut out meat and dairy.

Unfortunately, Serleena must have been following the same diet. Zed's one-two blows, capable of decking a platoon of teamsters, didn't even knock her off balance. She crossed to where he stood; she was no longer smiling.

"So very feisty," she said before kicking him in the head. It only took her one try.

Leaving Zed lying there, out cold, she shifted her gaze out to the main hall of MIB Headquarters, spread out below her. She could rest easy; all things were as she had left them when she first took over.

Or were they?

Her brows came together. Her eyes focused on the body of the dead alien. It wasn't acting dead enough. Something inside it was moving. The crease between Serleena's eyebrows deepened. It was dead and it was moving and it wasn't supposed to be doing that. First she would know the reason why, then she would stop it.

As Zed would testify, if he weren't unconscious, Serleena was very good at stopping things.

SIXTEEN

Newton lived in the apartment above Tapeworm Video. His bedroom was a chaotic jumble of UFO clippings, fake alien artifacts, model spaceships, signs that advised TRUST NO ONE, and a painfully neat display of perfectly organized, meticulously labeled, filed, and cross-referenced videotapes. As soon as he had led Jay, Kay, and Hailey safely within the restricted area, he shut the door and swiftly engaged several locks.

"Newton, is that you?" came an older woman's voice from somewhere in the apartment.

"Yes, Mom!" he called back. "I'm up here with some friends."

"I wanna have your baby!" Hailey screamed, loud enough for Mom to hear. Jay could tell how much she enjoyed obeying her Inner Anarchist by how wide she grinned and how high Newton jumped when she did that.

Unflapped and unflappable, Mom's voice replied, "Would you like some mini pizzas?" Plainly, she knew her little boy, and she was more than confident that her son would never indulge in premarital S-E-X. Not while he was living under *her* roof and *her* rules. Newton was a *good* boy.

Newton looked inquiringly at Jay, Kay, and a clearly

disappointed Hailey. "Mini pizzas?" He repeated the offer,
trying to be friendly, the way he'd seen mundanes do it on
TV. They just stared at him. With an *and-they-call*-me-
antisocial shrug, he yelled back: "Thanks, we're cool!"
And then, to his guests again: "Over here."

They followed him through the limited landscape of his
bedroom, past tabloid tales of alien autopsies and mini
shrines to Roswell and all its secrets, to where the tapes
waited in their obsessively organized rows.

"There it is," Newton said, immediately homing in on
one among hundreds, and handing it to Jay.

It was labeled MYSTERIES IN HISTORY: THE LIGHT OF
ZARTHA, with the subheading NARRATED BY PETER GRAVES.

"At last," Jay said. "Some hard evidence." It was tough
to tell whether or not he was kidding.

"Play it," Kay said, and somewhere the ghost of
Humphrey Bogart smiled.

Immediately Newton gave them the run of the VCR. He
was more than willing to do so. It was as if, for the first
time in his life, he had the feeling he was actually accomplishing something. And these weren't his usual sort of
guests. These guys in the matching black suits, they
weren't at all like the regulars who came into Tapeworm
Video. They looked normal; street-normal.

Newton knew how street-normal people generally
viewed people like him. Street-normal people thought he
was crazy to believe that there was more to the universe
than Oliver Stone movies, while he thought they were ar-
rogant to believe that, as far as life in the cosmos went,
they were It. Whether you were a Creationist or you bet
all your chips on the Big Bang, Newton believed in his
heart of hearts that Creation cried out for variety! For the

love of Pete, didn't these people think things *through*?
How could there only be *one* world populated by sentient,
self-aware creatures when the universe offered *four* kinds
of Coca-Cola?

For the moment, though, he got a grip on his emotions
and rolled the tape.

It was the sort of video that brought to mind such cinematic greats as Ed Wood and that weird kid who used to
live down the block who once got his hands on Dad's video
camera and convinced his pals to dye their skin green with
food coloring so they could play Martians. There's one of
those in every neighborhood. Aluminum foil wrapped
around a water pistol makes a nifty ray gun. When your
production values are on a par with *Plan 9 from Outer
Space* and your budget is the price of a pack of construc-
tion paper, a busted-down cardboard box, and a carton full
of Lego building blocks, your audience is assured to receive a quality viewing experience.

The first shot up was of an office that was standard
to these quasi-scientific "documentaries." The furniture
was cheesy; everything had the air of having been bor-
rowed from people who had day jobs. There were shelves
and shelves of important-looking books in the background, to bestow the illusion that corroborative research
had been done. It would have helped the video's credibility
if most of the spines hadn't looked like painted pasteboard
dummies.

Peter Graves walked solemnly onto the set and sat on
the edge of the desk. It had been many years since *Mission: Impossible*, but he still had that dramatic abundance
of silver hair, those intense blue eyes, and the ability to

speak with conviction, persuasiveness, and sincerity. It was a mercy that he hadn't decided to go into politics.

"Although no one has ever been able to prove their existence," he began, romancing the camera lens, "a quasi-government agency known as the Men in Black supposedly carries out secret operations here on Earth in order to keep us safe from aliens throughout the galaxies. Here is one of their stories that 'never happened,' from one of their files that 'doesn't exist.' "

Jay watched, marveling at the beauty of it all. It was Edgar Allan Poe's gambit from "The Purloined Letter": There's no better place to hide than in plain sight. Make a videotape that reveals the truth about the Men in Black, but make it to look like the lowest of low-budget sci-fi featurettes, and no one would ever believe it, except for the eccentrics, cranks, nut cases, and "woo-woos."

The television screen filled with a starfield that looked like a black cloth dotted with glow-in-the-dark paint. Peter Graves continued his narration:

"Nineteen seventy-eight. The devastating War of Zartha had raged on for fifty years. The Zarthan people, good and pure. Their enemies, Kylothian invaders . . ."

Books are written about those moments in cinematic history when the creative spirit was willing but the budget was weak. In the great American tradition of making do with what you've got when you can't get exactly what you want, duct tape in mass quantities is always involved, and you can usually see where it's being used.

At best, this results in such moments as when a Roman centurion raises his hand in salute, and you can see his Timex wristwatch, plain as day.

The battle scenes from the War of Zartha "documentary" were a combination of the Holy Grail, *Paradise Found*, and the Big Rock Candy Mountain for self-righteous blooper gleaners everywhere.

Yes, they were *that* bad. Compared to what Agents Jay and Kay saw on Newton's TV screen, Ed Wood was in the same class as Steven Spielberg. The manner in which the producers of this visual atrocity had chosen to portray a flying saucer attack was—was—was—

"Sparkler on a Frisbee," Jay remarked. "Scary." He sat down next to Kay as Peter Graves droned on:

"But the Zarthans had a great treasure: the Light of Zartha. A source of power so awesome, it alone could mean victory and restoration for the Zarthans . . . or complete annihilation if it fell into the hands of the Kylothians. A decision was made to hide it on an insignificant blue planet, third from the sun. A group of Zarthans made the journey, led by the Keeper of the Light—"

"Lauranna," Kay said quietly an instant before Peter Graves said:

"—Princess Lauranna."

Jay and Newton both turned to stare at Kay, who was now totally transfixed by the story unfolding on the little glass screen. The soothing, sincere voice of the narrator continued:

"Lauranna beseeched the Men in Black to help her hide the Light on Earth. But they could not intervene."

The video showed a gaggle of actors badly costumed as Men in Black, Zarthans, and Kylothians standing in one of those nondescript, generic cornfields that are a staple of sci-fi, horror, and action/adventure flicks. When in doubt, rendezvous somewhere in the middle of the Grain Belt in broad daylight. You never know what's lurking in your cereal, even when it's still just growing out in the fields. It could be a secret decoder ring; it could be a bunch of secret government agents and the aliens they deal with on a daily basis. Only difference is that the secret decoder ring's gonna have some resale value on eBay someday.

Kay gazed at the sun-drenched scene on the glass screen. "No," he said distinctly at the television set. "Night."

Something flashed inside his head.

He was there again, there in the heart of his restored memories. It was all so vivid—painfully so.

It was nighttime and he was standing in the middle of a cornfield, somewhere in the Midwest. The stalks towered above his head, tall enough to completely hide from prying eyes the MIB van and the golden, teardrop-shaped spaceship in the clearing. A grain silo loomed in dim relief nearby. The other agents accompanying him were no longer bit players in cheap, third-grade polyester suits but the real deal, slick, sharp, professional. The Zarthans and Kylothians were just as genuine as Kay's returned memories could conjure them, the Kylothians all hideous tangles of neural roots mercifully swathed in long, hooded robes, the Zarthans far closer to humanoid, and Princess Lauranna—

Princess Lauranna . . .

She was beautiful. The word at once said too little and more than enough. Her face, framed in the bell of her midnight-blue hood, held an exotic loveliness that could not be attributed to any one feature—luminous eyes, full lips, gleaming raven hair—but was instead the breathtaking effect of all her aspects taken together.

Another flash filled Kay's mind. This time it was lightning, the image of the same bolts that had seared the skies over that cornfield twenty-five years ago. It was raining as Kay and the other agents gathered to deal with the latest threat to the security of planet Earth.

From somewhere an infinity away, in Newton's bedroom, Kay heard himself say "raining," as he sank ever deeper into his memories.

The rain came down hard. He could almost feel it, in his hair, on his face, trickling down the back of his collar, even after twenty-five years. He was young and strong and new to the Men in Black, but ready to do whatever was necessary.

Whatever was necessary.

A hooded figure detached itself from the ranks of the Kylothians and approached him. Deep within the bell of the hood, a tangle of neural roots spoke with a deep voice, reminiscent of Serleena's, saying, "You've been very wise." Its tone smacked horribly of satisfaction and triumph.

"Kay. Please. I beg you—" Another female voice filled his memory with the force of a bullet through his heart. It was Princess Lauranna, and the raindrops of that lost night were running down her lovely face like tears. "—if they have the Light, it is the end of our entire civilization."

The young Kay turned to her, his expression the same adamantine mask that had become his trademark within the agency. Agent Kay: Know the Rules. Stick to the Regulations. Everything by the Book.

Always.

"Ambassador Lauranna," he said. "If we expand protection beyond Earth, we would jeopardize Earth itself. We have no choice. We must remain neutral."

"Where is it?" the hooded neural root creature de-manded, greed, eagerness, and a thirst for blood dripping from every word.

Kay addressed the creature in precisely the same businesslike tone as he'd used with Lauranna. "You didn't think we were going to give it to you," he said. "We're neu-tral. You want it—"

The silo in the distance split open like a milkweed pod and a spaceship erupted from it in a blaze of fiery exhaust, rocketing toward the vast and trackless darkness of inter-stellar space.

"—go find it."

"No!" The creature's cry of rage and frustration almost drowned out the thunderous roar of the fast-escaping ship. She raced to her own spacecraft, but before she slammed the entry port and took off in pursuit of the vanishing prize, she stopped and turned in the doorway. A weapon glittered in her grasp. It was ridiculous in appearance, a snarl of shiny golden tubes that sprouted into a bouquet of brassy, trumpetlike cups, a thing straight out of John Philip Sousa's worst nightmares.

But this abomination didn't make music; it dealt death.

The creature fired the weapon with lethal accuracy just as Kay cried out in anguish:

"Lauranna!"

Too late; the warning came too late, and the Kylothian's shot was too sudden, too accurate to avoid. Lauranna fell, dying, even as the other Men in Black agents fired futilely on the fleeing spacecraft.

The rain fell, soaking Kay as he knelt in the cornfield, cradling Lauranna in his arms. He never felt it. His face was wet with more than raindrops. Perched on the bed in

Newton's room, images long effaced by self-neuralyzation overwhelmed him, and the pain they brought in their train was all the worse for having been suppressed for so many years. He wanted to look away and knew he could not. There was nowhere to hide from memories.

The younger Kay knelt in a Midwest cornfield, Lauranna's body in his lap, and looked down at his hand, clutched into a fist. Slowly the fingers uncurled. A bracelet lay in the hollow of his palm as the rain continued to fall; a bracelet he remembered seeing somewhere before he had forced himself to call back all this pain.

The memory ended. Kay was fully back in Newton's bedroom—memories and all—gazing at the television screen while Peter Graves's voice-over concluded:

"Never knowing it happened, the people of Earth were once again saved by a secret society of protectors known as the Men—"

Kay stopped the tape.

"I shouldn't have—" he began.

"You didn't send it off the planet," Jay said, realizing the full significance of what he'd just seen. "You hid it here. That was your plan with Lauranna."

"I went offbook," Kay said. For him, it was the worst offense an agent of the Men in Black could commit, the worst sort of self-condemnation.

But he didn't have the chance for further recrimination. There was too much to be done, and as for the time to do it . . .

The Pulsar's bright red display was a blinking, irrefutable reminder that time was running out.

Huddled together, holding hands and sniffling loudly,

Hailey and Newton were indifferent to the sense of urgency that suddenly gripped their guests.

"So sad," Newton sniveled.

"So beautiful," Hailey concurred, crying softly.

"The bracelet," Kay said to Jay, who didn't need to wait for the penny to drop either. "Worm Guys." He ran out of Newton's bedroom, leaving his partner to tidy up loose ends.

Jay slipped on his Ray-Bans and held his neuralyzer in front of the weeping couple. They had clearly been made for each other, even if cynics everywhere would chime in with *Yeah, out of spare parts*. Maybe it was because he'd allowed his own sense of loneliness to take the helm, maybe it was just because he'd opted to listen to his inner yenta, but Jay decided what the perfect postneuralytic suggestion for this unlikely pair would be. He remembered what Hailey had said back downstairs in the video store, about her heart's dearest wish.

The neuralyzer flashed and he said: "Take her out for a lobster dinner."

It wasn't much of a start, but it was a helluva lot more doable than taking her to Cambodia. Besides, when a guy like Newton got his foot in the door of a relationship, sometimes the rest of him followed. It was what scientists call gravity, or inertia, or Survival of the Geekiest, or something.

Jay wondered whether Cupid ever had second thoughts about setting up matches that seemed like a good idea at the time.

Then he dashed out after Kay.

SEVENTEEN

Almost as soon as he and Kay leapt into the Mercedes, Jay was on the line, using the car communicator to call Laura. She was still in the Worm Guys' apartment when the call came through over the communicator Jay had left in her care.

"Hello?" she said, answering the device's insistent summons.

"Laura, it's me." Jay's voice came in loud, clear, and urgent.

"Jay!" Laura sounded genuinely pleased to hear from him. If she'd picked up on the dead-serious tone in his voice, she didn't let on. "We're playing Twister."

They certainly were. The worms were an impossible tangle of lithe little bodies, with Laura's own body knotted right into the middle of the squirming, contorted mass.

The Worm Guys were *not* complaining. It was the closest they'd gotten to anything female since all the escort services in town had put them on their Too-Weird-Even-for-*Us* lists.

"Hi, Jay!"

"Jay!"

"Quit touchin' my butt."

"Sorry, I thought it was your face."

Laura was taking the whole thing, including her snarled-beyond-belief position, with a huge dollop of good sportsmanship and humor.

"They're really pretty good at this," she told Jay.

"Laura," he said. "Are you wearing a charm bracelet?"

"Uh, yeah." Laura was somewhat taken aback by this unexpected inquiry. With some difficulty she managed to get the appropriate wrist free of the Worm Guy bundle and looked at the bracelet in question.

It was the same twinkling object the beautiful Princess Lauranna had pressed into Agent Kay's hand with her dying breath.

"Ben gave it to me," she said. "I've had it since I was—" Something about it caught her eye, something new and different, and disquieting.

The charm shaped like a little pyramid was—was—

"Is it glowing?" Kay cut in brusquely. It wasn't exactly a question, more like an expectation of something inevitable.

"It's glowing." Laura's confirming voice filled the Mercedes. "It's never done that before."

"Don't let that bracelet out of your sight," Jay ordered.

"Jay, what's—?"

He didn't have time to answer. He felt as though he didn't have time for anything but racing to her side, protecting her, setting her mind at ease, making everything all right for her. For both of them.

"We're on our way."

He cut off communication as the Mercedes took off at top speed in a squeal and screech of peeling rubber. Another click and he opened the channel to Frank.

"Frank, we found the Light." Jay's voice came through to the little pug's communicator back at MIB Headquarters with a distinctness that would turn cell *and* digital phone system execs bright green with envy. "We're on our way to the Worm Guys' apartment. See if you can get to the Sub Control Panel and deactivate the lockdown." There was a click and Jay's voice cut out before Frank could acknowledge the call.

But Frank wasn't in a position to acknowledge anything. He was bound and gagged into a neat little bundle of pissed-off pug, while his communicator rested in Serleena's hand. She gazed at it for a moment, digesting the precious information that Jay's reckless message had dumped right into her lap like the biggest and best birthday present ever. Then:

"Scrad!"

While Serleena's strident command rang through the halls of Men in Black Headquarters, Kay and Jay tore through the darkened streets of New York City.

"Why didn't you say 'I love you'?" Kay asked his partner.

"I don't even *like* Frank," Jay replied. He was dodging the question, and he knew it, and he was too smart to honestly believe that he was fooling Kay for an instant.

He wasn't.

"Laura," Kay said. "You're sweet on her, and as long as you're MIB, that's a mistake."

"You're trippin'." Jay did his best to hold on to the illusion that he was deceiving Kay, that he could put him off from the truth.

"It's why you didn't neuralyze her," Kay persisted. "You got soft."

"Like you?" Jay shot back. Maybe the best defense *was* a good offense. "Like you did with Lauranna?"

Kay didn't deny it. He wasn't one of those types who believed the pop-psych Golden Rule, that any offense you ever committed was A-okay and not your fault at all as long as you found the means to shift the blame to someone else. He took full responsibility for what he'd done all those years ago.

"I put our entire planet in danger by going offbook." He gave Jay a hard look. "Don't go soft on me, kid."

It took what felt like a million years for them to drive from Tapeworm Video to the Worm Guys' apartment. Kay's old Pulsar displayed beyond any argument that time was still ticking away at the normal rate, but for Jay it felt as though the blinking seconds were stretching themselves out like strands of liquid rubber. He wished that in all the alien technology the MIB had received there were some device that would have let him transport himself from place to place in the blink of an eye.

Actually, there was, but the extraterrestrials who owned the patent had refused to give it to Earthlings after some idiot at headquarters had allowed them to watch *both* movie versions of *The Fly*. The Cronenberg one put them off their lunch for fifteen years, and the offer of a Global Translocator was decisively withdrawn.

It was a physical relief when Jay finally reached the Worm Guys' apartment door and knocked.

No answer.

The little dudes were probably too tangled up in their game of Twister to let Jay and Kay in.

But if that were the case, why hadn't they yelled something like "Come in" or "Wait a minute" or—?

Jay's sense of relief vanished like a drop of water on a hot griddle. He leaned back and kicked the door in.

What lay behind it confirmed his every fear.

The Worm Guys' apartment had been transformed from swingin' bachelor pad into the aftermath of a war zone. Everywhere Jay looked he saw destruction and smoldering ruin. The echoes of the noise he'd made when kicking down the apartment door were the only sound in those demolished rooms, a sound that faded fast. The silence and all it implied fell like a great weight across his shoulders.

"Laura!" he called out into the devastation.

"Over here." The only answer he received was from Kay, summoning him to see what he'd discovered.

Jay moved quickly and saw a horrible sight: The floor of the apartment was littered with the bodies of the Worm Guys. They had been cut to pieces, each one brutally slashed in two by a creature whose vocabulary had no word for *overkill*.

It was a good thing they'd installed linoleum flooring. It was tough enough to get ordinary spills out of carpet, let alone assorted bodily oozes.

"Neeble!" Jay exclaimed, gazing down at the bisected body of one of Serleena's victims. They might be worms to the rest of the world, but to him they were comrades, coworkers, and friends . . . even if he *did* have to lock up the good silver when they came over for dinner.

A moan rose up from one of the slashed bodies. The worm named Neeble opened his eyes and looked around groggily. One of the first things he saw was the other half of his mutilated body. It couldn't possibly have been a comforting sight. Jay stood ready to offer what comfort he could, to ease what must be Neeble's last moments.

"Ho boy," said Neeble. He sounded less mortally wounded than miffed.

At the sound of his voice, a pair of eyes sprang open at one end of his severed lower body. Neeble stared at his other half as it became its own person.

"Neeble?" he inquired tentatively.

"Neeble?" the now fully independent entity responded.

The same thing was happening all around the wrecked apartment. One by one, the halved bodies regenerated everything they needed to complete themselves.

"Mannix?" one ventured.

"Yeah, I'm Mannix," came the reassuring reply from what had once been Upper Mannix's lower torso.

"My brother!" Upper Mannix exclaimed happily, raising half a hand. "Gimme a high two and a half!" Lower Mannix gleefully complied, slapping spindly palms with his former upper self.

Inwardly, Jay was just as glad as the next half worm to see his coffee-swilling, office-supply-filching buddies alive and well—and then some. But any celebration would have to wait.

"Where did they take Laura?" he demanded of the restored Worm Guys.

"MIB," Neeble provided willingly enough. "Some dumb two-headed guy."

"He was in a real hurry," said one of the two worms that now answered to the name Sleeble. "But he stopped for a few minutes to catch the end of *Everybody Loves Raymond*."

"They're using an impounded ship at MIB to go back home," Geeble chimed in.

"But they have the bracelet—" Jay began. He felt a passing pang of helplessness, and did his best not to let it show.

"We have thirty-nine minutes to get the Light off this planet or we go nuclear," Kay said, snapping him back to crisis mode. "Wanna chat about it?"

Chat, no. Get ready to rumble, yes.

Before they could take back MIB and save the Light of Zartha from Serleena and her crew, Jay and Kay both knew that they'd have to get their hands on the right tools for the job.

Time to go . . . "shopping."

The history of the Men in Black has borne witness to some frightening things, but nothing could properly prepare Agents Jay and Kay for what they found when they opened the door to Kay's old apartment.

Martha.

Of all the sentient life-forms in all the planetary systems in all the galaxies in the universe, why did it have to be Martha?

Jay took a deep breath as he and Kay walked through the door. In his time with the Men in Black, he'd made diligent inquiries concerning Martha and her minions, but had been unable to discover any link between that woman and any insidious intergalactic conspiracy, despite the fact that she possessed an uncanny ability to make every woman on Earth feel somehow inferior, largely because they didn't have room in their lives for accomplishing proper decoupage.

All that he'd managed to turn up was the frightening revelation that there was a cell of Martha fans at MIB—and not all of them were women.

Clearly the woman seated on the sofa in Kay's former digs had fallen under her influence. The man—the husband, no doubt—wore the glazed expression of someone who was just along for the ride. A little girl shared couch space with them, probably for no other reason than that she'd been told it was either watch this show or go to bed. Oh, the ordeals children were willing to suffer through just so they could stay up late! So she sat there, equally expressionless, but no doubt plotting all manner of payback scenarios that she would be sure to initiate the moment she became a teenager.

The three of them had all fallen into such a deep state of TV-induced hypnosis that they hardly noticed when their front door swung open, though they *did* look up from Martha's demo of take-no-prisoners sponge-painting as Jay, Kay, and the worms stepped into their apartment.

"Don't worry about a thing, folks," Kay said. "I used to live here. Came back to pick up a few things."

It might have been the element of surprise, the outright shock of this home invasion, or the fact that Martha had, indeed, broken their proud spirits, but the happy family didn't utter so much as a peep as they watched Kay cross their living room to the thermostat on the wall above their television set. He spun the dial with the sureness of a professional safecracker. In response to his actions, the entire wall behind the couch flipped open, revealing a cavernous room crammed to the gunwales with a lovely assortment of lethal-looking MIB weapons.

Under the stunned, silent gaze of the family, Kay and Jay raided the stockpile, selecting their weapons of choice, then tossing fission carbonizers and neural destabilizers to the eager Worm Guys. The little wrigglers were ecstatic to have been entrusted with heavy artillery.

"Lock and load, baby!" they crowed. It was a mercy that they didn't lapse into bad Arnold Schwarzenegger accents, or threaten to go medieval on someone's hindquarters.

As Kay returned to the thermostat and dialed the proper combination to lower the wall to its original position, Jay slipped on his Ray-Bans and confronted the catatonic family, still frozen in place on the couch. As the after-dazzle of the neuralyzer flash cleared away, Kay stepped in to provide the mental replacement data necessary for planetary security and civilian peace of mind:

"You did not see a room full of shiny weapons," he recited. "You did not see four alien nightcrawlers. You *will* love and cherish each other for the rest of your lives."

Duty done, he headed for the door, leaving Jay to add:

"Which could be the next twenty-seven or twenty-eight minutes, so y'all should get to loving and cherishing."

He was backing out the door after Kay and the Worm Guys when his glance fell on the little girl. A mischievous afterthought tapped him on the shoulder and he said: "Oh yeah, and she can stay up as late as she wants and have cookies and candies and cakes and junk and stuff."

Maybe the world would end that night, maybe it wouldn't, but somehow Agent Jay felt a vague sense of comfort in knowing he had done something to repay that child for what she'd been forced to endure.

Martha!

Some parents.

Damn.

And on that happy note, he left.

EIGHTEEN

There wasn't a lot of traffic en route from Kay's old apartment back to Men in Black Headquarters, and there weren't any passersby in that part of Manhattan at that hour of the night. It was all good, saving a whole lot of wear and tear on the ol' neuralyzer. Jay and Kay ditched the Mercedes and went racing up to the monolithic entrance to headquarters, locking their weapons into place as they ran.

Kay looked over his shoulder. "You guys ready?" he demanded.

Behind him, the Worm Guys were busy strapping on bandoliers and knives, their rubbery faces already streaked with camouflage makeup. Somewhere on the Other Coast, Sylvester Stallone had a lot to answer for.

"Lookin' for a few good worms," Neeble said grimly.

"Ho-aw!" Gleeble affirmed, and his combative, straight-from-the-gut cry was taken up by his brothers:

"Ho-aw!"

Whatever the hell it meant. But it sure *sounded* cool.

"You ready, kid?" Kay asked Jay.

"Kid?" Jay repeated resentfully. "You know, while

you were off delivering packages and getting chased by poodles, I saved the world from a Kreelon invasion."

Kay wasn't impressed. "Kreelons," he said. He even had the nerve to sound as though he were repressing a snicker. "The Backstreet Boys of space. What did they do, throw snowballs at you?"

Jay decided that, in view of impending full-planetary destruction, he would table all further arguments with Kay about his status within the agency. He remembered the words of the wise old sage who had once said *Never get into a pissing contest when Earth is about to be vaporized by extraterrestrial forces beyond your immediate control.* Maybe it was Socrates.

Whoever. It was time for less talk and more action.

"Age before beauty," he told Kay as he raised his bazooka and took aim at the front door. There was more than one way to end a lockdown.

"Wait!" Kay cried. He was too late; Jay fired, and the door was blown away.

"For what?" Jay asked.

"Depressurizaaaaaaa—"

Kay's reply was swallowed by the loud *whoosh* of air being sucked into MIB Headquarters, along with Kay and Jay, the Worm Guys, leaves, papers, and an entire Sabrett hot dog cart off the street. The whole ungodly mess landed right in front of the security guard, still at his post under one of the two huge fans in the entryway.

He continued to read his newspaper as if nothing much had happened. When he turned a page, the chains holding him to his chair clinked softly. It was a good thing to be prepared, yes it was. Just because some thoughtless young whippersnapper goes busting open the lockdown on the place, depressurizing everything all willy-nilly like that, hot dogs carts flying in on a body uninvited, wasn't any reason for *him* to get sucked out of his comfortable old chair.

"Depressurization?" Jay repeated.

"Code One-Oh-One lockdown," Kay explained. "Nothing comes in, nothing goes out. You sleep during orientation?"

The security guard turned another page. "Wondered when you two would finally show," he remarked, calm, composed, and unruffled. "Nice-looking young lady inside causing all kinds of hell."

He didn't bother looking up from his newspaper as Jay, Kay, and the Worm Guys went barreling past him, headed for the elevator. Those fine folks at the MIB paid him a good salary and nice benefits, but they sure as blazes didn't pay him enough to go getting all het up about nothing, nuh-uh. Leave that to the younger men. After all, they did their jobs, he did his.

He did kinda hope they had the smarts to do their jobs half as well as he did his, but he wasn't going to bet the pension fund on that.

No sirree.

Up on the roof of Men in Black Headquarters, Jarra was tending to the work that Serleena had commissioned him. This section of the building doubled as a launch pad, as well as a holding area for any alien spacecraft the agency had impounded, had confiscated, or was simply keeping safe until its original owners might want to use it again. It was the intergalactic version of valet parking.

There was no Earthly equivalent for the technology that

kept such goings-on invisible to the civilians whose office windows offered a bird's-eye view of the headquarters roof. Suffice it to say, it made the hoopla surrounding the stealth bomber seem pathetic and ridiculous.

There were going to be a lot of disgruntled former owners of approximately a dozen spaceships, when the time to reclaim them rolled around. And it wouldn't help to tell them that this, too, went along with it being the intergalactic version of valet parking. When it comes to their beloved vehicles, most drivers have a limited sense of humor and find absolutely no attraction in sacrificing their property in the interest of completing the perfect metaphor. Go figure.

Jarra had cannibalized all of them for parts to constuct the incredible ship he had put together at Serleena's behest. They were now little more than gutted hunks of interstellar junk, dismantled like so many Tinkertoys, their discarded portions littering the roof, transforming it into a spacecraft graveyard where the buzzards had been busy.

Jarra was just putting the final touches on his creation with a blowtorch. He was still cloaked neck-to-feet in that long black cape, the whole ensemble giving him the air of a blue-collar Dracula. At last, satisfied that he had done his best, he turned off the sizzling blue-white flame and stood up.

"We're ready," he announced.

Contrary to appearances, he had not taken the conventional Mad Scientist route and gone 'round the twist, bonkers, crackers, insane, or—for want of a better term— mad. He was not talking to himself, and he was not referring to himself in the royal plural. An internal surveillance camera caught his face and the image of the finished starship, along with a shot of Laura, bound hand and foot and already stowed inside.

In Zed's office, where she was overseeing the project remotely, Serleena received Jarra's message on the big Egg Screen. Scrad/Charlie was with her, and both of his faces registered deep, sincere relief to see that, for once, she was happy.

"I'm on my way," she informed Jarra. Turning to her two-headed minion, she said: "My one regret in getting the Light off this planet is that it saves Earth from destruction." She handed him a shiny metal orb and added: "Proton imploder and its detonator. Powerful enough to blow up MIB Headquarters. Once I'm gone, use it."

Before she could go, a loud *ding* announced the arrival of the elevator. Serleena glanced down from Zed's office to the main hall, only casually wondering who could have come calling at this late hour.

Not that it would make any difference. Anyone who took that elevator wouldn't be getting off it under his own power. Oh, he might *fall* out, maybe *crawl* out, definitely *leak* out, but *walk* out—? No. Not after that "special" assignment she'd given the little Gatbot when she'd first taken over MIB Headquarters.

Gat: A noun derived from *Gatling gun.* An Earth underworld slang term for a pistol.

Gatbot: A fine example of alien robotic technology, heavy firepower, and proof that somewhere out in the vast reaches of space there was a market for old Jimmy Cagney/George Raft/Edward G. Robinson gangster films.

As if on cue, the elevator doors opened to reveal an interior that was riddled with hundreds upon hundreds of bullet holes. Bullets were still spewing loudly from the wildly spinning alien robot.

Apart from the Gatbot, though, the elevator was empty. *Looked* empty.

Serleena was a seasoned warrior. She knew better than to go by appearances alone, especially when one was dealing with the Men in Black.

"Looks like there's someone I need to eat," she remarked as she headed for the door.

Someone with less martial arts training than Serleena might have asked *Where?* But anyone with that small a share of battle smarts generally didn't live long enough to ask anything beyond *Did you get the number of that truck?* before he went up in a puff of ray-gun-induced particles.

Bottom line: Never underestimate your enemy.

Inside the elevator, Jay, Kay, and the Worm Guys had followed that excellent piece of advice, which was why they weren't presently piles of bullet-riddled meat on the elevator floor.

They were a cluster of bullet-free fighting men who had taken the precaution of leaping up at the first ballistic hiccup out of the Gatbot and plastering themselves to the elevator ceiling.

"Get to the launch pad on the roof," Kay ordered Jay, while the Gatbot continued to spew out round after round beneath them. "Get the Light. The bracelet shows the departure point. No matter what, don't come back for me. Saving me destroys Earth—"

Jay opened his mouth to speak, but Kay didn't give him the chance.

"I'm your superior. That's an order. Saving me destroys Earth," he told him.

That was it. That was all. Jay's training was good, too good. Those were the words he would never be able to argue with, or take a stand against, no matter what his feelings told him otherwise.

"Okay, guys," he said to the worms. "Give me cover."

With the cold steel nerve and raw guts of veteran combatants, the Worm Guys immediately—

—did nothing.

Okay, they shook more than a gelatin-marshmallow salad in a hurricane and clung to the ceiling like a bunch of baby baboons holding on to Mama's belly for dear life, but aside from that . . .

Nothing.

"Too scared," Sleeble quavered. "Can't move."

Jay gave Kay a disgusted look. Kay just shook his head.

"What do they do for MIB anyway?" Jay asked.

"Accountants," Kay replied. "Go!"

Kay thrust both legs out straight to either side, feet pressed to the elevator walls, and swung down. Dangling in an upside-down split that would make stalwart men everywhere go *Owwww,* he blasted away at the little Gatbot, two-handed, weapons blazing.

The barrage of deadly fire drove the alien robot back, giving Jay the opening he needed if he was going to reach the Light in time. Dropping to the floor of the elevator, he made a break for it, shooting as he went. He raced across the main hall of MIB Headquarters to reach a second elevator, the one that would take him to the roof and the launch pad.

He made it; the doors closed.

No sooner was Jay safely away than Kay did the

stomach crunch to end all stomach crunches, lifting himself out of the Gatbot's line of fire.

"Limber," Geeble the Worm Guy remarked, taking time off from being scared spitless to express genuine admiration.

"Get to Sub Control Panel Seven R Delta," Kay ordered. "Shut down all power to MIB. They won't be able to launch."

"Too scared," Sleeble repeated. "Can't—"

Wordlessly Kay opened the ceiling hatch of the elevator.

"Oh, *that* way." Geeble nodded. *That* way was better because it was—

"*Away* from the bullets," Sleeble said. No one had to tell him that this would be a Very Good Thing.

"No problem," Geeble said cheerfully. He got his game face back on. "Ho-aw!"

The worms swarmed up and out of the elevator through the ceiling hatch. It wasn't possible to tell whether they were eager to do their damndest for good ol' MIB, or simply eager to get the hell out of the line of fire.

Kay didn't much care. He had other worries.

The little robot he'd managed to drive out of the elevator was heading back, prepared to finish its interrupted job of perforating anything that moved without Serleena's sayso. Kay watched it come, made some quick, clean mental calculations, and took out a grenade. Just before the robot whirred back into the elevator, he hit the BASEMENT button and swung out of the car, over the top of the Gatbot, tossing the grenade backward over his shoulder. The elevator doors slid closed behind him. There was a pause and then . . .

Boom!

Smoke seeped out through the crack between the doors. Kay didn't stay to gloat. Gloating was for villains. He was needed elsewhere. He turned and ran.

A branch of tough green neural root snaked out and clotheslined him, tendrils lashing themselves around his throat. Jerked back like a dog on a choke chain, Kay's eyes met Serleena's.

"Nice to see you again, Kay," she said.

She was gloating.

NINETEEN

Jay emerged from the elevator just in time to hear a computerized voice announce: *"Launch in four minutes."* He was heading for the waiting spaceship when suddenly his path was blocked by Jarra. The eight-foot-tall alien didn't *walk* so much as he seemed to *float*.

"Jarra," Jay said, on guard but keeping up a cool front. He'd been the one to take Jarra down, bring him in, see that he was locked up all nice and safe. He knew what this guy was capable of, and it wasn't pretty. A man who'll steal your ozone won't stop at anything. "You're cruising around smoothly these days."

"Bored," Jay's nemesis replied dismissively. "Had a little time to tinker, down in solitary."

His cape dropped like a theater curtain. Beneath it, his body no longer ended in legs but in a gleaming metal disk. He was half Jarra, half flying saucer. As if that weren't enough, a hatch in Jarra's new, improved lower torso opened and five smaller but identical Jarra/saucermen came flying out like hornets from a hive. Only instead of stings they had clutches of metal tentacles dangling from the bottoms of their little spacecraft. They looked like a miniature fleet of high-tech Portuguese man-of-war jellyfish.

"Paper clip here, piece of wire there," Jarra went on. He sounded a lot like one of the regular guys down at the corner bar, proudly explaining to his pals how he'd managed to fix a leaky pipe without needing a plumber, using only chewing gum, shellac, and duct tape.

Of course, very few regular guys have tentacles, even on the advanced episodes of *This Old House*. One of Jarra's limbs whacked Jay hard across the face, sending him reeling.

It would take more than a tentacle-delivered smack in the chops to take an MIB agent out, though, especially someone like Agent Jay. "Need to take the girl with me," he told Jarra matter-of-factly, as if it were all settled.

Not according to Jarra, it wasn't.

"Over our dead titanium bodies," the alien replied. At his words, the five smaller Jarras began spinning like tops, tentacles outstretched, a flock of bantamweight buzz saws surrounding Agent Jay and then, slowly, tightening the circle.

This was going to be messy, but obviously that was okay by Jarra. Like all good hands-on—or tentacles-on—guys, Jarra didn't mind when it got down-and-dirty. Jarra *liked* messy, but only when he was on the mess-*making* end of the process.

From his point of view, messy didn't get any better than this, when the mess-ee was one of his most hated enemies. He smiled.

Deep in the warren of air vents that ran throughout Men in Black Headquarters, the Worm Guys proceeded with caution. Now that luck had given them the opportunity to help their old friends, Agents Kay and Jay, without the nasty inconvenience of getting their rubbery hides shot full of holes, they were the most gung-ho gang of spineless action heroes on the face of the planet.

Ho-aw.

"Approaching J-Five intersection above Sub Control Panel Seven R Delta," Geeble reported into his communicator. This was *so* cool, getting to relay nifty hardcore tech information, being an integral part of a big-deal rescue-and-release op. To his mind, he sounded just like Tom Cruise or Bruce Willis or—could there be a greater thrill this side of heaven?—William Shatner.

"Jay? Kay? Over?"

He got no response. That might have been worrisome if not for the fact that he didn't have time to worry. Up ahead, Sleeble heard something and came to an abrupt halt. He held up one hand, listening intently. The rest of the worms stopped in their tracks and did likewise.

It would have been the perfect moment for someone to remark *It's quiet . . . too quiet,* only it wasn't. The metal walls of the air vent rattled and clattered with the sound of scores of tiny footsteps. Geeble motioned for the worms to get down. Tension filled the air vent like two-day-old turkey gravy.

Just ahead, a beam of light poured down into the shaft from an opening overhead. The worms stared at it, transfixed, waiting . . . waiting . . .

The light vanished as the opening flooded with dozens upon dozens of fully armed alien insects. Crickets, Serleena's minions. Their weapons chattered and roared and flashed, filling the confines of the vent with wildly ricocheting shots, a storm of shrapnel, a deluge of destruction, a monsoon of mayhem.

The Worm Guys fired back, but they were no match for the crickets, who had them outnumbered by at least a dozen to one. All they could do was defend themselves as best they could. Even so, they found themselves being pushed back, back, farther and farther from their goal, down the unfeeling gullet of the air vent system into a dead end.

Dead and *end* being the operative words of the moment.

Their carefree lives as swinging bachelors flashed before their eyes. To a worm, they felt the deep pangs of regret. If they survived this, they knew beyond the shadow of a doubt that they would live their lives differently, afterward.

For one thing, they would get the hell out of Accountancy. Sure, there was the glamour, the perks, the groupies, but *sheesh*—! It was just too damn dangerous.

In the main hall, Kay was having a reunion with Serleena that was only slightly less amicable than the one she'd had earlier with Zed. The beautiful alien picked him up and threw him against the wall with all the considerable strength in her.

He hit with a sickening, bone-jarring crash and slumped against it, fighting to recapture the breath she'd slammed out of his body.

Serleena's assumed human face writhed with unholy bloodlust, neural roots pulsing visibly beneath the surface of her skin.

"I should've taken care of you when I had the chance," Kay managed to tell her.

She responded by punching him full in the face.

"You wouldn't be in this mess if you had done what you were told, and she'd still be alive," she snarled at him. All of the frustration, the bitterness, the unnecessary *inconvenience* he'd put her through over this business of hiding the Light of Zartha welled up inside her, choking her with rage. Why this stupid, puny, Earthling scum had ever dreamed he could keep her from her goal—! The *nerve*. The unmitigated nerve of the creature.

But he had managed to do that, even if it had only been a stopgap strategy. He'd sent her off on a wild goose chase that had consumed years. Twenty-five long years. He'd forced her people to defer the destruction of Zartha, made all Kylothians dance to his tune, and worst of all, he'd made her look like a fool in front of a goodly share of the galaxy.

No one embarrassed Serleena in public and got away with it. She could kill him now—that would be easy—but first she was going to make sure he suffered.

"You did love Lauranna, didn't you, Kay?" she hissed, slipping the invisible knife deep into his heart and twisting.

He leapt for her throat, hands closing around her windpipe. But Serleena's body wasn't what it seemed—he'd forgotten that in his blind anger. His hands sank through what should have been solid flesh, becoming enmeshed in the network of neural roots that lurked just below the counterfeit skin. They sprouted up around his wrists and spread, growing, slithering, enveloping his body in a brambly green nest that would become his tomb.

Serleena's smile was every bit as smug as Jarra's.

*   *   *

As for Jarra, up on the launch pad the Kylothian's henchman was enjoying himself, playing Napoleon as he commanded his mini armada of flying replicas to circle Jay and move in for the kill. The five small Jarras whirred around the MIB agent, sharp metal tentacles deployed and spinning. They rushed in and retreated, sometimes taking individual turns at pummeling him, sometimes attacking in pairs or all together.

It was clear to anyone watching that their "father" was merely toying with his foe. Jay did what he could to fight back. His deadlier weaponry had been knocked far out of his reach, but the rooftop was strewn with the remains of Jarra's mechanical dabblings. He ducked down and grabbed a piece of pipe from the floor, swinging wildly at the little saucermen, like a man beset by a swarm of determined mosquitoes. It made one hell of a flyswatter.

And it was just about as effective. The little Jarras backed off from Jay's flailing pipe, then zipped in at him again whenever there was an opening, their tentacles scoring hit after hit. Jay finally got lucky and connected with one of the persistent pests, slamming it with the pipe so hard that it went flipping away, end over end, before going down with an awesome crash.

Jarra was only mildly disturbed to observe its demise, and his irked expression quickly vanished. After all, there were more where that one had come from. As far as he was concerned, great minions were made, not born. Give Jarra enough duct tape and he could rule the world.

Scrad/Charlie had been born, not made, but that only went to prove Jarra's theory: The two-headed alien wasn't exactly burning up the charts or heading—no pun intended—for the Minion Hall of Fame. If success was all about teamwork, you'd think that a creature that already was its own team would be destined to do well.

And you'd be wrong.

Somewhere within Men in Black Headquarters, Scrad/Charlie was running through a hallway, the glittering orb of the proton detonator cupped securely in his hands. He looked like a man who had been given his mission, and was hastening to accomplish it, but appearances could be quite deceiving.

"We can*not* set that detonator," Charlie was arguing.

"We were given an order," Scrad replied, as if that settled everything.

Not for Charlie, it didn't.

"By who? Worm-lady?" His recent, painful interview with the Kylothian had left its mark on his attitude, as well as on his face. It had turned him into a real Question Authority kind of guy, as opposed to the unscarred Scrad, who was apparently the sort to claim he was "just following orders" no matter how dirty the deed.

But all he said to Charlie was: "Shut up."

Charlie felt very strongly about his convictions, in this case, and he wasn't going to take *no* for an answer. He wasn't going to take *shut up* for an answer either, come to think of it.

"I love you," he told Scrad, "but you've given me no choice."

Concentrating fiercely, Charlie bent his mind to the task of overpowering his bodymate. Scrad stared, shocked, as his own hand began to act independently of his will, rising up in response to Charlie's hostile takeover and grabbing him by the face.

The hand yanked, and Scrad/Charlie flipped over, doing a beautiful midair cartwheel and landing—for a miracle—on his feet.

"You no-good son-of-a-bitch!" Scrad bellowed, and punched Charlie right in his already much-abused nose.

"My sinuses!" Charlie howled, and the battle was on in earnest.

Actually it was more like a *Best of the Three Stooges* marathon than any battle the world had even seen. The nameless pop-psych guru who counseled *don't be too hard on yourself* would have fled the sight in sensitive New Age tears. Many hands make light work, but one pair of hands shared by two minds—no matter how tiny those minds may be—is going to become *very* confused when it comes to beating the living daylights out of the Other Guy.

In this situation, who *was* the Other Guy?

Damned if Scrad/Charlie's body knew.

The same hand that smacked Scrad across the face turned like an angry viper and poked Charlie in the eye. The same hand that twisted Charlie's ear became the fist that clobbered Scrad. Someone obviously knew jujitsu, because the two-headed alien was throwing himself all over the place in a series of flips, twists, and somersaults that would have earned him a gold in gymnastics at the Olympics.

In the air vent, the besieged Worm Guys didn't need to worry about being hard on themselves. The vicious horde of armed-and-deadly alien crickets was taking care of that for them.

Though the worms were heavily equipped with enough weapons to make each of them a walking armory, it didn't help matters when the enemy had the capability to over-power them by the sheer force of numbers. The Worm Guys hadn't read a lot of Earth history, but if they had, they could have scared up any number of instances where man-power, not firepower, proved to be the deciding factor in ultimate victory. It was the same principle that decided the outcome of most encounters between elephants and army ants.

So it was that the Worm Guys developed a gut feeling about their chances for survival. It was mighty like indi-gestion, and no one had thought to pack the Pepto-Bismol.

The crickets pressed on, firing their weapons, backing the Worm Guys tighter and tighter into the dead end. It was all over but the bloodbath.

Suddenly, the crickets stopped firing. They lowered their weapons ever so slightly and stared in disbelief at the sight that met their goggling eyes.

Either the worms had gone insane, or they had decided that since they were bound to die anyway, they might as well rob their enemies of the pleasure of the kill.

That was certainly what it *looked* like, for the worms ap-parently had given up the struggle and, instead of re-turning fire, they were turning their weapons on each other. The crickets gaped as the worms swiftly and me-thodically cut themselves in half. Their severed bodies fell to the metal floor with echoing clangs.

Funny thing about worms.

Funny thing about Worm Guys.

New eyes opened. Limbs regenerated to replace missing arms and legs, completing half bodies, making them whole. While the dumbfounded alien crickets watched, the mass of Worm Guy segments became a mass of Worm Guys. The halves that had been holding on to blasters and ray guns and assorted other armaments tossed their spares to their newly reconstituted brothers.

They stood tall, they stood proud, and they stood to outnumber the alien crickets at last.

As for the crickets, their maternal egg casing hadn't raised any fools: They did a rapid head count of their opponents, and reasoned that the Worm Guys might even repeat that slick little trick of divide-and-regenerate-and-conquer as many times as they liked. Then they concluded that this wasn't the healthiest place on Earth for a bunch of crickets to be.

They dropped their weapons and ran like merry hell.

Their pounding feet set up such a resonant racket throughout the ventilation system that it was impossible to tell if the worms, victors of the field, were filling the air ducts with a jubilant chorus of *Ho-aw!*

Hopefully, they weren't. It was damn annoying.

Annoying or not, Jay wouldn't have minded having a *Ho-aw!* moment of his own just then, but it didn't look as if that were in the cards. The hand that Jarra had dealt him was out of a marked, stacked deck, with the murderous, ozone-pirating alien holding all the aces.

Even though he'd managed to take out one of their number, that still left him facing four of the mini saucers, not to mention the original, full-sized Jarra himself, and every one of them was sporting a deadly, whirling fringe of sharp, metal tentacles. Individually, those things packed quite a sting, and together, they could rip a man to shreds.

They circled around Jay, trapping him in their midst, and moved in for the final maneuver.

"Kill me," Jay conceded. "Let the girl go."

Jarra smirked. "Such a deal," he said scornfully.

One of the little saucers darted out, then zoomed in low, knocking Jay off his feet. The MIB agent took a pratfall, landing hard on his ass. Jarra's mocking grimace widened. He was having fun.

"Launch in ninety seconds," the starship's onboard computer decreed.

Jay clambered to his feet just as two of Jarra's tiny creations came racing in at him from opposite sides. Their tentacles could do more than sting and shred, as Jay discovered. Sometimes they could indulge their master when he wanted to drag out an enemy's death.

This deadly pair of saucermen chose to wrap their tentacles around Jay's body and fling him with great force into the jagged metal edges of one of the cannibalized flying saucers. It was like being dropped from a great height onto a coral reef.

Bruised and bleeding, Jay picked himself up and confronted the little saucers. "Like to see you two try that again," he gasped, taunting them through the red-hot hell of his pain.

Jarra never could resist a challenge. His mini minions were no different. Playtime was over: Killing time was here and now.

The two saucers pulled back and set their tentacles to spinning so fast that they became a death-dealing blur. They revved up and took off straight for Jay at a speed so high that when they hit him he'd experience firsthand what a papaya feels like in the instant before it gets shoved down the throat of a blender and transformed into a fresh fruit smoothie.

But there are some things a man won't stand still for. That's the major difference between a man and a papaya.

As the two hellbent saucermen converged on him, Jay waited until the very last second, then leapt high into the air, straight up. He heard the crash just below him as the little Jarras missed their prime target and rammed each other instead. They blew up with a satisfying explosion.

He'd been able to take out three of the small saucers, but that just meant that there were two remaining—three if you counted full-sized Jarra.

The surviving trio stopped fooling around. They moved into delta wing formation, big Jarra riding point, his two smaller versions taking the flanks, a flying wedge of death and destruction with tentacles twitching.

They barreled in on Jay, who ducked at the last possible moment. Overshooting the target, they pulled to a halt a goodly distance away and regrouped, once again setting themselves into a V shape. Their engines raced, their tentacles flicked hungrily.

"I want him in *pieces*," Jarra growled to his followers.

"Launch in fifteen seconds," said the computer as Jarra and his two surviving replicas began their approach, gaining speed, homing in on their target.

Jay knew from experience that he wouldn't be able to evade them the same way twice: Jarra was too sharp for that. The smaller Jarra-saucers were somehow linked to their creator in such a way that he didn't need to tell them what to do; they knew. They knew, and they would respond to their master's unvoiced directives just as if they were his own arms and now vanished legs.

Jay locked eyes with his enemy, saw the evil delight reflected there, saw the light of ugly gratification glowing in

Jarra's face. The two miniature Jarras wore the same expression, gloating-times-three.

Jay looked away, scanning the rooftop for something, *anything* that could help him come out of this with his skin intact.

That was when he saw the first miniature Jarra, the one he'd taken out of commission at the start. The saucerman was unconscious, his vehicle useless . . . to him.

Jay did a fast tuck-and-tumble, scooping up the incapacitated saucer as he flipped back upright. With the same smooth aim-and-release that had made him the terror and reigning champion of the Men in Black Annual Intramural Frisbee Competition, he shot the saucer off, edging it toward the small gap that lay between big Jarra and the saucerman who was taking the right flank.

It was the sweet spot in any bowling-pin setup, the place you wanted the ball to go if you were aiming for a strike. It worked like a charm.

Jay's saucer hit big Jarra, who in turn whammed into one, then the other of the smaller saucers. It was the most beautiful demonstration of the ricochet effect he'd ever seen, pinball combined with Bowling for Aliens.

All three saucers spun wildly out of control. The two smaller ones hit each other dead-on in midair and blew themselves to smithereens in a glorious fireball, while their creator crashed headlong into a pile of discarded spaceship parts.

Jarra hadn't stopped bouncing before Jay raced into the waiting spacecraft, found the control panel, and hit a bunch of switches. The whine of warming engines died, and the computer voice announced:

"Launch aborted."

It might have been Jay's imagination, but even the mechanized voice sounded relieved.

He untied Laura and helped her to her feet, then escorted her off the spacecraft. Together they approached the mound of spare parts where Jarra lay. It had been a damn hard landing. One of his own tentacles had torn a huge gash in the bottom of his no-longer-flying saucer. Fuel poured from the hole.

Highly combustible fuel.

"Take the girl," Jarra said groggily to Agent Jay. "Let me go."

Jay just looked at him. Man steals your planet's ozone, man's gonna steal your lines, too. Might as well steal his.

"Such a deal," he replied.

He gave the discarded welding torch an easy little kick, sending it rolling toward the shiny streak of leaking saucer fuel. A spark twinkled and ignited the trickle, running quickly, greedily along the inflammable trail all the way back to Jarra and up inside the evil alien's breached saucer hull.

There was a pause, then a blast that sent Jarra flying every which way in a shower of hot shrapnel and former extraterrestrial.

"Paper clip here, piece of wire there," said Jay, escorting Laura away from the blaze. He was either mocking his late opponent, or simply taking stock of the bits and pieces of Jarra as they came pattering back down to Earth.

While Jay had been turning his opponent into a shower of metallic odds and ends, Serleena had been choking Kay to within a single breath of his life. The roots springing from her hands tightened around his throat as she held him off the ground and happily watched him struggle.

Alas, even the greatest pleasures had to come to an end.

"Have to run, Kay," she said. Sharper, nastier roots extended from her fingers. She shifted her grip, seizing Kay in the middle of his chest while other roots continued to wrap themselves around him. For a moment it looked as if she were about to indulge herself in a little game of Aztec High Priest, and rip the heart right out of his body. It was probably a good thing for Kay that Serleena had never found Earth history relevant to day-to-day living.

Just because she wasn't going to tear his heart out didn't mean she was going to spare it, though.

"But before I squeeze you like a tube of toothpaste," she said, "the last thing I want you to think about is all the carnage and destruction that's about to happen because of your stupidity."

"Didn't happen then," Kay countered. "Not going to happen now."

She rolled her eyes. *Oh, puh-leeze!*

"You can't stop us," she said.

To her surprise, her prey didn't accept the helplessness of his situation, or beg for mercy, or even shut up.

Instead, as if it was he who had the upper hand—or upper root, or whatever—Kay said, "I'll give you one last chance to surrender, you slimy Kylothian invertebrate."

A ferocious smile parted Serleena's lips. Her expression spoke volumes. *Oh, really, this was just* too *good,* too *delicious! The nerve—the stupid, blind* nerve *of this— this—this puny Earthling!* She'd clearly cut off the flow of oxygen to what passed for a brain in this meat-creature. He was either insane, damaged, or living in a fantasy world.

He wouldn't be living anywhere much longer.

"What're you going to do to stop me?" she asked, leering.

"Not me," Kay said. "Him."

He pointed up. Serleena couldn't help but follow where his finger indicated. Her eyes widened.

There were Zed and Frank, both free, looking down at her from Zed's office. Zed was holding an old-fashioned over-and-under shotgun in his hands. As she stared, he dropped it—

—right into the waiting hands of Agent Jay, who stood in the doorway with Laura. All of them were wearing expressions that declared: *You lose.*

There was the loud, distinctive sound of the old-fashioned gun being cocked, followed by the double blast of both chambers being fired.

Serleena never had the chance to say a word. She was blasted to chaff and splinters where she stood.

"Keep her under the desk in case of intruders," Zed said, nodding at the antique shotgun still smoking in Jay's hands. The chips of Serleena were falling down where they might. It was the old, old story: Today, a born conqueror; tomorrow, bark mulch. "Gift from Chuck Heston. Go."

At that, Jay and Kay lit out of there, taking Laura with them. With luck, there'd be time to hand out commendations and cleanup assignments later. Right now, the clock was ticking, the Pulsar was blinking, and Earth's salvation or destruction was a matter of minutes away.

It was at that very moment that a Worm Guy named Mannix slid down a chute from the air vent system, landed in a chair in front of the keyboard for Sub Control Panel

7 R Delta, and typed a rapid-fire series of keystrokes while
his fellow worms watched from above.

"Code One-Oh-One deactivated," Mannix announced.
"We saved MIB!"

The worms cheered.

The main hall of Men in Black Headquarters went totally black.

"Worms," said Kay, by way of explanation to a non-
plussed Jay and Laura.

Jay's key chain beeped. The Mercedes pulled into the
blackened interior of the main hall with its headlights on,
luckily for everyone. The inflatable autopilot sat in the
driver's seat, but as soon as the car came to a stop in front
of Jay, Kay, and Laura, he was sucked back into his storage
compartment.

Both Jay and Kay headed for the driver's side at the
same time. Again they did it without thinking, a reflex. For
a beat they stood there, staring at each other, facing off. It
looked as if they were getting ready to argue again.

Then, without a word of debate, Jay flipped Kay the car
keys. *He's back. Gotta take him back the way he is. The
way he was, who he was. My superior officer. My partner.
My friend.* He walked around the car, headed for the passenger's side. It felt good to have Kay back. For that, he
could get used to giving up driving privileges. It was a
small enough price to pay.

As Jay headed for the passenger's side, he told Laura,
"Give me the bracelet."

"I'm going with you," she said. She sounded ready to
make a stand, to stubborn it out with him if that was what
it took. Mentally Jay cursed. They didn't have the time
for this.

"*Please* give me the—" he began again.

"Everyone in," Kay said.

Jay threw him a questioning look. He got back nothing.

Everyone in. Orders are to be obeyed. No time to squabble about it.

No time.

They all got into the Mercedes, and Kay threw it into gear. It sped forward, across the main hall of MIB Headquarters, and dropped from sight down a tunnel that suddenly appeared there. The tunnel led back up to the city streets.

Shooting out the other end, the Mercedes got air and came jouncing down onto the pavement, then took a corner in a screech of tires, and was gone.

In the main hall, all was darkness, all was silence, all was peace. Zed and Frank were busy elsewhere, doing what it took to get MIB back on its feet and functional once more. The Worm Guys were crowded into the room with Sub Control Panel 7 R Delta, indulging in an orgy of self-congratulation for quick thinking, heroism under fire, and self-bisection above and beyond the call of duty.

No one was watching the main hall. No one needed to. They'd taken care of everything down there.

In the darkness, a thin, small scratching sound was heard, soft as a butterfly's belch. Or *would* have been heard if anyone were there to listen.

On the floor, amid the scatter and splatter of woody fibers that had been Serleena, something stirred.

A neural root moved. Stopped. Twitched. Twitched again.

Paused as if considering its options and then—

—grew.

Clearly the old Earth saying was accurate, but incomplete: You can't keep a good man down. *Or* an evil Kylothian neural root creature.

TWENTY

The black Mercedes tore through the streets of Lower Manhattan, Kay at the wheel once more, back where he belonged. He reached back to where Laura sat, never losing control of the car even when he took her hand in his and said, with quiet gallantry, "May I?"

She allowed him to draw her hand forward and look at the glowing charm bracelet.

"I can't believe this charm bracelet is what everybody's after," she remarked.

"You'd be surprised how often it's something small like that," Jay told her. He could have added a score and more of illustrative tales from the files of the Men in Black—all of them coincidentally featuring himself as the hero—but before he had the opportunity, Kay cut in and took the wind right out of his sails.

"The bracelet is telling us the departure point," Kay said.

He, Jay, and Laura all gazed at the one charm on the bracelet that was glowing steadily, like the late, unlamented firefly that the subway-dwelling Jeff had devoured. The charm was shaped like a little pyramid.

A *pyramid*? The departure point was a *pyramid*? If they were in Cairo, okay, maybe, but in New York City?

Jay frowned. He knew of an obelisk in Central Park, a sphinx or two, *plus* an entire Egyptian temple inside the Metropolitan Museum of Art, and all the mummies you could handle if you sneaked into the Yale Club, but a pyramid—?

And if that pyramid was the all-important departure point Kay was talking about, which was somehow connected to the ticking clock and the fate of the entire Zarthan civilization, it was a landmark Jay couldn't zero in on mentally if his life depended on it—

Oh. Wait a minute. His life *did* depend on it. His and every other life on Earth.

Right, he thought grimly. *No pressure.*

As if to make Jay's state of mind even more cheerful, Kay went on to say: "It's also a fail-safe device. If we don't get to that departure point in eleven minutes and fifteen seconds, that bracelet's going to go nuclear, and destroy all life on Earth."

"What?" Laura exclaimed, as in: *I've had a miniature Three Mile Island dangling from my wrist for* how *many years now?*

Before either of the agents could respond, something bumped the speeding Mercedes. Something big enough to make a conspicuous impact. Something fast enough to catch up to a car with that kind of land speed capability, and make its presence felt.

Something that could be nothing good.

"What?" Kay exclaimed, as in: *What the holy hell now?*

Behind them, riding their tail, swooping in to bump the Mercedes again, harder, was the spacecraft Jarra had confected for Serleena's getaway. A fully regenerated Serleena sat at the controls, ramming the nose of her spaceship into the Mercedes again and again.

Inside the car, Kay checked his watch. Time was flying faster than Serleena. He glanced from the winking digital display to the infamous little red button on the Mercedes's dashboard. He knew what it could do. That was one memory that had come back to him intact. One touch of that button and the Mercedes would tear out of there so fast that Serleena would be left to chew their dust and choke on her own bile.

He reached for the button.

"No!" Jay screamed.

Too late. Kay moved fast. He hit the button and braced himself for what he knew was coming.

He got it.

He got more.

When you've been away from the office for a while, you've got to expect a few changes.

The Mercedes took off down the street in a streak of light just as the entire dashboard, including the steering wheel, was swallowed up whole. Outside, slick, glossy panels clamped down over the gleaming black exterior, transforming the vehicle into the hybrid offspring you get when you cross a top-of-the-line luxury car with a space shuttle. It was the sweetest piece of aerodynamic perfection ever spawned, with the sleek lines of a shark, and an allover look that would have given it the illusion of zipping by at jet speed even if it was only standing still.

Of course, it *wasn't* standing still just now. Not after Kay had gone ahead and pushed that little red button.

Jay just had time to say, "Modified to hyperspeed,"

before the vehicle's full potential for acceleration *really* kicked in, jerking their heads back in what might have been the worst case of whiplash on record.

The transformed Mercedes hurtled through Manhattan in a blur that rode ten feet off the ground. Yet Serleena's spacecraft was right behind them. Their initial burst of speed might have put her off, but only for a moment. A craft meant to traverse the unimaginable spaces between the stars wasn't going to let an upstart MIB jalopy get away that easily, no matter how souped up it was.

Inside the Mercedes, Jay, Kay, and Laura were plastered back against the seats, snugger than a cabbie's jeans. The denuded dashboard suddenly sprouted a stalk-like steering device.

"This is—?" Kay managed to force the words out of his distended mouth.

"At hyperspeed you need to fly it by the navigational stalk," Jay explained.

"Okay." Kay grabbed the stalk with determination, grit, and not a whole lot of stalk-jockey experience. The Mercedes did a wild barrel roll around a corner that sent everyone inside flying. Somewhere in the universe, the well-meaning originator of the Always Wear Your Seatbelts/Buckle Up for Safety campaign wept openly.

Jay did a flip out of the passenger's-side seat and landed on top of Laura.

"If we die—" she began.

Jay wasn't listening; he was too busy being freaked out of his mind by Kay's handling of the Mercedes. The way the old man was flying this baby, he might as well be working for Serleena.

"Triggers operate right and left ailerons," he shouted at Kay. "Toggle switch—stabilizers and rudder."

"Oh" was all Kay said in thanks for this tidbit of in-flight training. He hit the switches and promptly flipped the Mercedes upside down like a big, shiny, hyperspeed pancake.

In the backseat, Jay and Laura flipped over along with the car, landing her smack on top of him.

"—I want you to know you're the only person I've ever loved," she finished.

"Really?" *Now* she had Jay's attention. He gazed up into her eyes joyfully. "That's amazing. I feel—"

The Earth moved. They saw fireworks and were shaken to their very cores. The raging blaze came near to consuming them utterly.

Actually it was Serleena, firing a torpedo at the racing Mercedes. It exploded in a ball of flame. The Mercedes shot right through the fire, but began to spin out of control. Inside, Jay, Kay, and Laura were all screaming their fool heads off, and when the situation was bad enough to make MIB agents scream, you knew it had to be *bad*.

Jay began to inch his way back into the front seat, fighting the staggering G-forces every micrometer of the way. Turning back to Laura, he said, "I'll get back to you on that," before continuing his man-against-gravity struggle. She loved him, and that was wonderful, but it wasn't going to do either one of them a lick of good if they died in a hyperspeed car crash, or if they didn't make it to that wherever-the-hell-in-this-city-it-was pyramid before the fail-safe device kicked in and all of Earth went up in a blast of cosmic dust.

"Communicator!" Jay commanded. "Worms!"

Back in the main hall of MIB Headquarters, the Worm Guys and Frank were lazing around in front of the big Egg Screen, smoking cigars, trading war stories, and feeling really good about themselves. Frank leaned in to get a light, then resumed his tale of how he'd dealt with Serleena:

"So I said, 'Listen, bitch, if you don't want me to kick your skinny Zone Diet ass—' "

"Worms!" Jay's frantic voice cut short Frank's account of unusual bravery in the face and/or skinny Zone Diet ass of the enemy. "Where are you?"

"Main hall," Sleeble reported, setting aside his cigar. "Egg display."

Serleena's pursuing ship swooped in under the flying Mercedes and fired another torpedo. It missed, but just barely. A miss was supposed to be as good as a mile, but try telling that to the target. Jay was betting that Serleena would use that near miss to help her get their range, so that next time—

He didn't want to think about that *next time*. He could feel time itself slipping away, along with the last of his lucky breaks. He had to do something before it was too late to do anything; something for himself, for his partner, for MIB, for Earth—

—for Laura.

"Lost control," he told the Worm Guys. "Being fired on. Kay pressed the red button. Computer at MIB can lock on and destroy bogey. I'll walk you through it—"

Sleeble turned to the Egg Screen, ready and willing to do what it took to help his friends and save the Earth again. No way could Frank top that! He reached confidently for the controls . . .

But there on the Egg Screen, a row of bars was blinking brightly along the bottom. COMPUTER SHUT DOWN IMPROPERLY. RECONFIGURING HARD DRIVE. SEVEN MINUTES REMAINING.

"Uhhh, Jay—" Sleeble began. "When we turned off the electricity we may have—"

The blast of a torpedo came in loud and clear over the communicator, so loud that it shook the Worm Guys where they stood. Frank shouldered his way up to the microphone and gravely said:

"Jay? Frank. You were the best darn partner a Remoolian could ever have. Godspeed." He hung up. Sometimes you just didn't want to be there as a witness, even long distance, when a friend of yours was about to buy the ranch.

In the Mercedes, while Jay fumed over Frank's defeatist dismissal, Kay wasn't just sitting idle, waiting to be rescued. That wasn't Kay's style.

His eyes searched the largely unfamiliar controls of the transformed Mercedes until they lit on one particular button. He'd seen Jay use it, he knew what it was for, and he was sure it was the right one for saving them all and regaining control.

When you don't know how to operate a vehicle, call in someone who does.

Kay hit the button and the inflatable automatic pilot deployed right into his lap. Unfortunately, instead of taking the wheel and getting the Mercedes back under control, the inflated dummy just sat there, arms dangling uselessly at its sides.

"He's not piloting," Kay announced, a man betrayed.

"Not designed for hyperspeed," Jay explained.

Like *that* was going to make it all better.

"I could use a steering wheel!" Kay shouted. He groped blindly around the inflated, ineffective autopilot, reaching for the navigational stalk, and only succeeded in pushing the dummy down onto the controls. The Mercedes spun around crazily, like a flaming pinwheel escaped from a Fourth of July fireworks display.

Jay slipped under the dashboard and fought his way up again, battling to reach the controls as he was flung this way and that inside the car like a Ping-Pong ball.

"Left paddle!" he directed Kay. "Not the trigger, the top left—"

The two MIB agents struggled to switch seats, fighting the inflated autopilot every step of the way. At last they made it, leaving Jay in the driver's seat where he could do the most good. He laid hold of the controls in triumph.

"Mama never buy you a Game Boy?" he asked Kay as he took over.

With Jay mastering the helm, the Mercedes righted itself smoothly and did a fast, elegant barrel roll out and away from Serleena's pursuing ship. It was too bad that the MIB agent couldn't hold on to that little lead. Serleena's ship still had the greater speed capability, and it soon closed the gap.

The Kylothian warrior bore down upon them relentlessly, the Mercedes pinpointed in her sights, and fired another torpedo. Jay caught sight of the deadly missile on their tail and gave the controls a tiny flick of the wrist, sending the Mercedes into a hard right turn. The torpedo overshot its target and exploded just beyond them.

It was a good maneuver, but Jay wouldn't be able to use it more than once. Serleena was a fast learner, and someone who passionately believed in *fool me once, shame on you; fool me twice, I'll kill you.* The next time she fired a torpedo at them—

No. Better not think that way. Better think of how to get away from her, get to the departure point, get the Light off Earth while there still *was* an Earth.

But how—?

And then Jay happened to look down at the New York City streets below. Something caught his eye. A memory stirred, a thought clicked, inspiration struck, and his whole mind lit up like Christmas with a wild, triumphant: *Yessss!*

"Hang on," he told his passengers. "Straight down!" He turned the Mercedes so that it was heading nose-first for a terminal date with the sidewalks of New York.

"No!" Laura screamed. "Down is *bad*. Straight down is *idiotic!*"

Jay didn't argue. He simply pulled back ever-so-slightly on the stick.

The Mercedes nosed up just enough to go zooming right down the welcoming mouth of a subway entrance, without an inch to spare.

If Jay hoped to lose his pursuer by going to ground, or underground, it was a hope soon dashed. In the street above, Serleena's spaceship hardly missed a beat before flying into the subway after them.

The commuters standing in the Chambers Street Station glanced up from their newspapers to see if that roaring sound was their long-awaited train. It had been a tiring day, and, man, would it ever feel good to get home and take their shoes off.

It wasn't a train; it was a tricked-out, sleeked-down,

teched-up flying Mercedes, quickly followed by a spaceship that took out a chunk of cement wall and part of a CHAMBERS STREET STATION sign.

The commuters didn't even bother to shrug as they went back to reading their papers.

Down the tunnel, the Mercedes's high-powered halogen headlights turned the darkness to brightest day. In her spacecraft, Serleena couldn't help but remark, "Nice. Very nicely engineered."

Her appreciation didn't deter her from her purpose. She gunned her vehicle and gave the car another bump, harder than the previous ones. Her assault knocked it sideways, tearing out a big block of concrete-and-rebar wall. Serleena eased up slightly on the throttle, the better to survey her handiwork. It was pretty impressive: She'd smashed in the rear end of the MIB vehicle as easily as a frat boy could crush a beer can on his forehead.

"The bumpers aren't great over three hundred," she commented, as though making mental notes for the intergalactic edition of *Consumer Reports*. Pleased, she hit them again. Sparks from the damaged electrical wiring flew everywhere, gouging through the tunnel.

"Subway doesn't seem like the best place to lose her," Kay observed.

Jay wasn't listening. "Where is he?" he muttered. "Where the hell is he?"

"He?" Kay echoed.

A shape, large and lumbering, loomed out of the darkness just beyond the reach of the Mercedes's headlights.

"Jeff," said Jay.

The gigantic worm-thing screeched in rage and recognition as soon as he caught sight of Jay in the driver's seat of the Mercedes. The only force that coursed through Jeff's body more intensely than his all-consuming appetite was his ability to carry a grudge. He remembered what Jay had done to him, remembered it perfectly, and it made him hungry for the one thing he couldn't digest: revenge.

The sight of Jay was provocation enough, but the MIB agent went on to make things worse, waving cavalierly at the creature, deliberately taunting him. Jeff screeched again, madder, and opened his titanic jaws wide, eager to engulf the miserable human being who had been responsible for having him moved back to this less-than-satisfactory hunting ground. Revoke *his* travel privileges, huh? He'd show him! He'd swallow him whole. If that didn't teach that lousy son-of-a-Terran a lesson, nothing would!

Teeth glittering, throat red and pulsing, Jeff stood poised to gulp down the recklessly onrushing Mercedes and all who rode in it.

Come . . . to . . . Papa.

"Jeff," Laura repeated, staring down the scarlet gullet that stretched before her like a straight-to-hell water slide.

She was almost calm, the same sort of calm that overtakes people in the instant after the car shoots over the edge of the cliff, or the sizzling fuse vanishes into the keg full of gunpowder, or the bobbing barrel comes within sight of Niagara Falls. That ruthless alien who'd killed Ben was right behind them, right on top of them. One way or another, they were all going to die. No sense in getting worried about the inevitable.

At least she'd told Jay she loved him. At least she'd have that to take with her into whatever was waiting on the other side of . . . Jeff?

An abiding sense of peace and surrender settled over

her like a well-worn stadium blanket. Bye-bye, World. It was nice knowing you.

And then, breaking through that unnatural barricade of serenity, she heard Jay shout: "Hold on!" and he cut the throttle dead.

The Mercedes stopped.

Bam.

Snap.

Period.

No skid, no slide, no such thing as momentum, nothing. Dead in place. It stopped, it dropped to the subway tracks like a stone, and Serleena looked out the front of her spacecraft in time to see *not* the damaged rear end of the MIB vehicle, but—

"Teeth?"

She flew right over the Mercedes and directly down Jeff's open gullet.

It was over in an instant. The monster gulped, flicked his tail, and disappeared down the tracks into the darkness. Yummers. Heavy but nutritious, the worm equivalent of sauerbraten.

Somewhere inside his tiny mind the hulking creature reached the conclusion that Serleena's spaceship was Jay's attempt at a reconciliation gift, his way of saying he was sorry for what he'd done to Jeff earlier. Nice of the MIB agent to think of doing that, Jeff reasoned. *Mighty* nice. Jeff might be a gigantic extraterrestrial worm-thing, but his mama had raised him with an appreciation for good manners, before he'd grown large enough to devour her.

So if the man had made an honest effort at restoring cordial relations between them, the least that the worm could do was accept it graciously. All was forgiven.

Miss Manners would have been pleased.

Jay, Kay, and Laura looked at one another. Kay's eyes surveyed the interior of the Mercedes. He nodded, satisfied.

"Still a Ford man," he said. "But a very decent ride."

TWENTY-ONE

The Mercedes flew through the subway system that honeycombs New York City, emerging at a stop near the foot of Manhattan Island. In the distance, the Statue of Liberty raised her golden torch against a night sky all atwinkle with stars.

The car climbed the air to one of the many surrounding rooftops and roared to a stop within plain sight of the famous monument. The rooftops of New York are more than pigeon refuges. They are a kingdom in the clouds, a realm unto themselves, a conglomeration of individual sites as culturally diverse as Disney's Small World ride. New York City rooftops can encompass anything from simple swaths of tar, purely utilitarian, to the elaborate penthouse garden playgrounds of the rich and show-offy.

This particular rooftop looked as if it had once been more than just the topmost layer of a building, for it still boasted vestiges of a less practical, more owner-indulgent past. There were hints of an attempt at crafting a Zen garden, including one of those large, decorative rocks so popular during the 1980s heyday when all things Japanese were in. Having a lump of stone that size on the roof not only helped the owner meditate on the transient nature of material goods, it also proclaimed that he had the bucks necessary to haul something that big and useless all the way up to Pigeon Central.

In the open space below, a glass pyramid twinkled by the lights of the lofty buildings. The Mercedes's doors opened and Jay, Kay, and Laura got out.

Jay took a moment to glance over the edge of the rooftop to double-check on the glittering pyramid that lay beneath them. Mentally he congratulated himself for having recalled—before the clock ran out—that there was, in fact, such a structure in New York City. It was hell on his nerves, but *damn*, he really did work best under pressure.

Departure point located and secured: Check.

Now he looked around avidly, seeking the one thing they needed if they were going to save the world before time ran out. He knew his partner could be tight-lipped, but when you're the only guy on the planet who knows how to actually *use* the only thing that can save the planet, it's time to stop playing Yup-Nope-Gary-Cooper and start chattering like *all* of those ladies on *The View* put together.

"Runnin' out of time, Kay," he said. "Where's the Light?"

Kay took Laura by the hand. Around her wrist the bracelet that could save the Earth caught the city lights and twinkled, the pyramid charm still blinking.

"A code, Laura," Kay said to her with a quiet tension. "Think, Laura. A combination . . . Anything. Did Ben ever say anything to you about a code? A special date? Anything?"

Laura's brow creased in thought as she struggled to deal with his line of questioning. She stared down at the bracelet, still coping with all the things that had happened to her in such a short span of time. Out of everything she'd seen and experienced, of all the impossibilities she'd been asked to believe, this was the hardest: to accept the fact that the fate of her planet and of another world whose existence she'd never even suspected were dangling from her wrist. How could it be? The bracelet looked like just another piece of borderline kitsch, something a female out-of-towner might pounce on as the perfect souvenir to commemorate her once-in-a-lifetime trip to New York City. She thought of that time back at the pizzeria when she'd been dealing with a plumbing problem and almost lost it down the toilet. An icy chill shook her to the bone as she realized what *that* would mean now.

It was weird enough to comprehend that the trinket she'd cherished for years was the fabled Light of Zartha, but to suddenly be told that it wouldn't be enough just to hand it over, that two whole worlds were depending on her memory to dredge up the way to activate this thing!

No pressure, right?

A code . . .

She thought hard, refusing to let the urgency of the situation make her freeze up, keep her from remembering . . . remembering. . . .

"There was . . . a song," she said. "Ben used to sing to me when I was little. A lullaby . . . 'four, three, two, I love you; seven, eight, nine, ain't that fine.' I still sing it to myself when I can't sleep, but that can't be—"

Kay didn't wait for her to finish. He grabbed the bracelet and manipulated it rapidly, keying in the numbers.

"It's the code," he said. "It will activate the Light."

While Kay worked feverishly over the bracelet, Jay

pulled the napkin he'd taken from Ben's Famous Pizza out of his pocket and held it up, looking from the flimsy piece of paper out across the water to where the Statue of Liberty stood guard over New York Harbor. Looking at the beloved monument, he couldn't help remembering a time when his whole life was simpler, when he didn't have to deal with aliens, or the Men in Black, or—or—

—or finally finding someone to love.

His gaze shifted back to the napkin in his hand. Then it hit him. Every symbol on it aligned perfectly with the scene that lay before him now. Ben's Famous Pizza. The napkins. The pizza boxes. Everything that could carry the store's logo, printed with the images of a slice of pizza that pointed upward to the Statue of Liberty, who in turn aimed her torch straight for the stars. But it wasn't a slice of pizza, was it?

The glass pyramid in the plaza seemed to wink up at him as if to say *Took you long enough, slick. Oh, you were close, closer than you knew, back when you guessed that the slice was supposed to be an arrow pointing the way. Only then you thought it was pointing the way to a can of anchovies.*

Well, surprise, Junior! It ain't anchovies.

Laura looked at him, her eyes following his gaze. She had spent years of her life working in Ben's Famous Pizza, surrounded by copies of that logo. She recognized it right away, as the glass pyramid continued to glow like its miniature counterpart, its point indicating Lady Liberty, as Lady Liberty's torch came into direct alignment with one particular star just as Agent Kay keyed in the final digit of the code.

That's when the atmosphere snapped and sizzled.

The star above the golden torch flared, blazed, then shot out a beam of pure energy that lanced through the air to strike the large, decorative rock on the roof beside them. There was a blinding flash, and the rock transformed beneath a rippling skin of electricity.

Then the light was gone; the rock was gone. In its place, a space capsule sat waiting.

Kay looked at Laura, his expression clearly indicating that he wanted her to place the Light of Zartha in the vessel that would carry it safely away to fulfill its destiny before its fail-safe device could turn Earth into a gaping black hole.

She nodded, silently accepting the honor, and began to move reverently toward the space capsule. It was a beautiful moment, poetic, and, in its own way, unutterably heroic.

But there's always someone in the audience who seems to live solely for the purpose of spoiling moments like that.

With a hideous roar from below, Jeff's massive wormy body came crashing up out through the glass pyramid on the plaza. His roar echoed and re-echoed through the abandoned streets.

"Jeff!"

Jay hated having nice, romantic moments ruined. He hated it when some geek had a coughing fit during Juliet's death scene at Shakespeare in the Park. He *really* hated it when some moron suggested that they reshoot the end of *Casablanca* so that Rick got to keep the girl, and he really, *really* hated it that the big subterranean-dwelling worm had chosen this opportunity to screw up his own romantic moment with Laura.

"I am *so* not in the mood for you!" Jay shouted at the tactless worm. "Get your long ass back to the subway, or I'm gonna tranquilize you with something you won't wake up from!"

There was a loud, moist, deeply disturbing *rrrrrrrrriiiippp* sound from the plaza. You might say that Jeff had decided to ignore Jay's threat, but then you wouldn't be saying nearly enough. Jeff wasn't feeling like himself anymore, to put it mildly. Jeff's skin was what had made that ripping sound as it split wide open, like an exploding banana shucking its own peel, revealing a core of nightmare.

It was Serleena, but Serleena hideously transformed, a Serleena that was part worm, part cluster of twitching, lashing, dripping neural roots, with just a smidge of Victoria's Secret supermodel clinging to the whole ungodly package.

Jay stared down at the unspeakably ghastly vision below and couldn't help but mutter: "You are what you eat."

"That's not good," said Kay. He grabbed Laura by the wrist and pulled her away, toward the capsule. There was no longer any time to treat the Light of Zartha with the reverence it deserved, not with *that* thing on the playing field.

If there was any question as to whether the horror show creature was Jeff after an overdose of Serleena or Serleena after a binge of devouring Jeff, it soon vanished. The monster spied Laura on the rooftop and lashed out one writhing neural root to seize her.

Yeah, that was Serleena, all right.

Jay's combat-trained reflexes kicked in without a second's hesitation. He threw himself between Laura and the monster's brambly tentacle, shoving her out of harm's way. The neural root missed its original target, but Serleena was willing to make the best of things. The root lashed itself around Jay's neck and pulled him back, screaming, as more and more roots sprang up, wrapping him in strand after strand of twisting, immobilizing bramble.

Laura couldn't help it: She stopped dead in her tracks and stared in disbelief at what was happening to the man she loved.

"Jay!" She called out his name in vain as Serleena's roots engulfed him completely.

"Kay! A little help!" Jay called out desperately from deep inside the belly of the beast.

Kay whipped out his weapon and fired. The blast knocked Serleena back, though it didn't stop her.

"Laura! Get the bracelet to the pod!" Kay ordered as he fired another round at the monster. This one tore a gaping hole in Serleena's side.

Jay's head popped out of the hole like a meerkat on speed, only to be quickly sucked back inside.

Kay squeezed off another blast at the monster, then one more for good measure, doing his best to cover Laura, who was still hypnotized by the horror before her.

Serleena shook off the effects of Kay's assault, regrouped, and came back at him and Laura with a vengeance. Kay fired at the monster again, ripping open a fresh hole through the snarl of neural roots. This time one of Jay's shoulders popped out of the monstrous alien, his dapper black suit jacket smoldering like a badly doused bonfire.

"*Aaaaahhhhgh!* Aim . . . *higher!*" came the deeply annoyed directive from inside the creature.

"He's fine!" Kay called out for Laura's benefit, and fired right into the monster's face. The impact knocked her down.

But she was a warrior. And clearly she felt warriors don't stop just because some puny Earthling with an overdeveloped death-wish smears their mascara. Warriors kill. *Then* they check a mirror and reapply.

Serleena staggered back, recovered, and advanced once more, lurching forward toward Kay and Laura.

"He does this all the time!" Kay shouted at Laura, desperate for a way to get her moving again, before it was too late for them all.

"Laura, the bracelet!"

She snapped out of her trance and moved toward the pod. Kay said a silent prayer of thanksgiving and laid down a fusillade of covering fire. He fired volley after volley at the ever-nearing Serleena with a steady hand, a sharp eye, unimpeachable aim. He hit her again and again and again, but it didn't stop her; it only slowed her down, and not enough.

It also ripped a lacework pattern of holes throughout her brambly, worm-shaped tangle of a body.

Jay's head popped out of one of the holes, upside down, and declared: "You're just making her mad, Kay!"

Bang!

Kay got off another round before Jay was yanked back inside.

You can't keep a good man down. His head popped out again, from another hole, and added: "We need—"

Bang! Bang!

Kay fired two more blasts into the monster.

Yoink!

The creature sucked Jay out of sight.

Not for long. Like some freakish, demented Whack-a-Mole game, Jay popped out of yet a *third* spot in Serleena's multiperforated body. He was just able to shout: "—a bigger—" before Kay opened up her brambly hide with a triple shot and she absorbed him one more time.

"—weapon!" Jay yelled at the top of his lungs. Damn, seemed like he'd *never* get that sentence finished. It was hard to get a word in edgewise when Kay got his game face on.

As Kay continued to wage a losing war against the doggedly oncoming Serleena, a misshapen figure stepped out of the rooftop shadows. Above the sound of repeated blaster reports, the monster's roars of rage, and the warm-up hum of the still-stationary space capsule, a familiar voice inquired politely:

"Proton bomb?"

It was Scrad/Charlie, who had somehow managed to trail the Light of Zartha and the Men in Black to the pre-arranged departure point. Now the Scrad entity held out the brightly shining metal orb, thrusting it toward Kay as if it were some kind of a peace offering. Obviously Charlie had brought his bodymate around to seeing things his way when it came to Serleena.

This time Jay's head popped out of Serleena's mouth like one of those curly paper noisemakers. "Thank you!" he exulted. It was just what the doctor ordered, if you had the right HMO. That deceptively small silver sphere packed megatonnage like mama used to make. Jay's hands reached out of Serleena's mouth as Scrad literally tossed him the long bomb.

"Hey! Where's the detonator?" Jay cried. This wasn't the kind of surprise he liked.

"We broke it," Charlie admitted sheepishly.

"Kay, shoot them! Shoot them!" Jay shouted in anger

and frustration. He didn't really mean it. It just made him feel better to say it.

Okay, maybe he *did* really mean it, but Kay wasn't listening.

But this was no time for playing the Blame Game. Kay opened fire on Serleena again as Jay did a back-flip out of the monster's mouth, then leapt back up and slam-dunked the proton bomb down her throat, landing at Scrad/Charlie's feet.

"We request asylum as political prisoners of the tyrannical Kylothians," Scrad recited formally.

Charlie's head sprang out of the knapsack in time to add: "We love New York. It's the only place we've ever fit in."

While Scrad/Charlie was pledging allegiance to the Big Apple, there was still a Big Worm infestation that needed to be terminated.

Jay and Kay weren't wasting any time. As the Light began its departure, they made a beeline for the trunk of the Mercedes where the *really* serious firepower was stowed.

Serleena's grotesque head swung away from Jay and her defecting minion, back to where the little space capsule had finally lifted off from the rooftop. The tiny craft flew through the sky, heading for the still-shining star-beam piercing the darkness from just above Lady Liberty's torch.

Either Serleena didn't notice what Jay and Kay were doing, or she knew that even MIB's most heavy-duty weaponry was no match for her. She had other fish to fry, specifically one twinkly little charm bracelet–shaped fish that was in immiment danger of becoming the one that got away.

No one and nothing got away from Serleena. Not twice.

She headed off after the escaping Light of Zartha at a gallop. The capsule had already risen beyond her Earth-bound reach, but she regarded that as just a temporary advantage for her prey. Extremely temporary.

Wings sprouted from her back and the immense bulk of her part-worm, part-bramble body soared into the air.

Jay looked to Kay. Both of them were armed now. Jay nodded. They slammed down the actions of their weapons in unison, a sweetly synchronized movement that only went to show that a great partnership is a thing of beauty.

"Kid?" Kay said.

"Yeah?"

"Thanks for bringing me back."

Jay gave a little half smile. "No problem." He sneaked a look to check on Laura. She was standing by the car, looking stunned by everything that was going down around her but otherwise okay.

There was no time for further talk.

Serleena was airborne and gaining on the capsule. Together they raised their weapons, sighted along the barrels, and tracked Serleena's flight as if she were the biggest, ugliest clay pigeon that the fine sport of skeet shooting had ever known. It was all that Jay could do to keep himself from shouting, *Pull!*

Two shots burst from their weapons and hit Serleena squarely where it counted, just as her neural roots were beginning to wrap themselves around the fleeing sphere. The Kylothian's hold on the capsule broke as she paused to survey the two smoking wounds in her massive body. She was only marginally concerned, though. Her whole attitude seemed to sneer, *Oh, really, like* that's *going to stop me?*

But when she glared back at Jay and Kay, something was wrong. Though she was still aloft, they didn't look at all distressed.

They didn't look the least bit worried that victory—and that damn elusive Light of Zartha—were almost within her grasp.

They looked . . . happy.

They weren't supposed to look happy. Didn't they know when they'd lost? What did they think their miserable weapons could do to stop—?

That was when Kay gave her a little wave.

Buh-bye.

And Serleena exploded in a breathtakingly beautiful pyrotechnic display that would have had the geniuses behind the Macy's Fourth of July fireworks show taking notes. Of course, no one could ever hope to duplicate the effect. That would take another proton bomb, and a couple of crack shots to set it off in lieu of its broken detonator.

Not exactly the sort of thing you can budget for, even at Macy's.

Then a second brilliant burst of light filled the air. The sphere carrying the Light of Zartha was engulfed in the full glory of the energy surge that transported it instantaneously off Earth. Back it flew to a world awaiting its power, its salvation. All who witnessed it shielded their eyes from the overwhelming radiance.

When they could see again, it was over. The sphere was gone. The last telltale glory of Serleena's explosion fell over the city in a beautiful, ethereal glow more wonderful than a thousand sunsets.

All was silent.

The crisis was averted; Earth—and Zartha—were saved.

Jay was the first to break the silence.

"What was it like?" he asked Kay. "On the outside?"

"It was . . . nice," Kay replied after only a little reflection. "Slept late on weekends. Watched the Weather Channel . . ."

He paused, and slowly, leisurely let his gaze drift all around the full panorama of the familiar New York skyline. "I did miss the city, though."

Then he caught a glimpse of Jay looking at the still-dazed Laura. Kay turned to his partner. "I went offbook twenty-five years ago, and it almost destroyed the planet." He looked at Laura, then back to Jay again, and quietly said: "It's your decision. You'll do the right thing."

For a time, Jay just stood there, drinking in the sight of the woman he loved, thinking about the job he'd just done. It would be so easy to call in past favors, to get Kay to free him from being one of the Men in Black, to take his own place on the outside.

But where could that place be? He remembered how it had been for Kay—the vague longings he couldn't explain, couldn't satisfy, the sense of there being something more to his life than a nine-to-five job, sleeping late on the weekends, watching the Weather Channel.

Sure, he'd gone back to marry his long-suffering fi-ancée, but it hadn't lasted. She'd left him because she couldn't compete with a dream, even a dream Kay could no longer really remember. A neuralyzer flash worked only on your mind, but there were some things a man carried in his soul.

Agent Kay was MIB through and through. Was Agent Jay any different? If he left the agency and married Laura, would her love be strong enough to fight his buried dreams, or would it only be a matter of time before she left him, too?

Would he be strong enough to look at the stars and see only . . . stars?

We are who we are. Jay knew the words, and he truly knew their meaning. He walked toward Laura, slipping on his Ray-Bans and pulling out his neuralyzer.

"I just want you to know you're the only person I've ever loved," he told her just before the blinding flash of memory-altering light dazzled her eyes.

"The City of New York would like to thank you for participating in our . . . architectural survey," he concluded lamely. It was the best he could do on a broken heart.

Before the after-flash of the neuralyzer completely faded from the air, backup MIB agents were suddenly there to escort Laura away, back to a life where the only alien monsters she would have to deal with were safely confined to the realm of science fiction. As they led her off, Jay called after her:

"Maybe we can have pie sometime."

"Hey, what about us?" Scrad/Charlie piped up, breaking the mood of Jay's wistful farewell as thoroughly as they'd broken the detonator on the proton bomb.

"There's always an opening at the post office," Kay told them.

"Post office?" the two-headed alien repeated. *"Yes!!"* Both heads wore big, goofy smiles.

As Serleena's former minion dreamily contemplated the joys of a rewarding career in public service, Jay and Kay took a long, searching look at one another.

"Come on," Kay said. He wasn't good with words, and he knew that there really wasn't anything he could say to Jay now that would make him stop hurting. All he could do was get him back to work and let time do the rest. "Let's get going." He turned his back on the Statue of Liberty and began to walk away.

Jay fell into step at his partner's side. "Get going?" he echoed, incredulous.

For the good of the planet, he'd been forced to say good-bye to the love of his life. Now he was back in full MIB mode, burying the hurt deep in the demands of his work. And one of the prime duties of that work was effecting swift and certain cover-up for any and all instances of alien activities on this planet.

It was the only remedy he could come up with for such a big loss on such short notice, turning himself into as big a by-the-book, pain-in-the-ass stickler for regulations as Kay was. When you're bitching and moaning about how badly someone else has screwed things up, you don't have the time to think about a broken heart.

"Thousands of people in New York and New Jersey must've seen our little event," he declared, trying to make Kay realize that this wasn't something they could simply walk away from. "Plan needs to be *totally* thought out. A plan needs to be cool. How the hell are we going to explain—?"

"Kid," Kay interrupted him. "I'll get you trained yet."

He raised his ancient Pulsar watch and pushed a button on it. Behind them, the golden torch on the Statue of Liberty flared up in a blinding flash that could only come from the biggest neuralyzer the world had ever known.

The glare of light flooded the rooftop, flooded the city, surged out over the entire tri-state area in an inundation of controlled forgetfulness. No one would ever be able to remember seeing a space capsule flying toward the Statue of Liberty, or an unthinkable monster pursuing it, or—

Or anything at all connected with the Light of Zartha. And that was exactly as it should be.

"You didn't really think I put Earth in jeopardy without a back-up plan, did you, slick?" Kay asked.

Dazzled in the giant neuralyzer's backwash, Jay stood gaping for a moment, and then said:

"I *want* one of those."